Frederick Arnold

Robertson of Brighton

With some notices of his times and contemporaries

Frederick Arnold

Robertson of Brighton
With some notices of his times and contemporaries

ISBN/EAN: 9783337196912

Printed in Europe, USA, Canada, Australia, Japan

Cover: Foto ©Raphael Reischuk / pixelio.de

More available books at **www.hansebooks.com**

ROBERTSON OF BRIGHTON.

WITH SOME NOTICES

OF

HIS TIMES AND CONTEMPORARIES.

BY THE

REV. FREDERICK ARNOLD,

B.A. OXON.

London:

WARD AND DOWNEY,

12, YORK STREET, COVENT GARDEN.

1886.

TO THE

REV. S. J. STONE, M.A.,

VICAR OF ST. PAUL'S, HAGGERSTONE.

MY DEAR STONE,

I was busy with this book during some of the many visits which I have made to your hospitable home, and when I have been privileged to take some little share in your arduous East End work. I do not wish to identify you with my own views of the character and teachings of Robertson, although I venture to feel quite sure that you will love and honour him as a good man, with many of the highest qualities of a great man. I have a desire to associate this volume with my memories of a sympathy and helpfulness that have never failed me during many years, of a friendship which I have learned to prize as one of the highest blessings and privileges of my life.

Yours ever,

FREDERICK ARNOLD.

November 23rd, 1885.

CONTENTS.

CHAPTER VII.

CHAPTER VIII.

CHAPTER IX.

CHAPTER X.

ROBERTSON OF BRIGHTON.

INTRODUCTION.

It has so happened that, during a prolonged residence extending to nearly seven years in the neighbourhood of Brighton, it was my lot to make the personal acquaintance of many persons well acquainted with the late Frederick William Robertson. The number of those has become less and less since I began to make notes of their impressions and recollections. In Brighton itself he is fast becoming a faded memory; and indeed the Americans who visit our shores, and make pilgrimages to visit his tomb in the Lewes Road Cemetery, are the most faithful to his memory. I have been greatly impressed by the extraordinary influence which Robertson almost unconsciously exercised upon those who were brought within the range of his personal influence. I know many persons who have been brought into close personal relationship with celebrated men. But I have

B

known no case in which the influence has been more profound and lasting than in the case of Robertson. His, indeed, was one of the most rare and radiant natures that, with all its errors and imperfections, has ever adorned humanity. He has left hardly anything which he distinctly designed for publication, but the letters, lectures, and sermons which he threw off, and which have been mainly preserved through the devotion of his friends, make up some eight volumes, which increasingly invite and repay analysis and criticism. But the man himself is infinitely greater than his utterances, and affords a study of the utmost pathos and interest.

Continuously, from the time of Robertson's Brighton ministry to the present time, we have evidence of the influence of his writings—an influence which seems, both in extent and intensity, not to be diminishing, but increasing. The sermons have been translated into several foreign languages—they are classical in America and our colonies, and have immensely influenced all contemporary theological thought. The effect of these wonderful sermons, great as it is in the perusal, is little compared to the effect they produced at the time of their delivery. All those who heard Robertson preach, declared that he was the greatest pulpit orator—perhaps the greatest of all orators—of his time.

The present writer remembers to have heard Dean Stanley say, at one of his clerical meetings at St. James's Rectory, Piccadilly, that he looked upon Robertson as the greatest of modern English preachers. It is remarkable that the last article which the Dean wrote, which appeared in an American periodical a short time after his death, was one on Robertson. In this brief paper he gives two instances which showed him the wide appreciation in which Robertson was held. We quote a passage from *Scribner*, as it has much interest, both as respects the Dean and Mr. Robertson :—

" Once in travelling from the South of France to Paris, we entered the railway at Macon, and found coiled up on the opposite side of the railway carriage a rough, shaggy, wayworn traveller fast asleep. He was, with us, the only occupant of the carriage. After a time he lifted up his head and began to speak to us. He was a wild, revolutionary, unbelieving surgeon who had been attached to a regiment in Algeria, and who was then on his way to the army in Mexico. We entered into conversation which lasted through the livelong day till we reached Paris. In the course of this conversation he asked—not knowing that I was a clergyman—whether I had ever known or read the sermons of Frederick Robertson; he had himself fallen in with a copy and been struck with them, and he was eager to know anything that I could tell him about them. We parted at Paris; he went to Mexico, and I have since lost all trace of him. This was one end of the scale. On the next day, in Paris, I went as usual to see a man whom in his best days I greatly respected and loved, Augustin Cochin, who afterwards became Prefect of Versailles in the troubles which succeeded the Franco-German war, and he died of the fatigues which in that war had fallen to his lot. He was a devout Catholic, liberal indeed, and open to all kinds of questioning about England and Protestantism; of the school of Montalembert and Father Gratry. He, on the occasion to which I refer, asked if I could tell him anything about an extraordinary preacher whose name was Frederick Robertson. Thus, in the course of forty-eight hours, I had evidence of the effect produced in two extremes of French society, and that by an English preacher."

The Dean goes on to give some criticism of two great English preachers—Dr. Arnold and Cardinal Newman—and pronounces that as a preacher he considers Robertson superior to both.

The influence of these sermons is indeed most astonishing. Repeated instances of their effect, like those recorded by Dean Stanley, are to be found in books. In the biography of Lord Lawrence we read how, on the Sunday before he died, he caused Robertson's sermon on the "Victory over Death" to be read aloud to him. In the

Letters of the Princess Alice we see how greatly the Sermons were esteemed by the Princess and her Royal Mother. In the latest of Bishop Oxenden's works there is a citation from his writings. Sir J. T. Coleridge, in his "Life of Keble," quotes one of the hymns of the "Christian Year," saying that it was a favourite with Robertson of Brighton; and in one of his last letters, Keble has a reference to Robertson. A very striking evidence of the sort is to be found in a story, entitled, "The Life and Womanhood of Helen Tyrrell," by the authoress of "Brampton Rectory." The opening inscription is—"To the memory of Frederick William Robertson, sometime minister of Trinity Chapel, Brighton, these pages are humbly dedicated, by one to whom his teaching was light in darkness, relief in sorrow, and the impulse to a higher life." One of the principal characters is obviously drawn from Robertson himself, endeavours to reproduce in a popular form some of the leading features of his doctrines, and uses some of Robertson's vivid illustrations. I observe that the author of a valuable volume of sermons[1] says frankly that the whole of them are thoroughly imbued with Robertson's teaching, and that some of them are bodily taken from him. Some of our best modern essayists—M. de Pressensé pre-emi-

[1] Rev. M. Fuller's "Vox Clamantis in Deserto."

nently—have occupied themselves with the man and his writings. Indeed, it may be said that hardly any Sunday passes without Robertson's voice being heard in many pulpits of the land. It may be truly said in his case, that being dead he yet speaketh. This happens in two ways. Many a clergyman, overborne by parish duties and unable to meet the excessive demands for sermons which is often made on him, simplifies matters by giving his people a sermon of Robertson's. *Qui suadet, sua det*, is a true proverb; but if he has nothing of his own ready, he may as well give Robertson, especially if he has the moral courage to say whose sermon it is. Sometimes there has been among the copyists a great run on Cunningham of Harrow, or Blunt, famous for his divisions, or on the golden-tongued Melvill; but of late years we believe that there has been a greater run upon Robertson than upon any other preacher. The indirect influence of Robertson is probably still greater; in the greater manliness, freshness, and robustness of clerical tone; in the ever-increasing number of those who, instead of labelling themselves by party names, are content to call no man master, but to follow Christ only. To multitudes of preachers, both in the Church and Nonconformist pulpits, and consequently to their people, Robertson has been a great factor in quickening the spiritual and intellectual life.

The "Life and Letters of F. W. Robertson," edited by Mr. Stopford Brook, is one of the most admirable biographies, and the best known. It is no imputation on Mr. Brook's masterly work to say that it owes its chief charm to Robertson's own letters. I would here desire, once for all, to record my deep obligation to Mr. Brook's most interesting and instructive pages. I cannot but think, however, that it is well worth while that Robertson's character and career should be biographically viewed from another point of view, and after the lapse of a generation. It may well deserve fresh study from better writers in still distant times. The present forms an opportunity also of gathering up many interesting facts which might otherwise be lost. We may say that there are two great defects in Mr. Brook's work ; a failure to bring out the full and real character of the man, and also what we cannot but think an inadequate and one-sided view of the character of his teaching. He only brings out the ministerial character of Robertson : τὸ σεμνόν is stamped upon all of his that has been selected for publication. The private character of the man— brilliant, humourous, many-sided—seems hardly to have been taken into account. His remarkable individuality is to a great extent lost sight of. There is another error that arises, perhaps uncon- sciously, in the minds of many readers of the " Life and Letters " which is not so much due to Mr.

Brook as to his readers themselves. This is the tendency to identify Mr. Robertson's teaching with that of Mr. Brook. I venture to say that those who carefully study the body of Robertson's writings and compare them with Mr. Brook's own remarkable writings, will be conscious of a large divergence. That divergence is very sensibly broadened since Mr. Brook left the Church of England and surrendered the great distinctive doctrine of Christianity. Before Mr. Brook took that step he spoke with some distrust concerning Robertson's teaching. " Considered as a theological teacher I doubt if his influence will be permanent. I do not see how it can last in the rapid advance of the river of religious thought in England." Mr. Brook goes on to say, "The moment a man, having used Robertson as a means of determining his position, becomes a declared Liberal, or retires into the opposite ranks, Robertson, as a theological teacher, though not as an ethical or religious teacher, ceases to be of any use to him. Therefore, when Liberal Christianity, assisted as it is by the march of social, scientific, and political events, becomes the regnant form of Christianity, Robertson will cease to possess his present widespread influence as a theologian."

From language such as this, I must express my utter dissent. Both on the religious side and on the personal side there are new lights and new readings for the examination of the character of

Robertson. In his own time and among his own contemporaries, Robertson was censured for audacity of expression and inorthodoxy of opinion. But it is surprising to see by how very slight a line Robertson was separated from the earnest-minded men of his time to whom he so often seemed to stand in an antagonistic attitude. There is much reason to believe that in the last months of his life Robertson reverted more and more to the opinions of his earlier years. We do not for a moment believe with Mr. Brook, in the preface to the last edition of his "Life," that Robertson will be left behind in the expansion and development of the Church of the future. Mr. Brook in his secession from the Church of England, on that one cardinal point which involves the Christ of Christianity, has indicated the so-called advance which he means. The careful students of Robertson will be able to affirm, with the utmost confidence, that with such an advance—or retrocession—Robertson could have had only the scantiest measure of sympathy. Neither can we believe with Mr. Brook that the volumes associated with his name will ever lose their charm and interest and unique place in the literature of theology. We can as well believe that the writings of Butler and Pascal, the poems of Byron or Keats, will become obsolete and out of date. As long as the deepest problems of morality and religion, as long as the practical and contemplative life endure, so long will Robertson's teachings prove helpful, suggestive, and inspiriting.

Mr. Brook brings out in a way that few others could have done, the mode in which Robertson exercised his *prophetic* or teaching office. The most serious criticism on his work is that he has failed to bring out the light and shades and tones of the man as he really was. We see the great preacher distinctly enough, but of the man himself, with his infinite variety and play of character, his moody fits of depression, and then his flow of fun and fancy, of wit and wisdom, we see comparatively little. I have been favoured with the perusal of a large number of his unpublished letters, in which these characteristics are exhibited to a remarkable degree. They are marked alternately by intense depression and by the utmost gaiety of heart. He seems to take a delight in revealing to friends whom he loved most the variations of his own mental history and each incident and feeling of his own daily life. "I do not care to be looked upon even as your clergyman. Take me just as I am, as a man." Robertson was a born letter-writer as well as a born orator. His letters remind one of Eugenie de Guerin, or of Cowper. A message may have come from a neighbour living only a few streets off, and in reply he flings off side after side of note-paper full of fun and raillery, or perhaps deepening into sad and even morbid feeling. He was not unaware of his gifts as a letter-writer, and we have somewhere heard that he once had intended to bring together a collection of his letters. How admirable these are may be seen in the copious selection that has been published. But this selection fails to bring out the other side of Robertson's character, his love of social life, the fact that he was a wit and oracle of society, his manifold interest in individuals, the absolute fun and frolic of his nature, and alternating with all, the pathetic touches of gloom and despondency. His life, indeed, constitutes an intensely interesting psychological study, of some complex and discordant elements, but marked by a fearlessness, a love of truth, a tenderness and elevation of character, which for weak natures and in evil days may prove a shining beacon both for warning and help.

I have also made an attempt, by a careful analysis of his remarkable writings, to exhibit something of the changes and growth of this many-sided mind, to show the intellectual history, to exhibit what may be called his manner and his method. He was a master of clear, incisive speech. All his ideas are fully thought out to their extreme results. Many of his paragraphs are built up of sentences that have the regularity and precision of mathematical demonstration. He once said to a friend, who reported to me the incident, "These are my present ideas; I am not quite sure what they will be next year."

There were various opinions which he held in solution and on which he was anxious to receive light from whatever source it might flow. And because he was blessed with a passionate love of purity and truth, He to whom the search after truth must always be the most acceptable of services, honoured His servant by more and more revealing His truth to him. Doubtless it was a long process and an arduous struggle. It was said of him in his first curacy that he was unable to distinguish between a saving faith and a historical faith. We believe that he ultimately worked out the problem to a successful issue. To outward seeming in the first years of his life he was an Evangelical of the Evangelicals. Then there came a great revulsion. To some extent his nature became warped by a belief, which he afterwards found out to be altogether a mistake, that one whom in his early ministry he had especially loved and reverenced, had been unkind and untrue to him. In his brief sojourn in the Tyrol it is generally said his faith was shaken to the very core. In fact, however, all acute attacks are really chronic, and this unrest came from having long been tossed. But he came to firm ground on the other side. This spiritual experience has been divinely overruled to manifold good. He is a kind of link between religious experience and secular experience. Those came to listen to Robertson who ordinarily would never attend church or chapel. Those read his sermons who will read no other sermons. Those study his life who studiously hold aloof from all religious biography. The man thought and taught to the utmost of his energies and powers. Wherever he found truth he recognized it impartially, and sought to follow it. He desired to find the basis of truth that underlaid error, the soul of good in things evil. He so revolted against conventionalism, hard orthodoxy, and stereotyped forms of thought, that at times he hardly did justice to the truth and goodness that were involved in these. Being thoroughly earnest and courageous, men obtained courage and earnestness through intellectual or personal contact with him. If in some degree his simplicity of faith in the Gospel of Christ became obscured in his own mind and of others who were his closest disciples, there is abundant reason to believe that in his last days his entire, simple dependence was on the Cross of Christ.

It is always to be borne in mind, that in the case of Robertson it is a unique phenomenon that we are witnessing, the making of thought; that in his case we are not witnessing the homogeneous perfected processes of mind, but are, as it were, admitted into the laboratory of the soul, and witness the gradual evolution of opinion and experience. There are many whose happy lot it has been that their souls have never been darkened by a doubt. Thus Keble, writing from Bournemouth shortly before his death, says: "Robertson's 'Life' I have not met with, and I doubt whether I should like it; 'honest doubts,' as one calls them, are not very pleasant on a sick-bed."   But even such a saintly soul as Erskine of Linlathen, after all that he had done in the cause of sacred truth, was deeply troubled by doubt at the last, and the doubts departed before the end came. Those warrings of mind which we see in Robertson have, we think, a special value.   We are glad that, since the publication of the Brighton sermons, there has been a volume published of his earlier sermons, and we earnestly trust that nothing that he has written will ever be withheld, that we may grasp the spiritual history in all its proportions.   This is, in fact, the best compensation that can be made for the publication of writings which he never desired to be published, and which he had no opportunity of revising or bringing into definite shape.

In writing about Robertson we have a further object than dealing with the details of a life however interesting.   The personal incidents of his life have nothing abnormal about them.   And even of these, some of the most important have not been told, and probably never will be told ; nor is there any need.   But we trace in Robertson the growth of a mind, a school of the heart, a discipline of the soul.   The difficulties and sorrows, the hopes and encouragements of such a life, reproduce for us the

difficulties and sorrows, the hopes and encouragements of our lives, and more especially the lives of
those who have entered the ministry. The words
of St. Paul are in their way true of this intrepid
servant .of God : " And whether we be afflicted, it
is for your consolation and salvation which is
effectual in the enduring of the same sufferings
which we also suffer; or whether we be comforted,
it is for your consolation and salvation."

In the course of this volume it will be seen that
there were various opinions of Robertson's in which
those of the present writer do not at all agree.
Some of them appear to him to be hardly recon-
cileable with the deposit of sacred facts committed
to the Church of God. Some of these opinions
Robertson seems to have really held in solution;
some he revised; some, there is reason to believe,
he abandoned; some he retained. I have indicated,
in their place, what I look upon as the errors of his
teaching, and least willing of all would be this true-
hearted servant of God, that one single iota of
truth should be sacrificed, that the least tone of
compromise should be adopted in the discussion of
his claims and his teaching. No one would have
wished more than himself that the great verities of
the Christian faith should be upheld at whatever
cost.

Interwoven with the work there is some study of
Brighton as it was a generation ago, and of some

of Robertson's contemporaries. I have endeavoured to group various names of much interest around that of Robertson, more especially that of his tried and valued friend, Lady Byron. No apology is needed for this course. The interest belonging to Brighton is not merely local and provincial, but presents points of contact with great movements of thought, with general history and imperial interests. It was a time when Brighton presented an unusual galaxy of eminent people. The fashion and frivolity of the great watering-place seem at this period to be dominated by the commanding figure and strong, clear utterances of its most illustrious teacher. The facts, sayings, and brief inedited passages of Robertson will hardly fail to be received with much interest. I had intended to have mentioned fully my authority for every statement and incident; but though I find this impossible, I will ask my readers to believe that I have accepted nothing save from trustworthy sources, and have always sought to verify the statements. Two persons, who gave me much information, friends of my own and of Robertson, Mr. Bowdidge and Mrs. Sawyer, have passed away before the publication of these pages. Further thanks are due, among others, to the Rev. Morris Fuller, Miss Howard, the Misses (Horace) Smith, Prebendary Borrer, and Mr. Charles Boyd Robertson, the only son of the subject of these pages.

CHAPTER I.

I DO not propose to write a formal biography of Robertson. I shall seek to preserve a thin thread of narrative, for which I am mainly indebted to the autobiographical element in his writings, and bring together what information I can derive from an independent examination of those writings, and from extraneous sources of information. For fuller information, I must refer to the "Life;" but I believe I am able to bring out further points that have been overlooked in the "Life," and may be regarded as subsidiary to it.

The family is of Scottish descent. The name Struan in the family points to the Robertsons of Struan, of the clan Donnachie, who at one time held the principal part of Athol. The Struan Robertsons are stated to be the heirs male of the old house of Athol. The possessions of the Struan family were formed into a barony, but they were deprived of most of their possessions by the Earls of Athol. Their remaining possessions have been three times forfeited to the Crown, for the Robertsons have been associated with every insurrection thathas broken out in Scotland. Struan Robertson is one of the most famous names of the insurrection of 1715. He is said to have been the original of Sir Walter Scott's famous Baron of Bradwardine. In his novel of " Waverley," Scott quotes some verses of Struan Roberdson (*sic*), which shows that the man was in his mind. Robertson's great-grandfather was a cadet of the House of Struan. His grandfather was in a Scottish regiment, the eighty-third, or Glasgow Fusileers. His mother was the last of the Johnstones, of Castlemilk, Dumfries. An American visitor, who saw her after her son's death, speaks of her as a most lovely woman. Thus Robertson was thoroughly Scotch on both sides, and the *ingenium perfervidum Scotorum* shone forth conspicuously in him.

This grandfather of Robertson's performed a noble act of soldiership at one time, which obtained for him a just renown. He was at Jersey when the French made their famous attack upon the island. The Governor had virtually surrendered it, but the soldiers and the populace refused to assent, and gallantly fought and drove off the invaders. The gallant Pierson, who led them, fell. Copley's famous picture, a copy of which is found in so many houses in Jersey, reproduced his heroic death. · The second in command was also killed, and the command then devolved upon young Robertson, who in gallant style, and after severe fighting, achieved a victory, due in much to his own valour and conduct.

Robertson's father long survived him. In his later years he removed to Bath, to be near his eldest son, Struan; and at Bath he died. In his letter to Mr. Field, the American publisher, he speaks of his son, and makes mention of a remarkable supernatural event, which may be commended to the Psychical Society:—

"The last of the Napiers is gone. You recollect seeing the portrait of my friend, that glorious soldier, Sir Charles Napier, in our sitting-room. . . . In the early part of February, as I had taken my seat in the College Chapel, a little before 3 p.m., I had a mental vision that Sir William was at that moment dying. Next morning I said, 'Mark my words, Sir William Napier died yesterday afternoon, when I was in chapel.' . . . Tuesday morning brought a letter, saying that Sir William died on the Sunday afternoon, without a sigh. Two other instances in my life have occurred of this spiritual communication with me of departing friends, so that I can have no doubt of the intercourse of spirits in this nether world; and I think we may see from Holy Writ that even departed spirits have held communion with those not yet glorified. . . . Sir William said he had a second self following him continually, and essaying to be joined to him. I have no doubt that 'the second self' of which Sir William spoke was the one, to use the words of the sermons, attendant on a life of spirituality: 'A living Redeemer stands beside him, goes with him, talks with him, as a man with his friend.' . . . I have had some most interesting and extraordinary letters sent me, to be added to the forthcoming volume of my son's letters."

He was like "young Edwin," a marvellous boy. We have had the pleasure of inspecting some of the poetry and drawings of his youth. There were lines of feeling and promise, in his own hand, addressed to Mrs. Milner Gibson, the wife of the Cabinet Minister, who died in her Paris home this year (1885). There is a picture of Mazeppa with wild horses, the horses' heads being done with astonishing power and freedom. His Greek caligraphy is exquisite, and in his sentences there is never an accent omitted or misplaced. In French he was absolutely perfect; in France he could easily pass as a Frenchman. His German and Italian were excellent. His Schiller seems to have been ever by his side. In every school to which he went he was pre-eminent; and if his classical education had been better planned and more consistently carried out as a whole, he would have swept Oxford of the prizes.

A few notes on his early days, in regard to his training and education, should be made. He was born in London, in 1816. Besides some education at a country grammar school in England—and England

owes a vast debt of gratitude to the grammar
schools that have trained so many of her best
children—he spent various years of study in Scotland
and in France. It is not difficult to recognize in
his work decided traces of both his Scotch and his
French training, a combination more frequent in
history than at the present time. In the logical
faculty, in the elaboration and thoroughness of his
theological work, he reminds us of the best efforts
of the divinity schools of Scotland, and in the lucid
diamond-like brightness of his style he reminds us
of the writings of the school of the French historians. According to a law of heredity, which we
find widely dominant from his earliest years, he had
a passion for his father's profession of arms. This
did not meet his father's views, a deeply pious man,
who wished his son to enter the Church; but for
the Church, at this time, Robertson felt a decided
disinclination, and, indeed, at no time do his affections appear to have been thoroughly devoted to
that profession. It is not without a kind of pathos
that after such an elaborate and complex education
we find him settled in flat Suffolk, in the office of a
country attorney. At this time he began to develop
a strong poetical taste, and more even than Frank
Osbaldistone, he seemed to verify the lines of
Pope :—

> "A clerk condemn'd his father's soul to cross,
> And pen a stanza when he should endorse."

There are various passages in his writings which indicate that this measure of legal training was not thrown away upon him. His acquaintance with the profession did not impress him with much veneration for it. " Look at a *Nisi Prius* lawyer, with clearest notions of evidence, principles of law, &c., &c., and withal, how much of personal meanness and hatred, of pettifogging and professional lying!" In one of his lectures he quoted, with much approval, Burke's celebrated saying, that " no man comprehends less of the majesty of the English constitution than the *Nisi Prius* lawyer, who is always dealing with technicalities and precedents." Similar language of disparagement might be adduced, yet no doubt his legal training was a very useful element in Robertson's education. Somewhat careless in his own arrangements, he was a man of great promptness and exactitude in all that concerned others. He was distinguished for that close reasoning and keeping to the point which is the characteristic of the highest forensic minds. His indoctrination with the law helped to make him a good reasoner, and also, for a clergyman, an excellent man of business.

There can never have been any young man with a stronger feeling of duty than Robertson, and he persevered, in order to carry out his father's wishes, until his health broke down through the sedentary occupation which he detested. The good father accordingly summoned him home. The family, after some wandering, had settled at Cheltenham, and finally migrated to Bath. Many persons have visited Rodney House, Cambray, where Robertson resided for some years of his youth with his parents. The family used to go to the old parish church where the late Dean Close was Vicar, and at that time a living power in Cheltenham, and the Rev. Frederick Arnold, late Rector of Brimington, curate. There existed a deep vein of religious thought and feeling in his character, which expanded, side by side with his military predilections. His father, through his wife's family, who had rendered some service to the King when Prince William, had met his son's wishes by obtaining for him the promise of a cavalry commission in the Indian army. For years Robertson looked upon himself as a soldier. In a little unpublished poem of his, addressed to Mr. and Mrs. Milner Gibson, who had presented him with Lamartine's works, he says :—

> " And when, by chance or glory led,
>   In other lands I roam,
> When busy memory fondly turns
> With pleasing pain to home.

> "These volumes, when they meet my gaze,
>   Shall wake in every line
> The thought of her whose praise must grace
> A loftier harp than mine."

He would find plenty of military reading, and his

father could tell him many stories of the Royal Artillery, and of his great friend, Sir Charles Napier. He went to Chatham, to visit a brother who was in the Royal Engineers, where he would gain an insight into the practical work of a soldier. We have before us a copy of a translation of a German poet by him, which is dated Paris, December, 1835. There was probably some object of military education in this visit, which did not extend beyond a few months.

All these plans, however, were abandoned, and it was determined that he should make the Church his profession. His biographer says that his hopes were " doomed to disappointment," and that he was " apparently impelled by circumstances into the clerical profession." This was not, however, the case. Side by side with his desire to be a soldier there had grown up the desire to be a soldier of the Cross. Side by side with his military reading had been the theological reading. If one set of tastes impelled him in one direction, another set of tastes impelled him in a different direction. When the direct offer of a cavalry commission reached him he had just matriculated at Brasenose with a view of entering the ministry. If he had still clung to the army, the loving father would have given way to his wish, or at his age—he was older than most men that enter the University—he could have asserted his freedom of choice. He could at any time have returned to his first love, the army, and have given up the University. It is never said that he regretted his change of view, but he was delighted with the offer of a commission, " for it would not be said that he went into the Church because he could not get into the army."

There is a remarkable autobiographical poem of Robertson's which tells us of the workings of his mind in this matter. It was suggested by Wordsworth's immortal poem, "The Happy Warrior." It is interesting to observe that the date of Robertson's lines is prior to the offering of a commission and the Oxford matriculation. He shows that there were still higher phases of a soldier's life than Wordsworth had mentioned, though we may well believe that Wordsworth had them in his heart. It is to be observed that it is not on the old Pope couplet, but in the heroic measure of Wordsworth that these lines are written :—

> " No dreamy Painter !—other far is he,
> The happy Warrior I would wish to be,
> Amid the scoffs profane, the ribald jeers,
> And worse, the scornful silence of his peers,
> He dares to stand confest, not all untried,
> A lowly servant of the Crucified.
> The cost was counted. What he braved he knew—
> Ease, honour, glory, to the winds he threw :
> On the cold earth his master had his bed,
> Then why should roses lull the servant's head ?
> Shall he desire the favour of the world
> Whose bitterest malice on his Lord was hurled ?

Or shall his joys divide his blood-bought soul
With Him who died to save and now demands the whole?
    . . . And shall the hour of danger find him quail
When hurtles through the air the iron hail?
He, who in every shot that hisses by,
In every flushing sabre can descry
The friend that yet may herald him to rest.
Shall he be backward to expose his breast?
Oh! for a moment can this warrior dread
The few gore-drops that stain his bridal-bed?
    But in the heat of conflict. if a streak
Of sudden paleness blanch his manly cheek,
Stranger, believe it was no selfish fear
That seem'd to check his downward sword's career.
It was one sigh for thousands that around
In writhing torture press'd the gory ground,
And thousands more who reckless, unforgiven,
Stand suddenly before the bar of Heaven!
'Tis this, that in the fever of the strife,
While careless of his own, of other's life,
Makes him a miser—spares the suppliant foe,
Strikes but where Duty sternly points the blow,
Fans the fierce scene with Mercy's angel-wing,
And robs the tyrant War of half his sting!"

No doubt in the army he would have been a missionary and Christian teacher. It is interesting to observe that had Frederick Robertson accepted the commission he would have perished with the thousands who fell in Afghanistan. The path of Christian usefulness would have been closed by premature death.

In the October of 1837, the first year of the young Queen's reign, Frederick Robertson went up to reside at Brasenose. His rooms are still pointed out. A painted window, of much beauty, in the little chapel here preserves his memory, with the inscription, "The goodly fellowship of the Prophets praise Thee!" Here Robertson carried on with ardour his theological reading. "Bonus textuarias est bonus theologus," and Robertson is said to have learned both the English and the Greek Testament by heart. He is only a poor theologian who knows nothing but theology, and Robertson sought out all available paths of knowledge akin to the queen of sciences. He found himself in the midst of what is known as the great Oxford movement. He endeavoured to master the teaching of Mr. Newman and Dr. Pusey. He thought himself in a condition to refute the erroneous teaching of Tract No. 90. He could have put himself within the range of the personal influence of these great men, but there is little or no trace of this having been the case. He seemed to have kept his mind free, both from the turbulent party spirit and the intense fervour of those days. At this date he was an Evangelical of the Evangelicals, with a decided leaning towards moderate Calvinism. He interested himself in the practical work of the Church, and endeavoured to promote the interests of such societies as the Church Missionary Society and the Society for Promoting Christianity among the Jews. Such efforts have always met with a very languid response in the atmosphere of Oxford, at least on Evangelical lines. The Universities' Mission in Central Africa, started by Dr. Livingstone, has a better story to tell.

The writer has had the pleasure of examining some of the books which Robertson used at Brasenose. The books were not heavy, but they had the traces of having been thoroughly handled, and must have grown into the very fibre and structure of the reader's mind. We were especially struck with an interleaved copy of the " Republic " of Plato. It was full of analyses and notes; had evidently been read and re-read from cover to cover. We are told that his copy of the " Ethics " of Aristotle showed the same condition. The notes were quite in the style of a first-class honour-man. It is to be regretted that he did not take his first-class; but the peculiar good of the Oxford system he emphatically had made his own. That he had studied the historians and philosophers, the logic and mental science of the schools is apparent, we might almost say, in every sermon that he preached.

He was a member of the Union Society, which, with a great deal of pleasure and many conveniences attached to it, consumes a great deal of time in desultory reading, writing, and speechifying. He became Treasurer of the Society, an office that argues that he must have been a frequent and fair speaker, and also socially popular. The views which he expressed were at times thoroughly ascetic. He opposed both novel-reading and the theatre, and on the theatre question he was opposed by Mr. Ruskin in a sarcastic tone that elicited much laughter. We quote the entries relating to him in the reports of the Society :—

"*Feb.* 1*st*, '38.—'That the proceedings of the Convention, on the retreat of James II., was unjustifiable.' Robertson, of Brasen-nose, in the affirmative."

"*May* 24*th*, '38.—'That the reading of good and well-written novels is neither prejudicial to the moral nor to the individual character.' Robertson, B.N.C., in the negative."

"*Oct.* 25*th*, '38.—'That theatrical representations are, upon the whole, highly beneficial to the life of a nation.' Robertson, B.N.C., in the negative. Ruskin, Ch. Ch., in the affirmative."

"*Nov.* 8*th*.—Mr. Robertson moved, 'That the true objects of poetry have been more realized by modern than by ancient writers.' The motion was carried by a majority of two."

"*Jan.* 31*st*, '39.—Robertson, of B.N.C., Treasurer, in the chair.

"*Feb.* 7*th*.—   „   „   „

"*Feb.* 14*th*.—   „   „   „

"*Feb.* 28*th*.—Mr. Robertson moved, 'That in the administration of the affairs of India by a British legislature, a one-sided toleration has been in effect an intolerance unparalleled in the policy of heathen nations.' The motion was carried."

It will be seen that Robertson, at the Union, took everything *au grand sérieux*. On one occasion, when he was about to speak, he asked a friend to pray for him. The last subject mentioned in the report is one that indicates, as was undoubtedly the case, that he had the greatest interest in, and understanding of, the affairs of India, and of the relation of toleration to religion in that country. In all probability the imitative parliament of the Union, if, indeed, it represented its prototype in England, was too indifferent to an Indian question.

On one occasion, at the Union, an honourable member proposed, "That in the opinion of this Society, Eclecticism is the only true philosophy." To this an honourable member proposed as an amendment, "That this House is unable to grasp the idea of Eclecticism," which was agreed to almost unanimously. On one occasion we have seen members of the Union voting just as they happened to be sitting, scarcely one of them taking the trouble to cross the floor.

Robertson also wrote a poem for the Newdigate, which did not succeed, however, in obtaining the medal. It is very rarely, however, that Newdigate examiners select the prize poems. Tennyson obtained the English prize poem at Cambridge; but his friends have rather regretted it, and say that it was owing to an accident. One examiner, so the story goes, who knew a little about poetry, was sorely puzzled by it, and wrote on the back of the MS., "Look at this." The other examiner, who knew nothing of poetry, thought that was the selected composition, and voted accordingly.

We might say of Robertson, with some confidence, that it would have been easy for him to have obtained the highest honours of the University. His mind and tastes were in thorough accord with the Oxford studies. The only difference was that the University mapped out a precise line for him, whereas he preferred to work out a line for himself. We believe that the course prescribed by the University is in itself a wiser and safer course than any which an undergraduate would be likely to prescribe for himself. With the philosophy of Plato and Aristotle, with logic and mental science, Robertson was probably as much at home as any man of his time, and Mr. Dobson, the Head of Cheltenham College, *laus a laudato viro*, guarantees the excellence of his scholarship. It is to be regretted that he did not turn his abilities and attainments to practical account. In vain the examiners, having looked at his papers, entreated him to go in for honours. He was unwilling, and they had to content themselves with giving the honorary fourth, usual in the case of high promise

CHAPTER II.

WINCHESTER, CHELTENHAM, AND OXFORD.

Mr. Robertson was ordained deacon at Winchester, by the Bishop of Winchester, July 10th, 1840, and priest the Trinity Sunday of the following year. He seems to have much impressed Bishop Sumner on both occasions, especially on the latter. His title was given him by Mr. Nicholson, the Rector of St. Maurice. He did not complete the ordinary term of two years, being obliged to give up through ill-health shortly after taking priest's orders. The inner history of his life during his diaconate was of a very remarkable kind. He became thoroughly ascetic. He avoided society. He rarely partook of dainties. His whole life was passed in prayer, fasting, and his parish work. He combined the rigour of the Trappist with the religious system of those who held Trappists in abhorrence. At last he became ill and thought he was dying. He rather enjoyed the prospect, and determined to preach as long as he could stand. I made a pilgrimage to Winchester, which was full of interest, to see what facts I could glean about Robertson. I fortunately met the clerk, who recollected him clearly. The churchwarden, a worthy tradesman, knew nothing of his history after he had left Winchester. He thought him a very fine young man, he was quite ' soldier-looking,' they had a very good opinion of him, and expected that he would do well. The name of the clerk was Clarke; his father had held the office before him; they had had the office between them for sixty years. The clerk remembered going to speak to him on the subject of the Holy Communion. So impressed was the old clerk with his military bearing that he insisted that Robertson had been a soldier, and I could not succeed in divesting him of this impression. He was so fond, said the clerk, of military images. He was curate of the united parishes of St. Maurice, St. Mary Kalendar, and St. Peter's, Colebrook. These parishes are represented by the one church of St. Maurice, which is practically the only parish. There is just a trace of St. Peter's, Colebrook, in an old garden wall. He never actually preached at St. Maurice's. All the time that he was there the church was undergoing the process of being rebuilt. In fact it had been entirely pulled down, except the tower. The services were consequently held at the neighbouring church of St. John's, Lawrence. St. Maurice has some curious points about it. There is a right of way from the street, one might almost say through the church itself, to the cathedral precincts. The buildings on each side were church buildings. The entrance to the galleries is on the other side of this passage, and the gate of the passage is closed at night. This quarter of the town is one of the most picturesque in Winchester, with old gabled houses, a wooden colonnade, and a "butter cross." His former lodgings were pointed out to me, a room with a bow-window. It is now a public-house. There is a very pretty prospect looking towards St. Giles' Hill.

He seems, as was natural for a junior clergyman, to have undertaken a good deal of the surplice duty. His first entry of baptism was August 28th, 1840, his last May 23rd of the following year. He celebrated marriages, which, as deacon, was hardly in order. His last funeral was May 23rd. He made a singular mistake in inserting a number of entries on a wrong page, an error which was set right by the rector, Mr. Nicholson, in a note in the register-book.

This Mr. Nicholson was rather a remarkable man. He was a good man; in wretched health, indeed, almost in a' dying state, and was greatly beloved by his people. It is, I believe, quite a mistake that at this early date Robertson was much sought out. In fact, all the interests and sympathies of the people flowed towards Mr. Nicholson, the worthy, suffering rector. Between him and his rector there existed the strongest identity of feeling. One cannot but look upon Robertson's first year as one of the deepest import. Just as the boy is father to the man, so the first year in the ministry often indicates the colour and complexion of a whole career. Perhaps it is not until the close of a ministry, if even then, that the glow and freshness of feeling of that primal time returns. On the first day of his ministry the old clerk told me that he went and consulted him about receiving the Holy Communion. Other personal proofs of effective work done have come to my knowledge. One who knew his whole career says that his sermons were never more taking than during his ministry at Winchester. And yet during this time he was greatly puzzling himself about a matter which was on the very threshold of that religious life, the difference between an historical and a saving faith.

It has been sometimes said, and there is a great deal of truth in the observation, that the most spiritual part of the work of a church is done by its humblest members. The bishop has the claims of politics, society, and administration constantly upon him. His finest energies are sometimes exhausted upon matters of ritual and rubric, which, compared with the essential verities of religious life, are a mere hewing of wood and drawing of water for the congregation. One day a bishop went to visit a great city, where he had once laboured as a parish priest, and was the life and soul of a large social gathering. Presently there came a solitary knock at the door. It was a poor man, who used to be visited by the bishop when he was a parish priest, and who had been enjoined always to see him when there was an 'opportunity. The good bishop took the pauper by the hand and led him to his study, where he sat down and read and explained the Bible to him, and prayed with him, as in the old days. It must have been as refreshing to the bishop as to his humble friend thus to revert to the simplest and most delightful duties of the ministry. Similarly there is one of our bishops who has been heard to say that he could never shake off the influences of the world until he had been to read and pray with some sick neighbours. Similarly in the case of the beneficed clergyman of an important living, there are frequent deductions to be made from his spiritual work. He has often 'to serve tables instead of giving himself to preaching and prayer. He has the work of parochial organization and supervision. He has a multitude of social and public claims. He has the thought and literature of the day to watch, and the pulse of society to feel. He is almost inevitably removed from constant contact with the sick and poor, and often becomes surrounded with a stifling atmosphere of secularity.

All these conditions are happily reversed in the

case of the young man who has just taken holy orders. To him is assigned what is too often professedly regarded as the lowest rung of the clerical ladder, but which is, in truth, its highest duty and sweetest privilege, the work of visiting the sick and poor. If he is a true man, it is a work which he will never forego as long as he lives. He has to deal with the sick bodies and sicklier souls of the most degraded of his parishioners, with all that round of clerical duty which is the most common-place, and at the same time the most divine order of service. That "surplice duty," from which the rector very probably considers himself exempt, brings him into contact with the people, on the occasions when their hearts are most open and their sympathies most keen; the baptism, the marriage, and the funeral. His leisure time is spent almost necessarily in his preparation for the pulpit. He would rather give what comes of his own thoughts and labour than read the lithographed sermon or servilely copy out the thoughts of other men. So it often happens that the ardent young curate, far beyond his fellows, is a profound student of spiritual things, exercising day by day his ministry of reconciliation, and day by day living in the region of spiritual truth, and so living an isolated but spiritualized existence. He ventures to make trial of his own armour and to build up for himself his own conclusions. If he has a truly scientific spirit, he does so with diffidence and modesty, holding his opinions in solution, and still listening with reverence to those who are masters and rabbis. It is with a new sense of happiness and power that he finds himself able to examine truth with some degree of originality and independence, that he is able to confide in his own opinions, and that he is himself one of the company of scholars and thinkers. No doubt this stage of intellectual development has also its snares. Of all sciences it is least likely that originality can be found in theology ; whatever is opposed to the Vincentian canon, *quod semper, quod ubique, quod ab omnibus,* necessarily incurs some suspicion, and although there may be a true development of the religious *gnosis,* this must proceed in orderly lines, as derived from the treasure of truth.

In the path of Biblical criticism Robertson went very much further than is done by the average clergyman. He carried out here as in every other department of life, the motto *approfondissez.* The vast mass of Biblical expository teaching which he has left behind him, attest his powers and his studies as a student and explainer of divine truth. Teaching of this kind is by no means the most popular sort of preaching, and Robertson showed how far he aimed above mere popularity when he deliberately selected it as a regular vehicle of instruction. Not, indeed, for the intellectual interest of a fashionable and admiring crowd, but for the building up of the solidity of Christian character is Biblical study the one thing necessary. It may be said, however, that there are still larger regions of thought than those that are contained in theology, pure and simple. Indeed, a man who understands theology alone must be a very poor theologian. The one thing necessary for a true theologian is to attain breadth of interest and sympathy. Just as we have pure and applied mathematics so we have pure and applied theology. All the problems of life and character and society, of history and politics, of metaphysics and science, become inextricably mingled with religion. The key to the whole labyrinth is only to be found in Christ. Just as nature gives us wheat, and not loaves; wood and clay, stone and marble, but not houses; so revelation gives us the material from which the enlightened mind constructs its systems of truth. In the case of Robertson it would appear that gradually the idea of the relatedness of religion to every thought and province of life became more and more intense. He was a God-possessed man. He saw God, the working of His laws, the supremacy of His will throughout life, throughout the universe. He seemed to be ever making grander and fresher discoveries of divine character. Here was a field of exploration which was absolutely illimitable. There was no object of observation however grand or minute, no proposition that could be submitted to the human mind, but the thought of God both veiled and illuminated it.

There is yet another development in the character of a religious teacher. This is the growth of his own soul, the construction of his own character. It is quite possible for men to study theology, and even to study it profoundly, simply on the intellectual side and without any effort of the heart. There is such a thing, as the world has often seen, as godless orthodoxy. The heart may be as totally untouched by religious sympathy in the study of religious problems, as the vivisectionist may be devoid of sympathy in his process of analysis. Gradually he would feel his way. The first thing that a diligent young divine does is to select the spiritual teacher for whose thoughts and ways of expression he feels the highest degree of affinity. In the case of most earnest young men the preference is given not so much to some great dogmatic teacher—though there are preferences this way also—as to some expositors of Holy Writ. Just as all natural science finds the subject-matter in Nature, so all theological science finds the subject-matter in revelation. In Robertson's day young men drew much from Trench and Alford, just as Trench and Alford drew so much from Olshausen and Stier. Then our student goes on to the verification of authorities and the conflict of views. In all this there is a leaning upon authority. But the time passes away, during which the mind is to so large an extent passive. The scholar finds himself more and more thrown upon his own thought and insight and intellectual resources.

In his latter time at Winchester Robertson was very far from strong and well, and there were unpleasant symptoms which seemed to threaten consumption. Several of his family suffered from that complaint, which seems to love to destroy the young and brilliant: the " death of the chosen," as it has been called. One great means of cure in the first stage of such an illness is travel and change. Sir Henry Holland used to say that a man should change his residence, and if he could not change his residence he should change his room, and if he could not change his room he should change his furniture. Robertson started on the tour which is now so hackneyed, the Rhine and Switzerland, which is ever fresh and glorious to those who travel for the first time. This tour had very important consequences. It led to his intimacy with Malan, and through Malan to his marriage.

A few words may here be said about César Malan. The present writer had the privilege of knowing him, and made his acquaintance in his Swiss home in much the same way that Robertson did. Malan's prophecy to Robertson has often been quoted— " Mon très-cher frère, vous aurez une triste vie et un triste ministère." This was not, however, so much a prophecy personal to Robertson as a statement of the view which Malan held of the ministerial life. He told me, perhaps he was thinking of Robertson at the time, that within his experience very few ministers were happy men. This is what Robertson says of Malan's prophecy: "It may be so, but present peace is of little consequence. If we sin, we must be miserable; but if we be God's own, that misery will not last long. Misery for sin is better worth having than peace. I love old Malan from my very soul, and hate disputing with him, even though it is the dispute of Christian brothers."

Dr. Malan was descended from an ancient Protestant family of Provence, who left France after the revocation of the Edict of Nantes. He was the first-fruits of that remarkable revival in Geneva which attended the visit of Mr. Robert Haldane in 1817. The way in which he was expelled the Establishment by the "Venerable Company of Pastors," as the General Assembly of the Genevese Church is called, was very curious :—Disapproving of evangelical preaching, that degenerate body, in order, as they said, to secure peace and avoid scandal, ordained that every preacher should sign a declaration that he would not in preaching allude to the following points :—1. The union of the Divine nature in the person of Jesus Christ; 2. Original sin; 3. The operation of the Spirit of grace ; 4. The doctrine of election. The tendency of such an arrangement as this would be entirely to destroy all freedom of Christian teaching, and to eliminate therefrom some of the most precious truths of Revelation. Refusing to sign, Dr. Malan was expelled the ministry, as were afterwards those distinguished pastors, his friends Gaussen and D'Aubigné. Dr. Malan was one well fitted to be a confessor, and, if necessary, a martyr. His career, therefore, furnishes an important chapter in the religious history of Switzerland. His preaching in the first part of the century is associated with the revival of religion in Geneva, and the attempt of the Arian and Socinian party to crush the truth by means of persecution. But, in truth, the controversial character of Dr. Malan is that of which we most easily lose sight. His whole soul overflowed with love, tenderness, and earnestness. Those who made his acquaintance at once recognized the unconscious portrait which he has furnished of himself in his stories and in his hymns. That simple, childlike docility and faith, that constant realizing of the invisible world, that love towards the Saviour and the brethren, made him indeed a holy minstrel, "a sweet singer of Israel," and exercised the stronger impression for those brought within the range of his personal influence.

The writer of these pages well recollects the circumstances under which he had the happiness of forming the acquaintance of the late Dr. Malan. It

is with peculiar pleasure that he recalls a visit made
to him at his Genevan home about two years before
his death. There are many who used to think that
a visit to Geneva would be incomplete without
seeing and hearing César Malan.

A charming country drive of about five miles
brought me to the little hamlet in which the good
pastor had pitched his tent for the remainder of his
pilgrimage on earth. His home was quite destitute
of pretension, but it was of sufficient size, stored
with all necessary comforts, and even simple luxuries,
and had the advantage of a beautiful garden.
Nothing more beautiful than the site can be well
imagined. The kindly guidance of Providence had
literally placed the faithful pastor by green pastures
and still waters. He was within the neighbourhood
of the most beautiful of lakes, and the most majestic
of all mountains. I have rarely, I question if I have
ever, been more impressed by any man's appearance
than by Dr. Malan's. He was seventy-five years of
age at this time; but his eye was not dim, nor yet
hardly his natural force abated. The freshness and
earnestness with which he threw himself into conversation perhaps gave the idea of greater strength
than was actually the case. The venerable figure,
the bright, piercing eye, the snow-white locks, at
once suggested to me the resemblance to the de-
lineation by ancient masters of St. John the Evangelist. I had never seen him before, but he saluted

me with affectionate cordiality, and exclaimed, "Ah! whom have we here?" or words to that effect, and added, in tones which I shall never forget, " A poor sinner saved through Jesus Christ?" We sat down and talked together over many subjects. He spoke English, not quite accurately, indeed, but with great force and intelligence. He took me out into the garden to see Mont Blanc, visible enough on a clear day, but not on this occasion, on account of some haziness of atmosphere. Somewhat regretfully he reminded me that the mount was no longer Swiss, but French. He talked to me about Merle d'Aubigné and his work, and appeared quite exultant about the success to which it had attained in England. Of England, indeed, and of his English friends, he spoke as familiarly as of his own Switzerland. He told me that he still went into Geneva every Sunday morning and ministered to a little flock. " There were many," he said, with a happy smile and pleasant humour, "who did not know him, but looked upon him as an old fox." His whole being seemed suffused with peace and joy.

Dr. Malan long suffered from a dangerous malady, in which his advanced age afforded but little hope for recovery. He died at his beautiful residence, near Geneva, on Sunday, the 8th of May, 1864. Vandœuvres will long be visited and recollected by Christian pilgrims. He was born on the 7th of July, 1787, and was consequently in his seventy-seventh year. His end was perfect peace. He bore his illness with humble and courageous resignation. He would listen quietly to the prayers and exhortations of his friends and his sons, and humbly add his amen. When he expressed his resignation and trust, and desire to go to his Saviour, it was in words in which the great preacher and theologian had quite disappeared, and left only the humble and loving disciple.

The following letter of Malan's to a deceased sister of the author's will be read with interest :—

"Genève, Dec. 15, 1862.

"Amen! chère et vivante sœur en Jesus. Oui, qu'il plaise au Seigneur, de rapporter à sa gloire le beau et facile talent qu'il vous confie. Ah, c'est un grand honneur que l'Esprit Saint fait reposer sur mes faibles chants, quand Il les addresse aux âmes par le langage que vous leur avez donné. Et quelle bénédiction n'est-ce pas sur *nous*, qu'Il daigne ainsi se servir de nos bouches pour répéter à plusieurs que connaître le don du Père en Jesus, c'est avoir, ici-bas, déjà, des gages de l'éternelle joie. Je vous remercie donc, de nouveau et cordialement, et avec vous je demande à Celui qui seul bénit, qu'il fasse reposer sur votre belle et bonne ouvrage le regard de son approbation.

"Chère sœur, quelle allégresse sera la votre quand vous verrez dans la demeure paternelle des âmes que vos chants avaient unis à Jesus!

"Votre cher frère est joint, dans mon cœur, à

votre doux nom. Qu'il plaise au Tout Bon, de vous bénir l'un et l'autre, et aussi le ferait-il !

"César Malan."

Robertson married, at Geneva, Helen, third daughter of Sir George William Denys, of Eastin Neston, Northamptonshire, equerry to the Duke of Sussex.

He now began to look round for a curacy suitable for his delicate state of health, and where all duties would be shared. He obtained one at Cheltenham, where his family were residing. He first lived quite close to them, in Rodney Place, and afterwards removed to Park Place.

Christ Church crowns the moderate acclivity known as Bay's Hill. It commands a fine prospect, and the long range of the Malvern Hills. It was, at least until lately, the finest church in Cheltenham, and its tall, graceful tower dominates the landscape. It is a wealthy parish, but attached to it was the poor hamlet of Alstone. Here there were school-room services, which in their way were as important and as well attended as those in the parish church. The great preacher was the incumbent, Archibald Boyd, then in the prime of those powers which were afterwards so appreciated in London and in Exeter. Robertson sat at the great teacher's feet with intense interest. He heard with a kind of admiring despair. Yet even then there were probably persons who might have observed distinguishing intellectual characteristics which were even beyond Mr. Boyd. It is usual to suppose that Robertson's sermons formed the outcome of great spiritual and intellectual conflicts of later years. But the very sermons preached in Brighton in some instances had been preached at Cheltenham within the memory of people still living. The title of the last volume of his published sermons was derived from a sermon preached at Christ Church, which may hold its own in a comparison with the Brighton sermons.

There was a very handsome white stone pulpit, with a stone reading-desk beneath and the clerk's stone desk beneath that—the old three-decker style, which was then considered a bulwark of Protestantism. The modern innovation of the evening sermon was at this time unknown in the parish. There was the Alstone evening service at the schoolroom, which, as a regular thing, was undertaken by Mr. Boyd, and only very occasionally by his curate, Mr. Robertson. The afternoon service was not, as an afternoon service often becomes, one for children and servants, but comprised the orthodox people who dine late and also desire to attend evening song.[1] The best memorials of Robertson's Cheltenham teaching are to be found in his latest volume of sermons.

[1] Some interesting details are to be found in "The Golden Decade of a Favoured Town," by Contem Ignotus. Elliott Stock. 1884.

The late Vicar of Cheltenham, Canon Fenn, showed me a few scanty entries in the church books, but they are quite devoid of interest. In those days there were no sermon-books kept.

In his early years he always preached, and indeed apparently somewhat strictly, from his manuscript. Sometimes he preached extemporaneously, when called upon to do so through Mr. Boyd's absence from illness, but, in the judgment of his friends, not with very much success. Yet the faculty was as much in him as in Sheridan and Disraeli, who, failures at first, became such conspicuous orators. Yet one who watched him carefully at Cheltenham writes: "We heard him lecture extemporaneously at Cheltenham, at the Philosophical Institution in Cheltenham, with singular fluency, beauty, and power; and have also heard him speak at one or two public religious meetings with striking eloquence." A lecture of his has been published, but never included in his works, of a thoroughly Protestant character.

Cheltenham is a busy and prosperous place now. Its waters are regaining something of their old reputation, and the schools of Cheltenham have become famous. The Cheltenham of Robertson's time was in a state of still higher prosperity. Queen Adelaide and many royal princes stayed here at the Clarence Hotel, and multitudes of coaches stopped every day in the largest inn-yard

of England.   The pump-rooms, long deserted, but
at the present time once more beginning to be
frequented, were crowded every morning.   A single
individual had built the once splendid suburb of
Pitville.   There were two very different parties
at Cheltenham in those days—the fashionable and
religious parties.   Sometimes they blended insen-
sibly into each other, and sometimes they stood out
in the sharpest antagonism.   It is curious to compare with the records of religious life in Cheltenham
such a work as Grantley Berkeley's "Life and
Recollections."   He has an interesting passage on
the growth of the town : " Cheltenham, like
Brighton, began very soon to stretch out its arms
on the surrounding lanes, and to turn what used
to be the pretty by-ways and paths into streets and
roads.   The market was no longer held in the High
Street, shops spread themselves in all directions,
magnificent promenades and convenient places
for drinking the waters arose, and from a little
neat country, but rather hungry-looking town,
it became in size almost a city."   It is foreign
to our purpose to speak of the fashionable side
of Cheltenham life, or of the influence of the
Berkeley family upon the town, or the miserable
feuds and still more miserable scandals.   Earl Fitz-
hardinge, as he became, was for a long time the
King of Cheltenham.   He gave the town deer
and hounds, and led the huntsmen many a long

chase around the Cotswolds, and his doubtful
career had a sinister effect on the place. In his last
years he associated much with a nonconformist
minister, Dr. Morton Brown. This well-known
writer and preacher gave the writer an interesting
account of his relations with the earl. He, with a
deputation, had waited upon him on some public
business, I believe to ask him to present a petition
to the House of Lords. It so happened that the
earl and the minister were left alone in the room as
the deputation filed away. "I cannot forget," said
Morton Brown, turning to the earl, "that I am a
minister of God, and that you have a soul to be
saved; and therefore let me ask you whether you
have yourself ever given any thoughts to your
own soul." The earl then told the nonconformist
minister that no clergyman had ever spoken to him
in such a direct and straightforward way, and this
was the beginning of a long acquaintance and intercourse, which seems to have excited a good deal of
curiosity in the country.

There was yet another person living at Cheltenham at this time, of kindred character and kindred
genius, Sydney Dobell. "Frederick Robertson,
Sydney Dobell, and Alfred Tennyson were all
dwelling there together, and might have been seen
on the same summer morning or the same summer
evening, at different parts of the same town, weaving
that wondrous prose or composing that wondrous

verse, which was to help to raise them to the pedestals of the immortals. They were remarkably kindred spirits, and yet we are not aware that at any time they knew each other. We do know that Dobell and Tennyson met and knew each other as friends some time after the former had become famous. We remember himself telling us about a certain glorious walk that he had with Tennyson and Carlyle at Malvern. Dobell had been brought up in a very secluded and isolated way, and his home was generally out of Cheltenham, either between Cheltenham and Gloucester, on the glorious Birdlip Height, or on Chorlton Kings, between Cheltenham and Oxford, two miles out of Cheltenham, sheltered by clustering firs and encircled by the amphitheatre of the Cotswolds.

At this date, too, the town of Cheltenham had a kind of literary character.

Tennyson, with his mother, sisters, and brother Horatio, lived at 1, St. John's Square. "Like himself his songs are heard, but he himself is rarely seen." Nor was he much seen at Cheltenham. He was often in the habit, however, of walking and musing in what was then known as "Jessop's Gardens," which were quite contiguous to his mother's house, and no doubt many of the stanzas of "In Memoriam" were born there. That exquisite poem was published during the author's residence at Cheltenham. Tennyson is supposed to have had Cheltenham in view when he wrote the lines,—

> "A goodly place . . . .
> A realm of pleasure, many a mound,
> And many a shadow-chequer'd lawn,
> Full of the city's stilly sound."

It is interesting to find in Robertson's biography a personal reference to the town. Robertson himself thus speaks of Cheltenham : " The Cotswold Hills which surround Cheltenham, exhibiting a great variety of outline and rich in woods, were in extreme beauty from their colouring. Among those hills are some of the loveliest valleys I know anywhere. The building, too, of Cheltenham is far better in style than that of Brighton, greatly varied, and almost all the detached villas in good taste, some Italian, others Elizabethan ; but there is an air of lightness and grace about it which is quite different from cockneyism. This is much assisted by the abundance of trees with which the town is filled ; many of the streets like boulevards, one long walk of ancient elms, a noble avenue." Walking over to Leckhampton he particularly noted the farm of Major Macready, the brother of the great actor. " It was surrounded with beautiful iron rails, and a trellis-work of iron extending above them. Around it and in it is a garden border, full of most rare and carefully-tended plants : roses which bloom nowhere else were blooming there." Years after this was written, Macready the actor himself came to reside at Cheltenham, and in a letter to his friend Lady Pollock describes the place in very similar language.

Macready writes to Lady Pollock : " I presume you who 'have seen the cities and manners of many men,' have not omitted Cheltenham in your wide survey. If so you will not dissent from my opinion of its beauty. I do not think there is a town in England, or out of it, laid out with so much taste, such a continual intermixture of garden, villa, street, and avenue. The hills that encompass it are objects of interest and beauty, observable from almost every point; the conveniences of all kinds equal those of London, and with the shops and clubs and various institutions, gives the promise of a residence answering the demands of the most fastidious. So much for Cheltenham itself."

Another Cheltenham friend of his, who attained to a great reputation, was the late Mr. Brownlow North. The heir apparent to an earldom and endowed with many fascinating qualities, Mr. North had been one of the brightest and most fashionable figures in that bright and fashionable society. The curious fact is related by his biographer that one season he proposed to no less than nineteen young ladies, by all of whom he was accepted. One day he proposed to race a friend on horseback adown the road of that boulevard-like street, the Promenade, which is the special glory of .Cheltenham. His friend proposed that they should change sides for the sake of gaining some advantage of ground. Riding at full speed he came against a heavy vehicle and received such injuries that he died very shortly afterwards. So narrow an escape from death greatly impressed Mr. North. He was in some measure awakened to a sense of spiritual things. Frederick Robertson was at this time an undergraduate of Brasenose, and had frequent conversations with Brownlow North. By his advice, North entered Magdalen Hall. At this time he did not even know the characters. of the Greek alphabet, but he made such rapid progress that the college tutors thought that he might take honours. Many years passed, however, before Mr. North found his place in the ministry. It would be interesting to know. if there were any memorials left of any intercourse between him and Robertson, but we are not aware of any traces. Mr. North took the whole world for his field, and was accepted by the General Assembly of the Free Church of Scotland to act as an evangelist. He set forth with startling energy and pellucid clearness the truths which for so long formed a debatable ground in. the mind of Robertson.

It was at this time, too, that Robertson began in all seeming his especial epistolary correspondence in which he dealt with the difficulties of so many minds and unveiled his own so clearly. The following letter deals with the difficulties suggested by Socinianism, a subject which may be said, more or less, to have occupied his attention throughout his life. The enclosed letter was probably written in 1843.

"My dear Sir,—I have been looking out for some treatises on the subject of your difficulty, a list of which I subjoin, as I think they might be valuable to you. I should extremely like to spend an hour a day in reading some of them together, as this is much the most satisfactory way in such difficulties. I have been invited to-day to take part in a course of lectures which may possibly be given. As the subject is of great importance, if they be given, I should not be able to spare a moment's time, of course, having already to prepare for a lecture on the principles of the Reformation, which involves much reading also. But I shall know this more certainly in a day or two, and we can then make arrangements. I have been thinking much of your difficulty, and shall be extremely sorry if you are unable to enter the ministry. There seem two questions completely separable—whether Jesus was from everlasting and whether His Sonship was from everlasting. A denial of the first, of course, is Arianism, but a doubt of the second may be, and I think in your case is, only a metaphysical difficulty.

The fact is we do not know what we mean by son-ship or generation as applied to Jesus. And the metaphysical difficulty is this, how a communication which implies apparently something antecedent can have had no antecedent time, as it certainly had not if it were from eternity. I do not expect ever to reconcile this contradiction, yet it does not seem to me a greater one than that respecting objective right and God's Will, of which we spoke. We must be content with knowing the ὅτι without under-standing the διότι.

"Yours very sincerely,

"FREDERICK W. ROBERTSON.

"Pye Smith's 'Scripture Testimony,' 'Wardlaw on the Socinian Controversy,' Halden's 'Scripture Testimony to the Divinity of Christ,' Bull's 'De-fensio Fidei Nicaenæ.' "

There was one amusement at Cheltenham to which he was greatly addicted. This was riding. He was frequently one of a happy group of riders. Riding parties at Cheltenham are a special institu-tion. The sound of hoofs intermingled with silvery laughter are well known in the lanes and fields. He was a beautiful rider; his grace and skill this way excited much admiration. He appears to have relinquished shooting during his stay at Cheltenham, but to have resumed it after he had gone away. His great delight was to get away to Ireland, and thoroughly enjoy a shooting holiday until it was

time for him to return to his work. He would
vault upon his horse with the utmost ease, and
appears to have been a master of all manly and
athletic exercises. He had the habit of a close
observance of all natural phenomena, and was almost
a Thoreau in his acquaintance with bird life.

The lectures to which he referred were those on
poetry, which he subsequently delivered in a fuller
form at Brighton. It was characteristic of Robertson that there was always a wise economy in his
materials. The same subjects were again and again
used by him, and always with greater breadth and
added form and beauty. During his stay at Cheltenham he practised a severe intellectual discipline in
many departments of human knowledge, science,
politics, poetry, chemistry, languages. He seems
during this time to have been diligent in his visitation of the sick and poor. A great cloud seemed
during much of this time to have rested upon his
mind. But it did not prevent many days and hours
of exquisite happiness.

Still all this time he underwent great trial and
unhappiness. Part of this was personal. He had
the greatest reverence and affection for his vicar,
the late Dean Boyd, but he had reason to believe
that the vicar was no true friend of his. In this
Robertson did his vicar an injustice. In later years,
when he came to visit Cheltenham again, he came
to understand the facts, and to know that mischief

had been done by a slanderous, or at least by a careless tongue. Moreover, a deep dark wave of thought had passed over his intellectual and spiritual being. He had made some acquaintance with the language and literature of Germany. He seems to have studied, not only the biblical criticism of Germany, that deals so often in a destructive fashion with the most cherished and least disturbed opinions of the Evangelical party, but also to have familiarized himself with schools whose conceptions shatter even the bases of sheer deism. He examined, one by one, the foundations of belief, and one by one they seemed to give way. He commenced anew in life the search after truth. One result was that he threw off Evangelicalism as a system, and permitted himself to indulge in bitter taunts against his old friends the Evangelicals. Another result was that he resolved to terminate a false position, and a state of moral agony, by giving up the curacy which he held at Cheltenham.

Who will not sympathize with Robertson in such a position? I know those who have truly said of themselves, that the cold shadow of doubt has never passed over their spirits. And the special blessing is not to those who doubt, but to those who have not seen, and yet have believed. For those who are teachers and thinkers in our day it may be necessary to examine the whole armoury of scepticism. We may venture to believe that the humble, sincere search for truth cannot fail to be acceptable to the God of Truth. What father is there who would not be delighted with the loving, intelligent effort of his child to understand the truth, though his own thoughts may be crude and vague? At this crisis of his life Robertson found it necessary to recast all his old opinions, to examine the foundations of the most cherished beliefs, to pass all his ideas through the crucible. There might have been a moment in which, like the psalmist, his feet had almost gone, his steps had well-nigh slipped. It is at such time, if ever, that a man is tempted to speak unadvisedly with his lips. There was one thing which, amid all the conflict of his inner and outward life, kept Robertson safe and clear. He illustrated the words of the Word, that if any man wishes to do His will, he shall know of the doctrine, whether it be of God. This is the clear rule and canon by which we may attain to the certitude of truth. It is the purified heart that confers the clear, unbiassed mind. What one is greatly impressed with in Robertson, both at this period of life and throughout his career, is that he was an eminently righteous man. With his whole soul he thoroughly endorsed and made his own the declaration of the Divine Will. He desired, with every energy of life, to carry out that Divine Will; to be self-denying, pure, truthful, just, merciful; and because he thus longed with his whole heart to do

the Will of God, he was not left in the darkness,
but the truth of life was more and more revealed to
him. This is the Divine method by which we may
attain to truth. In these days past evidently there
is an unsetting of the old foundations. There is,
at the same time, an avowed desire to attain to
truth. We remember meeting with a judge who
said that he would willingly part with all that he
had gained, and begin life afresh, if only he could
gain certitude and simplicity of faith. We may
venture to feel sure that God never meant his
creatures to live in doubt and die in despair.
Christ has shown us the lines on which we must
move if we attain to the vision of God. Nor have
we ever heard in human experience of those who
have faithfully sought to do the will of God, and
yet have been left to doubt respecting the doctrine
of Christ, whether it really be of God.

It was a great tendency of Robertson's, so to
speak, to return upon his own steps; as when he
broke down at Winchester he left England, and
sought the mountain solitudes of the Continent. He
was by no means so unsettled as to give up his
profession during the period of seclusion. On the
contrary, he continued his habits of preaching and
theological discussion. We have visited the plain
old building at Heidelberg in which the English
Church service was at the time carried on; but we
have been unable to glean any traditions respecting

him. Nevertheless, here, as everywhere else, the personal effect which he produced was great. That he passed through a deep mental and spiritual struggle, of which we have spoken, in his later days at Cheltenham, and during his travels abroad, is evident from some autobiographic language which we shall have to examine later. But it is remarkable that these doubts did not drive him into absolute worldliness, or indeed cause any suspension in the active duties of the ministry.

Herein Robertson displayed both the scientific temperament and the religious temperament. Indeed, the scientific temperament and the religious temperament are essentially the same. The object of each is the attainment of truth. There is the same observance of method and registration of facts. There is the same patience and persistence. The man of science possesses a constructive method. He does not reject the only theory that appears to account for facts, just as many reject religion, though they have nothing to put in the place of religion. He adopts the theory as a working hypothesis. He eliminates all doubtful elements, he collects facts, he observes, he passes through the process of verification. He discovers the true law, and before the verification is absolutely complete he arrives at the condition of moral certitude. Before we reach a future state a verification of the truths of religion will not be absolutely complete ; but as the facts of religious life accumulate, as varying lines of truth converge, as the infinite adaptation of religion to the complex nature of man, and of man to religion is felt, we attain to a moral certitude, to the highest degree of probability respecting the things of faith. The path of scientific discovery is only possible to the man who adopts some working hypothesis, and treats it according to its own method and instruments. The sceptical, or agnostic spirit, is therefore contrary to the true scientific spirit. Robertson sought to do the will of God, that he might know the mind of God. He did not relax his grasp of the central truth, and so he was able to discern more truths.

It was when Robertson was in Heidelberg that he made the acquaintance of Mr. Henry Crabb Robinson, which subsequently ripened into the sincerest friendship. At Heidelberg, too, he made various other friends, who in after days " looked him up " at Brighton. From Mr. Robinson's diary we derive many interesting details respecting Robertson's career, and the impressions which he produced. Crabb Robinson shines with a kind of reflected splendour; he was famous for having been the friend of Goethe and of Wordsworth. The anecdotal and sporadic character of the " Diary, Reminiscences, and Correspondence " has done some injustice to Mr. Robinson, who, in the opinion of many well able to judge, was one of the most profound and intellectual men of his day. It is, we believe, to be regretted that a large mass of his papers still continues to be unpublished, and some of these might throw some further light on his connection with Robertson.

"1846. *October 23rd.*—Heidelberg.—I had an interesting companion at the table-d'hôte, in a young clergyman, Robertson, who has a curacy at Cheltenham, and not being in good health, has got a few months' holiday. He is now earnestly studying German literature. We were soon engaged in a discussion on the character of Goethe as a man, and of most points of morality connected therewith. He intimated a wish to take a walk with me next day, and we have since become quite cordial. He is liberal in his opinions; and though he is alarmed by the Puseyites, he seems to dislike the Evangelicals much more. I like him much.

"*October 25th, Sunday.*—Went to the English chapel—a room in the Museum—where I heard an admirable sermon from Mr. Robertson; one much too good to be thrown away on a congregation of forty or fifty persons. The subject was the revolution in Judea, when the people required a king, being tired of the theocracy, or government of the judges. He accounted for this offence, and showed that the people were drawn to the commission of it by the corruption of the priests (who appropriated to themselves a portion of the sacrifices—the fat-—

which belonged to God), the injustice of the aristocracy, and consequent degradation of the people. All this he applied to the Irish, and ascribed their peculiarly oppressed condition to the English Government—for enacting the penal laws. The picture he drew of the poverty even of the English was very striking and affecting. I was led to give twice what I intended."

This was a favourite subject with Robertson. He afterwards gave the same sermons with much effect at Brighton. We notice that the English clergy officiating on the Continent generally give their best sermons. The audience may be limited, but then it is generally a fit and select audience, through which a much larger circle may be influenced.

Coming back with a mind calm and satisfied, he was desirous of once more getting into harness. There were personal reasons why he should not resume clerical work at Cheltenham. The thought occurred to him that he would ask Bishop Wilberforce, with whom he had some acquaintance at Winchester, to find him some work in his diocese. He was very careful to explain to the Bishop that he did not hold the same views on the subject of Baptismal Regeneration as the Bishop held. Indeed, up to the last it is difficult to say with precision what were Robertson's exact views on this great subject. He had now come out of the

Evangelical body, and he never joined the High Church party. Bishop Wilberforce had his own way of dealing with ardent young men who placed themselves at his disposal. He gave such young men plenty of hard work, small emolument, but extended hopes and promises, which were often left unfulfilled. He explained to Robertson that he gave his clergy a wide latitude, and that unless they stepped beyond the mark he did not interfere. He asked him to be curate-in-charge of St. Ebbe's, Oxford. Robertson said that the stipend was miserable, and that a residence in Oxford would be depressing. He felt just what ~~John~~ Frederick Denison Maurice described himself as feeling, a hopelessness of contending with the conventionalities of the place. Nevertheless he thought it his duty to accept the Bishop's offer.

St. Ebbe's, Oxford, is a very plain church, but of considerable antiquity. In Robertson's time the living was of very slender value, only ninety pounds a year without a house. It was formerly in the patronage of the Lord Chancellor, and by the beneficent Act, which enables the Lord Chancellor to sell a living and increase its value, it has now the normal three hundred a year and a remarkably good house. For some forty years the parish was under a succession of curates, the rector, who lived away at Headington, being invalided. It is one of the poorest in Oxford. It is not exactly in " the slums," which may be said of one or two parishes, but the most important of the parishioners do not rise above the class of poor tradesmen. Men may pass many years at Oxford and not be aware of the existence of St. Ebbe's church and of Paradise Square, its most important department. At the present time the parish is in the gift of some Evangelical trustees (and helps to constitute a group of five churches) who, in sharp contrast to prevalent "Oxford views," vigorously maintain the platform of the Reformation, and adhere to all the traditions of Simeonism. Without doubt they do very effective work in portions of the city where there is much squalor and poverty when the colleges are "down," and where at all times the means of existence are precarious. Several very distinguished men have served St. Ebbe's. At one time two curates were labouring together who each rose to the Episcopate: Baring, who became Bishop of Durham, and Waldegrave, who became Bishop of Carlisle. Occasionally, but very rarely, does an undergraduate wander thus far afield to worship on Sunday—to whom the early college service is not adequate—missing the pulpit of the old parish church to which he was accustomed, and more than one has been known to proffer his services in the Sunday-schools, or at times to visit the sick and poor.

It was with peculiar interest that the present writer took some church duty in this interesting parish. A few entries of Robertson, but only a few, appear on the parish books, in his usual excellent caligraphy. I met a few old people with shadowy recollections of him, and one whose memory was most distinct. Robertson seems, so far as we can judge from a stay that hardly extended beyond two months, to have done a genuine work there, and to have stirred the parish to its depths. My aged friend said that it was necessary for her to be in her place half an hour before the service began if she wanted to hear Mr. Robertson. I imagine that Mr. Brook is mistaken in saying that at first the undergraduates dropped in one by one, and then rushed to hear him in crowds—for the very sufficient reason that in the latter part of his ministry it was the Long Vacation, and there were no undergraduates to hear him. Unlike Cambridge, Oxford has never encouraged the residence of undergraduates in the Long, and though there may be some slight change, at the present epoch of Oxford changes, there would be no undergraduates staying up in the Long to attend St. Ebbe's church. They certainly missed some very fine sermons. The five Oxford sermons, lately published for the first time in the latest volume, are equal to any in the series. For the first time Robertson as a *locum tenens* was practically in the condition of an incumbent. He was not, as at other times, acting as curate to one who took the lead. He probably enjoyed the freedom and responsibility of his power, and most curates aim at such a position as eminently desirable. But the *locum tenens*, or the incumbent, has often to regret the comparative restfulness of the curate days. The curate has his duties shared with him by the incumbent, and can take his holiday, and can limit his responsibilities. It had been Robertson's earnest wish that his clerical work should be of a light character, and that he should not have all the work on his own hands, but should share it with a like-minded vicar. But from the day in which he took the sole charge of St. Ebbe's to the end there was no fellow-labourer with him; the wise provision of the Master in going forth two and two was overlooked, and he eventually sunk under the weight of the burden.

He had hardly been two months in Oxford, when Trinity Chapel, Brighton, was offered him by the trustees, the Rev. James Anderson, Lord Teignmouth, and Mr. Thornton. A vacancy had arisen through the resignation of Mr. Kennaway, a Gloucestershire clergyman, who had gone back to his former parish. To many clergymen the better position and larger income of the Brighton living would seem preferable. Robertson, however, refused the tempting offer at once. It was not until the trustees renewed their offer, and Bishop Wilberforce thought it his duty to go, that Robertson accepted the appointment, and began those marvellous six years at Brighton which have made his memory immortal.

CHAPTER III.

FIRST YEARS AT BRIGHTON.

It was in the August of 1847, that Robertson went down to Brighton to take possession of the proprietary chapel to which he had been appointed. It was the dead season of the year. The Queen of the Watering-places may be said to have its season all the year round, but in the month of August the season touches low-water mark. The Robertsons had to do much house-hunting before they came to an anchor at Montpellier Terrace. They at once felt the cheering and restorative effect of the magnificent climate. As for his church, the revenues, which first went to pay a large rent to Mrs. Anderson, the widow of the proprietor, were a source of natural anxiety to him. The congregation he found consisted almost entirely of tradespeople and their families; it was like Winchester and Oxford rather than Cheltenham. At first he had almost an utter hopelessness of being listened to, but this feeling passed away as the pews filled up. It is ominous, however, to find that before he has been in the place six months, he is complaining of the excitement, which is "killing."

At Brighton Robertson found a proper environment for his character and genius. Many of his sermons at Cheltenham were as remarkable as any delivered at Brighton, but with the exception of hearers fit and few, they could hardly be said to tell. When Edward Irving was assistant to Dr. Chalmers at Glasgow, nobody thought anything of Irving. All public attention was concentrated on the great doctor. But when Irving came to London it was found that he had an oratorical magnificence peculiarly his own, and his success was in its way as great as Chalmers'. Robertson had been comparatively subdued and effaced while under Dr. Boyd. At Oxford for a brief time he had paused on the threshold of a new development of his career, as it were to poise his wings and to develop his strength. Then came the memorable ministry at Brighton, which, so to speak, summed up and included all his previous work. A similar development would not have been possible for him in any previous position. The secret of oratory lies in the audience. The influence of Brighton upon Robertson was in its way as great as the influence of Robertson upon Brighton.

Robertson's success was at first gradual. He did not take the place by storm. Indeed, when he first went to the chapel it was only slightly attended. Some people who were accustomed to the quiet ways of his predecessor, Mr. Anderson, were somewhat startled by the preaching and manner of the new incumbent, and after a time withdrew altogether. Others who came from curiosity to hear a new man were delighted, and continued to come ever afterwards. Before very long the tide set in very strongly in his favour, and the greatest public success that Brighton had ever known became his. The chapel became crammed to the utmost limits of its capacity. The resident Brighton congregation was almost overpowered by the influx of visitors. There were people who used to run down to the Brighton coast from the Saturday to Monday, that they might combine the change of air with the pleasure and profit of hearing Robertson ; others who avowed that they came for Robertson alone.

The great London people used to crowd about him. Of course his friends liked to see him. One day Lord Shaftesbury pays his shilling for a seat. The Marquess of Lansdowne comes and invites him to dinner at the "Bedford." Lord A. C. ventures to tell him in the vestry that he does not agree with something he has said in his sermon. Robertson comes down on him with the language of the original Greek. The noble lord knows nothing about Greek and succumbs at once. To Robertson these attentions would be irksome. They might have some value to him as indicating a popularity that itself indicated power, but that was all. He did not like compliments. No true-hearted clergyman ever did. His rule was never to reply to them. If the use of a carriage were offered to him, it was declined. If the use of an umbrella were offered to him, it was declined; he would rather get quite wet in walking home in the rain.

In the midst of all this blaze of popularity Robertson was neither satisfied nor happy. There was much in the popularity itself that was irksome to him. The pew system connected with the chapel could not fail to be offensive to him. He had his own private reasons for restlessness and dissatisfaction; but he manfully girded himself for his task. He knew that the weakness and failures of a pastor's life may be overruled for the strengthening of his people and the growth of sympathy. This, he tells us, was what St. Paul meant when he said that he counted not himself to "have apprehended." "And we know not how otherwise any minister could hope to do good, when he addresses men who are infinitely his superiors in almost everything. We know not how else he could urge on to a sanctity which he has not himself attained; we know not how he could dare to speak severely of weaknesses by which he himself is overpowered, and passions of which he feels in himself all the terrible tyranny, if it were not that he expects to have tacitly understood *that* in his own case which the apostle urged in every form of expression: Brethren, be as I am, for I am as ye are—struggling, baffled, but panting for emancipation." Every whole-hearted clergyman must have some such sense of his own imperfections and limitations, and the feeling how infinitely he may be exceeded in holiness by so many of those whom he addresses.

On another occasion he says: "It is apparently a proud and a vain thing for a minister of Christ, himself tainted with sin, feeling himself, perhaps more than any one else can feel, the misery of a palsied heart, for such an one to give advice to his brother-men; but it must be done, for he is but the mouthpiece of truths greater than himself, truths which are facts, whether he can feel them all or not." This was no mere forced expression, no rhetoric of humility. It was a grand sight, as men often said, to see his erect figure in the pulpit, a sea of faces before and around him in gallery and on floor. But the heart of the preacher was bowed down with the sense of infirmity and unworthiness. On one occasion he said to a friend: "When I get into the pulpit I feel thoroughly bowed down, and would cry 'Unclean, unclean.'" He writes to a friend: "I feel the wear and tear of heart and mind in having so constantly, and in so unassisted a way, to speak on solemn subjects. I would gladly,

joyously give it all up to-morrow for a calmer life."
Again: "How long will sermonizing continue?
With all my heart I hope not till the end of life,
unless life is very nearly done, for it is a kind of
mean martyrdom by a lingering death." Once
more, to quote some pathetic words: "If you knew
how sick at heart I am with the whole work of
'parle-ment,' 'talked palaver,' or whatever it is
called; how lightly I hold 'the gift of the gab;'
how grand and divine the realm of silence appears
to me in comparison; how humiliated and degraded
to the dust I have felt in perceiving myself
quietly taken by gods and men for the popular
preacher of a fashionable watering-place; how slight
the power seems to me to be given by it of winning
souls, and how sternly I have kept my tongue from
saying a syllable or a sentence in pulpit or on
platform, because it would be popular."

It may be mentioned that the great orator suffered greatly from nervousness in the pulpit. His
tongue would sometimes cleave to the roof of his
mouth through nervousness. All that he would
take would be a little water in the vestry.[1] Nervous-

---

[1] Some city vestries are liberally provided with port and
sherry for the clergy and churchwardens, according to
the bequest of distant benefactors, but no wise clergyman would "offer false fire unto the Lord." I may here
mention that having once remarked in a publication, that
many orators would be glad to know the secret of Mr. Glad-

ness is not a bad sign for an orator. It is reported that William Pitt once said, "I am going to make a good speech to-night because I am so nervous."

The function which Robertson filled was a most singular one, and at the same time most useful. People there were who complained, with some measure of justice, or injustice, that in the Laureate's phrase, he did not " preach Christ to simple men." They said that he did not succeed in bringing people to their knees. There are old women—of both sexes —who, if they hear sermons of an intellectual character, or outside their customary grooves, will go away saying that they don't call that preaching the Gospel. But wisdom is justified of her children. The work which he did was of a peculiar and valuable kind. Those went to hear him who would listen to " no one else." The Jew and the Jewess, the Unitarian and the unbeliever, would be found in his chapel. Just the same kind of cosmopolitan audiences, though on an infinitely larger scale, still listen to him as he teaches in his books. How many minds have won their way to the light through avenues which otherwise would have been closed to them! They have found in him a fulcrum for faith; they have gone, in so many instances, on

stone's flask, a gentleman sent it to Mr. Gladstone, and the Premier at once wrote to explain that it was egg and sherry, but that the egg was the principal ingredient, in case he should need physical support.

from less to more, from love to fuller love, from truth to higher truth; they flash back as a mirror the image of the Lord, and go on from glory to glory.

It is almost difficult for us at the present date to understand the theological hue and cry which was raised even by holy and kindly men against Robertson. He was simply in advance of his age. He was first to say what is constantly said now. Many of his opinions, which were once considered paradox or heterodoxy, are now accepted as truisms. Some of them were really never anything else. But Robertson thought out received opinions for himself, and as they came glowing from his mint with his own image and superscription he impressed people, and sometimes himself, with an impression of originality that did not really exist. To most people originality in the pulpit is an offence.

Like many other great speakers he was often carried away at the moment, and said things which he would not have deliberately written down and approved. One day a clergyman of great ability and insight came to hear him, and took note of what he considered questionable teaching. When this language was quoted to Robertson, he had no recollection of having used it. Such an experience is not uncommon among orators. There was a remarkable instance of this kind of thing in the life of **Dr. McNeill**, whose churchwardens once had seriously to remonstrate with him in the vestry on some fierce, intolerant language which he had employed respecting the Roman Catholics. McNeill had no recollection of what he had said. Occasionally in Robertson's sermons there were passages which he probably would not have used if he had had an opportunity of correcting the proofs.

It does not seem that his parish work was at any time very extensive. His one great gift was in preaching—that one talent which it were death to hide. In parochial visitation he does not seem to have done very much. At least that is the account which he gives of himself, very probably with an undue depreciation of his own work. I have met with several persons who have accompanied him in visitations of the poor. On one occasion a friend accompanied him to the cottage of a poor man in the last stage of consumption, whose wife had just given birth to a babe. Robertson rebuked him sternly for having been the means of bring a being into the world who, in all probability, would suffer from hereditary consumption. There was one portion of his work in which he took the deepest interest, and which is in truth one of the most absorbing and anxious of a clergyman's responsibilities. We meet with various references to this in his writings : " I urge upon many of you to spend the hours previous to your confirmation separate from friends, from teachers, from everything human, and to force yourself into the Awful Presence." "I am anxious that we should meet on Sunday next for an early communion at eight o'clock. I desire that the candidates may have a more solemn and definite communion of their own, with few others present except their own relations and friends. In silence and quietness we will meet together then. Before the world has put on its full robe of light, and before the busy, gay crowd has begun to throng our streets—before the distractions of the day begin, we will consecrate the early freshness of our souls—untrodden, unhardened, undissipated—to God. We will meet in the simplicity of brotherhood and sisterhood." I have seen a very earnest and affecting letter of Robertson's to a young lady before her confirmation.

Into the season society of Brighton Mr. Robertson entered very little. He knew indeed some of the very best people, highest in intellect, highest in rank, who came to Brighton, but he had no place in the fashionable movements of the gay watering-place. He was in the world, but not of it. They knew him, but he did not know them. He knew only a few people, but he knew them intimately, and they were of the best. He was not one of those who like to receive hospitality—and are careless of returning it. Sometimes, but rarely, he entertained his friends at dinner, but what he greatly liked was to persuade the chance visitor to stay and share the family meal. This is the true hospitality, the heartiest and without ostentation. One of these guests remembers how on leaving the table, when his wife was about to go to an evening party, he presented her with a beautiful bouquet. Trifles such as these represent the wholeness and tender-heartedness of the man's nature. If there was any one who seemed nervous, or neglected, or in any way thrown into the shade, that was the person to whom Robertson attached himself, and for whom he abandoned his own shyness and reserve.

On one occasion, and one only that I am able to discover, Robertson met Thackeray in Brighton. There is a well-known house at which both gentle-men were intimate. Thackeray used to send up his name as Mr. Pendennis, and would sometimes say that he had nothing ready for his next number that would be due in a week, and that he would be thankful for any hints. On the day when the two gentlemen met they had a discussion about Haw-thorn's "Scarlet Letter." The question was whether the clergyman did right in keeping his guilty secret for so many years. Robertson con-sidered that he ought to have made a full confession. He should have purged his bosom "of such perilous stuff." Thackeray took another view. He thought the unhappy clergyman would have done more harm than good. He would have distressed his people, and injured the cause of the Church. He was not

called upon to make a public confession before men.
The difference between the two men is characteristically shown. Robertson is the stern purist;
Thackeray, despite his cynicism, is benevolent and
easy-going. And the novelist seems to have the
best of the argument. Every congregation knows
that a minister is weak and fallible, and a sinner
like one of themselves. A clergyman may feel that
he is getting covetous, or passionate, or worldly.
Let him confess it to himself and to God. But he
does no good in getting up in the pulpit and talking
about it.

Perhaps the deepest utterance that ever came
from Thackeray's heart was addressed to one of the
Brighton ministers, though not to his acquaintance,
the minister of Trinity Chapel. Thackeray wrote
thus to Mr. Sortain : " I want, too, to say in my way,
that love and truth are the greatest of Heaven's
commandments and blessings to us; that the best of
us, the many especially who pride themselves on
their virtue most, are wretchedly weak, vain, and
selfish, and preach such a charity at least as a
common sense of our shams and unworthiness might
inspire to us poor people. I hope men of my profession do no harm, who talk this doctrine out of
doors to people in drawing-rooms and in the world.
Your duty in church takes them a step higher, that
awful step beyond Ethics, which leads you up to
God's revealed truth. What a tremendous respon-

sibility his who has that mystery to explain! What a boon the faith which makes it clear to him." This deeply interesting letter revealing the great novelist in the religious aims of his writings—for such they may be called—is found in a work now hardly to be procured, the " Life of Sortain."

Robertson, in his early days, seemed a being of air and fire, with less of the grosser clay than seemed the case with other men. He was a man who condensed his life into a narrow compass; who lived as much in an hour as an ordinary man does in a day. His physical appearance was very striking, and in harmony with what one would expect. In height he stood just under six feet; erect, sinewy, but with a chest less broad than should have been, giving an idea of delicacy. He was a man of tireless bodily activity. He always passed on his way with light, springy, elastic step. He would clear every obstacle with a bound. He would vault over balustrade in style, clear hedge or ditch, and keep straight across country on foot or on horseback with the best. He would tire out keeper after keeper in a day's shooting. Often he would be out in the woods before daybreak, not so much for the sport as for watching the habits of the denizens of the woodlands.

No doubt, in the crowded, active life of Brighton, Robertson found full scope for all his energies and activities. His physical endurance was remarkable.

When he travelled in the Tyrol, he wrote how he had tired out the hardiest guides. When he went shooting in Ireland, he told how he had knocked up one gamekeeper after another. He always walked down from his house to Trinity, and even when there was a heavy rain. Robertson thoroughly enjoyed social life. His acquaintance was large; his correspondence was large. He had some poor to visit, and he often used to visit them wrapt up in the great military cloak which he had purchased when he thought of going out to India as a soldier. He had his confirmation classes and his Bible classes. But with all these outlets for activity Robertson's existence was essentially isolated and self-contained. He lived in a region where only few friends could accompany him, and his chief society was the companionship of books. While there was no man of greater mental originality, his reading was also very broad and exact. It is a true saying of John Stuart Mill's, that in these days originality is to be looked for, not among those who read little, but those who read much. A man who reads little may have the mortification of finding that all that he regarded as most his own has really been anticipated by other minds.

All that Robertson has left us shows long solitary communings with his own soul. He loved in solitary rambles to wander on the uplands and the downs, and by the shore of the much-resounding sea. The sea at Brighton, without caves or wooded estuary, or rocky recesses, or neighbouring islets, such as make some ranges of coast so peculiarly beautiful, was full of attraction and meaning to that richly poetic nature. The most striking passages of his sermons and letters were due to the scenic surroundings of his Brighton home. But his was not "the harvest of a quiet eye." The eye was often unquiet. The heart was often perturbed. Robertson was not a happy man. He was so constituted, indeed, that hardly under any conceivable human circumstances could he have been a happy man. Old Malan's prophecy was continually being verified, "Vous aurez une triste vie et un triste ministère." There was a restlessness, a despondency, almost a despair at times. One day a friend drew near him as he was standing on the beach. "I have missed life," he was saying to himself in a mournful tone. "Life, like war, is a series of mistakes; but he is not the best Christian nor the best general who makes the fewest false steps." This, however, is opposed to a *dictum* of the Duke of Wellington's, that all generals make mistakes, and that he is the greatest who makes the fewest. Then came the inspiriting thought: "Forget mistakes; organize victories out of mistakes." Theoretically, no one felt more deeply than Robertson that a Christian ought to be a sanguine and happy man; but it almost universally happens that the theory comes first and the verification of the theory afterwards. It is the intense humanity of Robertson's that has been one of his highest gifts. When cast down, it has been for our sakes; and when comforted, that he might be a means of consolation to others.

It is interesting to notice how both the scenery and society of Brighton set their stamp and signature upon him. He speaks of those who have, in a sense, never seen the sea or the sky, or any of those occasions of thought, which, leaving vagueness on the mind, suggest the idea of the illimitable. He formed a very real companionship with the sea, a sympathy almost, as of the crowds who hung upon his accents.

There was another peculiarity of Robertson's of which I have been informed. Sometimes he would wander for hours at night, and even for the whole night through. For such wanderings Brighton is singularly propitious. Both the view of the sea from Brighton, and the view of Brighton from the sea, are equally splendid and effective. He would roam through the silent, deserted esplanade, watching the gleaming waves of the sea in front of him and the starlit abysses overhead. Sometimes some unhappy, lonely castaway would accost him with a tale of misery or solicitation. For her there would be gracious, solemn warning words and a helping hand to raise the lost one. Mr. Robertson has been known to speak with just indignation of those who

could gather up the skirts of their raiment that they
might avoid pollution from such touches, and yet
imagine themselves the disciples and followers of
Christ, who revealed Himself to the poor sinner at
the well-side of the city of Samaria, and gave pardon
and peace to the Magdalen, and would not, if we
may trust the authority of the received text, con-
demn the poor woman taken in adultery. Although
Brighton is an enormous place, it would be easy for
one active and alert as Robertson to get beyond the
congeries of houses. He would soon get beyond
Hove in the direction of the old harbour of Shoreham, to which Brighton officially belongs, and the
stately bridge which the Duke of Norfolk has thrown
over the tidal Adour. On passing Kemp Town he
might wander on to the two deans, Ovingdean and
Rottingdean, towards the modern harbour of Newhaven on the ancient, storm-beaten town of Seaford.
Or, climbing the heights behind the watering-place,
he would strike the downs, where he might wander
towards three points of the compass, a region as
solitary as Dartmoor or the Westmoreland fells. The
Greeks well termed night $\epsilon\dot{v}\phi\rho\acute{o}\nu\eta$, " calm night that
breedest thought." We are reminded of one who
was all night long on the mountain in prayer. Many
a profound, difficult subject would be thought out
and wrought out in these mystic, lonely hours.
When the last frequenters of the fashionable balls
were in the early dawn going home from the luxu-

rious Pavilion, the tall, erect form of the soldier-priest would rapidly flit by them on his way homeward from these midnight studies.

In the October of this first year at Brighton, Crabbe Robinson came down to stay there, and soon found out his old friend. "The only incident belonging properly to Brighton has been my finding settled here, as incumbent of one of the chapels-of-ease, the Mr. Robertson of whom you will find an account in my letter written from Heidelberg when I was last there—the eloquent preacher who delivered a remarkable discourse in favour of the Irish. This Robertson has already made a sensation, and is popular. He has already driven away some High Church ladies—no men —and he preached last Sunday in favour of the Irish and against the Protestant English in a way that has given great offence." One week later he writes: "On Sunday I heard Mr. Robertson preach, and was very much pleased with him. He is fully aware that his liberalism will make him many enemies; but he ought to rely upon it that for every enemy so raised he will make two friends. His eloquence is such as to seduce a large class who will be neutral on all points of doctrine that require consideration and intelligence. He has been several times to see me, and there is no abatement of his cordiality." Just one more week passes, and Crabbe Robinson again refers to Robertson, who is evi-

morning I heard Sortain, and in the afternoon
that very remarkable man, Mr. Robertson, of whom
I have written frequently of late. He is an admirable preacher, and every seat in his chapel is
taken. . . . I read early a speech by Robertson to
the Brighton Working Class Association, in which
infidelity of a very dangerous kind had sprung up.
His speech shows great practical ability. He
managed a difficult subject very ably, but it will
not be satisfactory either to the orthodox or the
ultra-liberal."

Another incident may be recalled belonging
to the first years in Brighton. The so-called
" Papal Aggression " of 1851 caused great excitement in Brighton as throughout England.
Lord John Russell's " Durham Letter " had fomented the excitement, and the Government eventually brought in an absurd bill on the subject,
which, though passed, continued a dead letter on
the Statute until its repeal. There was at this
time living in Brighton a namesake of Robertson's,
a man of considerable mark in literature, and most
estimable character, Mr. John Robertson, the friend
and associate of John Stuart Mill, and the first
editor of the *Westminster Review.* Frederick
Robertson had said in a speech, " The Sovereign
of England does no spiritual act whatever." John
Robertson wrote to Frederick Robertson, referring
him to the Statute 26 Henry VIII. chap. 1, which

says, "The Sovereign in England can correct 'errors' or 'heresies,' and do anything whatsoever which can be done by any manner of spiritual authority or jurisdiction." Robertson in reply wrote him the following very characteristic letter. It is very sad and significant to find him even thus early speaking of his "shattered state of nerves:"—

"60, *Montpellier Road,*

"*Nov.* 19*th.*

"DEAR SIR,—I do not think there is any contradiction between what I said and the Statute Law.

"'The correction of heresies and errors' is plainly an executive function. 'Any manner of spiritual authority or jurisdiction' are words, I think, which evidently imply the same spirit, but meaning there ecclesiastical in opposition to civil. Clearly it could not mean what is commonly meant by spiritual in ordinary parlance, for the lowest minister does acts which the sovereign cannot do. In that sense she cannot 'do whatsoever can be done by any manner,' &c. And hence it seems only fair to interpret the words in a natural sense.

"I will not undertake, of course, to say that the plan is a perfect one, or that the theory is carried out in an immaculate manner. In all earthly things I am content with much imperfection and much evil: nor does it require much sagacity to expose the evil. But on the whole, I am content with the noble theory of our Reformers, and prac-

tically I do not know, even in the awkward case of judging of heresy, whether a mode which, like ours, is liable to the charge of Erastianism, be not as safe, or safer, than any other. I would rather trust to the decision of lawyers than I would of theologians, episcopal or dissenting. A tribunal presided over by the Bishop of London, or Calvin, or Edward Irving, or even Professor Norton, after his bitter virulence against the heterodoxy of another Unitarian, James Martineau, would not be necessarily a wise or just one.

"Doubtless the theory of the Reformers is becoming day by day less real. But it was in itself beautiful; with them the Church was the State under another name, as a committee of the whole House is only the House of Commons after all. And they held that the nation, all Christian, resolving itself into such a committee in view of things heavenly, did delegate its ecclesiastical jurisdiction to, and express its will by, the highest magistrate. Of course this is becoming less possible in proportion as the body politic and the body Christian or ecclesiastical become no longer co-extensive. The Reformers did not conceive of this, and on that ground they were severe on all nonconformists, for nonconformity carried to excess would ruin the practicability of their theory.

"Nevertheless, I think you will admit that it was a noble idea, and I regret much when I see it utterly unappreciated. Men may rightly object to it, only I wish that its meaning should be fairly understood, and its practicability or impracticability estimated fairly.

"I am glad that you thought I replied with courtesy. I feared that from a shattered state of nerves I had spoken throughout so vehemently from agitation only that I must have been misapprehended.

"I remain, Sir,

"Your obedient servant,

"FRED. W. ROBERTSON.

"To John Robertson, Esq."

The year after Robertson came to Brighton the course of public events brought him prominently into notice in connection with some of the deepest questions of the time. That year of the overturning of thrones—1848—affected Robertson powerfully. He rejoiced in the wild wave that spread from Paris half over Europe. He rejoiced in the deep truths which, however perverted, are contained in the cry, "Liberty, Equality, Fraternity." Robertson writes: "The world has become a new one since we met. To my mind, it is a world full of hope, even to bursting. I wonder what you think of all these tumults:

'For all the past of time reveals
  A bridal dawn of thunder-peals,
Wherever thought hath wedded fact.'

Some outlines of a kingdom of Christ begin to glimmer, albeit very faintly, and far off, perhaps, by many, many centuries. Nevertheless, a few strokes of the rough sketch by a Master-Hand are worth the seeing, though no one knows yet how they shall be filled up. And those bold, free, dashing marks are made too plainly to be ever done out again. Made in blood as they always are, and made somewhat rudely; but the Master-Hand is visible through the great red splotches on the canvas of the universe. I could almost say sometimes in fulness of heart, 'Now let Thy servant depart in peace.'" The political wave spread to England and found expansion in the Chartist movement.

It may be set down to the credit of the Church of England that it was a set of clergymen in her communion who set themselves to understand what amount of natural justice and of religious truth were to be found in the cry of the Chartists. First of these, or among the first, Charles Kingsley, "Parson Lot," led the way. At that momentous date of the 10th of April, such clergymen as Charles Kingsley, Archdeacon Hare, Mr. Maurice, with various like-minded laymen, met in conclave to deliberate how best they might be useful at such a time. Charles Kingsley drew up an address to the "workmen of England." We would cite the first sentences: "You say that you are wronged. Many of you are wronged; and many besides yourselves know it. Almost all men who have heads and hearts know it; above all, the working clergy know it. They go into your houses, they see the shameful filth and darkness in which you are forced to live crowded together; they see your children growing up in ignorance and temptation for want of fit education : they see intelligent and well-read men among you, shut out from a freeman's just right of voting; and they see too the noble patience and self-control with which you have as yet borne these evils. They see it, and God sees it." Of those claims enumerated by Charles Kingsley, the want of a system of national education and the want of the suffrage have been removed. Still greater efforts, however, must be made to educate our masters. The complaint of filthy, overcrowded houses is as true as ever, and the evil has even darkened in malignity. Kingsley even thought in these days that the Charter did not go far enough. Perhaps even he himself went too far, and this was probably his own opinion when he came to be Canon of Westminster. But the error, if such it were, was a generous error, one on the right side, and with ever so much of justice and charity in it.

These good men betook themselves to practical work for the improvement of the people. Having their measure of light and sweetness, God's good gift, they sought to pass it on. Mr. Maurice took charge of a poor district in the parish where he lived, and set young students of the Inns of Court to make themselves of use. Mr. Maurice, known among his familiar friends as " the Prophet," was still more widely known among the public as " the Christian Socialist." Men went to hear him in the afternoon services at Lincoln's Inn Chapel, and how many recall with reverence the beauty of that noble head, the thrilling utterances of that vibrating and beloved voice! It is to this practical work that Lord Tennyson alludes in his lines to Mr. Maurice :—

> " Till you should turn to dearer matters,
> Dear to the man that is dear to God ;
> How best to help the slender store,
> How mend the dwellings of the poor
>   How gain in life, as life advances,
> Valour and charity more and more."

There appears to have been no kind of alliance and combination between Frederick Robertson and Mr. Maurice and Mr. Kingsley. No trace of the kind is to be found in the remarkable biographies of these two great men. Still there was a private friendship of a sort among them all. Robertson proceeded on identically the same lines as they did ; he discussed on pulpit and platform the rights and wrongs of things, and by assiduous practical efforts sought the material benefit and intellectual elevation of the people.

Running up to town, he writes to a friend :—

"9, *Montpellier Terrace, Brighton,*
"*Feb.* 5, 1849.

My dear Miss ——

*   *   *   *

" Last week we were in town for a day and three-quarters, during which I had made up my mind to have found you out; but the first day we were in the House of Lords from an early to a late hour, I going straight from thence to the Commons, to hear the debate on the address; and the next was a singularly marred day, in which we achieved nothing.

*   *   *   *

"I never felt the mockery and unreality of life more vividly than when the Queen opened Parliament, and the poor old Duke stood with a great sword, which he could scarcely hold, beside her. Men and women, grown up, seemed acting a play, we being the audience, which is but a miniature of life. It is all a phantasmagoria, and I shall be scarcely sorry when it all melts away into thin air.

*   *   *   *

" That arch-humbug, Alexis, the clairvoyant, has been here, and I tried his guessing powers with that picture,[3] among other things. It was a most signal failure, as everything else was which I saw. I wish the world would credit truth as readily as they will accept marvellous falsehood.

"Alexis guessed an animal with hands, then a

[3] A miniature of his son.

man, a woman, at last a child, but no relation of mine, that his name was the same as my own; then he wrote three or four names, and at last, the first letter being given him, he worked out 'Charles.' All this the wise people looked upon as quite supernatural.

*　　　*　　　*　　　*

"Ever most sincerely yours,

"FRED. W. ROBERTSON."

In the March of 1848, Robertson, as his custom was, selected the burning topic of the day. He spoke of Liberty, Equality, Fraternity: "These spirits make their voices heard in a cry for Freedom, for Brotherhood, for human Equality; and we must not forget these are names hallowed by the very Gospel itself. They are inscribed on its forehead. Unless we realize them we have no Gospel kingdom. Distinguish, however, well the reality from the baser alloy!" He then proceeds to speak of the freedom given by Christ and His truth, of the brotherhood of man, of the equality of all before God: "The man that is less wise, less good than I, I am to raise up to my level in these things; yes, and in social position too, if he be fit for it. And those that are above me, better than I, wiser than I, I have a right to expect to elevate me, if they can, to be as wise and good as themselves. This is the only teaching the Gospel knows." He denounced the galling, insulting spirit of demarcation, with which men separate themselves from the sympathies of the class immediately beneath them : " If we could but all work in generous rivalry, our rent and bleeding country, sick at heart, gangrened with an exclusiveness which narrows our sympathies and corrupts our hearts, might be all that the most patriotic love would have her." Thus Robertson, with courage and generous feeling; and after thirty years, his language is real and instructive for us still.

There is one subject which is constantly before the public, and will be so evermore so long as the poor continue in the land, the controversy between the rich and poor. From time to time the question assumes larger proportions, and emerges into sudden and almost violent urgency. At such periods the very basal principles of property and liberty are brought into discussion. Such a period is the present time, when violent contrasts between rich and poor are necessarily brought before those poorer classes who have now obtained some kind of intellectual and political training through the cheap press, and who now, through Reform legislation, have become the ultimate absolute depositories of political power in this country. The worst is to be apprehended when in one country there arise two distinct nations, the nation of the rich and the nation of the poor, of a rich class that is constantly growing richer, and of a poor class that is constantly growing poorer. It so significantly happens that at the present time there are two classes of publications, one dealing with rich men's houses, their architecture, furniture, and decorations ; and another giving expression to the exceeding bitter cry of outcast London, setting forth the state of the crowded filthy dwellings of the poor, with all the misery, degradation, and want belonging to them. No wonder that at such a time we go into the very roots and first principles of things. No wonder we find schemes discussed on every platform, and in every thoughtful periodical, that involve plans of Communism and confiscation, especially when the parliamentary precedent of the abolition of various rights of property in land has indicated a mode in which practical effect might be given to such speculations.

In Robertson's times such questions came, in an especial manner, to the front. It is one advantage in studying the records of his life and opinions, that we are dealing with the basal questions of our own time as they appeared in the last generation, and to the view of a singularly powerful and independent mind. It was that year of revolutions, 1848, which seemed to give a new dawn of hope to the *ouvrière* class all over the Continent. Robertson went ardently, as is the mode of noble aspirants, into the aims and promises of the new time. Such men as Coleridge and Wordsworth—of whom the latter became a Tory of the Tories—have framed schemes of political regeneration for the race, and have endeavoured to give them practical shape and result, by instituting new forms of life and society in distant lands.

Surely fundamental questions such as these have a most imperious claim—an absolute imperative—upon the teachers of religion, who profess to guide the thought and conduct of men in all their higher relationships. It is too often objected to clergy-men, that they stand aloof from the living interests of their time; that they avoid burning questions; that, content with the interest and appreciation of the cultivated, well-to-do classes with whom they are brought into contact, they overlook those igno-rant masses by whom they are surrounded. Those who know anything of the work-day life of the clergy in our enormous centres of population, also know well how such language is grossly over-charged. At the same time, no doubt, their ten-dency nervously shrinks from everything that would have the character of political, and still more of revolutionary opinion. Robertson dis-cerned that the religious truths which he taught must be vitally connected with the condition and prospects of Christ's poor in the world. It was only such a conviction that could have driven him to take an active part on the platform. To a man of his fastidious nature, a man of the drawing-room and the library, platform appearances must have been peculiarly distasteful. Indeed his speeches and addresses possessed so much subtle and delicate meaning, that they could hardly have been appreciated, save for their flow of eloquence and his knack of putting his points strongly. Robertson felt that the clergy lived a kind of cloistral life, shut off from the influences of the time, and he sought to stem this tendency in his own person and work.

Surely Christianity has much to say on this burning question of all time. The great example of Communism is found in the Acts of the Apostles. In the early days of the Church of Christ men had all things in common. Such circumstances cannot be literally reproduced under the altered circumstances and past development of the Church. But the motive and spirit of that era of the Church indicate a principle binding upon each generation of Christians. That principle, stated in its largest form, is the Law of Love. Each Christian man holds as a principle, a principle which he works out practically according to the extent of his Christianity, that he is not the absolute owner, but the trustee of the possessions that have accrued to him. Apart from the revelation of Christianity by the light of natural law, it may be discerned that every man born into God's earth has a right to so much fair share of his heritage that with honest labour may give him the means of passing his life under conditions of usefulness, comfort, and self-development. It is contrary to the dictates of natural religion that one man should be a *millionaire* and another die of starvation. The natural right includes a labour which should not be excessive, a leisure that may be turned to account, and the full opportunity of arriving at the best of which he is capable. If these rights and opportunities are not favoured and promoted by the rich, a great duty is omitted, and in the long-run terrible penalties are incurred. There was no subject on which Robertson felt more keenly than on the cruelty and selfishness habitually displayed by so many who are the possessors of wealth. The hardening and depraving effects upon the minds of these poor rich—making of themselves the poorest poor and most terrible losers, and inflicting injustice, creating discontent, and disturbing God's moral order and the very foundations of society—were ever present considerations in his mind. He spoke with emphatic earnestness against the worship of the golden image, which is as much set up in our own day as ever it was upon the plain of Dura, and with startling prophetic force denounced the sin of covetousness which is the modern equivalent of the coarse idolatry of ancient times.

The uses of leisure among the poor for the cultivation of the mind and the development of the moral and spiritual being were strongly felt and insisted

upon by Robertson. Thus he took a great interest
in the early closing movement at Brighton, and
earnestly sought to impress on the young men that
any time gained for them was not to be spent in idleness
and self-indulgence. It has been calculated, I believe
by Bentham, that if every one did his share the work
of the world might be done by four hours' labour on
the part of each individual. It is the duty of each
to labour as it is the privilege of each to rest. To
those who acknowledge the Divine law it is enough
that the same commandment which tells us to rest
on one day tells us to labour on six. It would
almost seem that by the marvels and discoveries of
this latest age, that have abbreviated the processes
of labour and made machinery do the work of
living hands, that the Providence of God was preparing for men a larger measure of rest from toil
and greater opportunities for cultivating the affections of home, the study of the Divine works, and
the development of human powers and faculties.
Here again human weakness and wickedness combine to frustrate the benevolent intentions of the
Creator of all good. The rapacity of the rich looks
upon the triumphs of invention as intended to increase the output of human things. The haste to
increase riches suffers no diminution. On the other
hand it must be owned that the labouring classes of
this country have not shown so much appreciation
as might have been expected of the benefit of leisure.

And indeed leisure is a perilous benefit to most men. Better the Travaux Forcés than the vice of idleness and the other vices which idleness brings with it. When there has been a thorough estrangement between rich and poor, between class and class, then, as the ultimate expression of a terrible social vengeance, there comes an age of catastrophes like the French revolution. There cannot fail to be an impending doom where the carcase is thrust where the vultures be gathered together. "The sword of heaven is not in haste to smite, Nor yet doth linger." The individual insolence of wealth may apparently go unpunished; the individual himself meet with no visible retribution. This may be understood as we believe in the awards of a future state, when with an absolute equity the crooked will be made straight, and the rough places plain. There is, however, no immortality for a nation. The corporate life does not survive. The main value of the study of history is to point out the ethical lines that pervade it in the vindication of the principles of the everlasting judgments of God. We see this on the largest scale in the French revolution of the last century, and the hundred years of anarchy and bloodshed that have followed in their train. That was the necessary issue of a state of society where the principles of brotherhood and justice had been ignored. It is to be hoped that henceforth society, resuming its natural inherent rights, may arrive at some of the benefits of the revolutionary era without going through a revolutionary era itself. On the principle of sumptuary law, it may restrain and limit overgrown wealth in order to assure to the humblest the conditions of health and well-being. That we have had no such revolutionary experience in England—that the Tenth of April was not like the Tenth of Fructidor or Fifteenth of Pluviôse—is owing to the continuous effort of the Church conformers and Nonconformists in this country. While the public conscience has been cultivated and developed, while a broad and ever deepening stream of charity has been fructifying the land, while the bonds of Christian sympathy and brotherhood have been recognized through all classes of society, and would that all this had abounded in still larger measure, there has been a safety-valve provided against the revolutionary instinct. This has stood between the Destroying Angel and the people. This has been the best evidence for the reality of the Gospel of Christ. This has softened and sweetened all the relationships of society. Those who have followed in the Master's steps, Who went about doing good, have been the conservators of society, and have built up the solidarity of our country. Those who, in the accursed selfishness of sordid wealth have shut themselves up from natural pity, are disintegrating influences, and, as far as in them lies, are unloosening the passions and crimes of men.

" To the great majority of the poor of this country there is no such thing as home. We dare not, cannot say that those two small rooms in which a whole family are huddled up together . . . we dare not, except in mockery, call that in a Christian land a *home.*"

These words of Robertson's, spoken a generation ago, are probably accentuated at the present time. Foreign writers, when they comment on the beauties of English homes, dwell also on the fact that for an immense proportion of our population homes are utterly non-existent. Just now there is much philanthropic discussion on the subject. The attention of the nation has been aroused to it, and our contemporary history has become a commentary on Robertson's pathetic language. We have had articles in the papers, public meetings, committees and societies, and Royalty itself has taken interest in the matter; but it almost seems as if the wave of generous emotion is subsiding, and sentences such as the above may lose their effect on regardless ears.

CHAPTER IV.

THE BRIGHTON OF ROBERTSON'S TIME.

AN interesting chapter might be written in the social history of our country on the Brighton of Robertson's time—a Brighton of only one generation ago. So much has the gay and brilliant town changed and expanded through the fleeting years, that to revive these past days requires some of the work of an historian, almost of the archæologist.

> "Eheu fugaces, Posthume, Postume,
> Anni labuntur, lost to me, lost to me,"

as poor Barham sang, with his usual happy mixture of rhyme and reason. The then recent introduction of the railway had begun to revolutionize Brighton. The place had entirely ceased to enjoy the smiles of royalty. Queen Victoria had found that at the seaside she could hardly get a glimpse of the sea, and that retirement and privacy were almost impossible. She found both at Osborne, and perhaps there is hardly an individual in the Isle of Wight who has not profited by her presence. Not as yet had the

New Pier been erected. Not as yet had the Dome been utilized for vast musical and social gatherings. Not as yet had Brighton flung out a long arm to the west and another to the north. But, though Royalty has retired, the full tide of fashion has set in steadily, and only in the dead summer months is there ever low water. The fashionable part of Brighton was then Kemp Town. There the Duke of Devonshire, the Marquis of Bristol, and Lady Jane Peel had their well-known residences. The fashionable promenade was on the eastern cliff during hours in which it is now left solitary and deserted. In that promenade there were constantly mingled men and women whose lives and influences made up so much of contemporary history.

Brighton will always be associated with the memory of the Prince Regent. No doubt he greatly demoralized the place. He built his huge palace with a chapel at one end and a harem at the other. The stories and scandals of his residence have never died out, or are likely to do so. There are also some stories not too many to his credit, which will be always recollected. But without him Brighton would never have been Brighton. He was the author of its existence. Brighton, however, might have intimated to the revered author of its existence that he might have set a far better parental example. That, however, was a wise instinct on the part of a worthy Mayor of Brighton, who, when

Mr. Thackeray wished to deliver his lecture on the Four Georges at the Pavilion, said that he did not approve of a man being abused under his own roof. Consequently Mr. Thackeray delivered his eloquent invective elsewhere. Once Thackeray said to a friend at a dinner-party that he would not send his daughters to Court lest they should be haunted by the ghosts of the Four Georges. Both Thackeray and Dickens were then in the habit of visiting Brighton,—I wonder if they ever attended Trinity Chapel,—and some of the most characteristic hits of their novels are scenes in Brighton. At one time Lord Macaulay visited Brighton a great deal, his sister having a house here. The artists and the novelists have found happy hunting-grounds in the town and neighbourhood.

Brighton has other regal associations besides the fourth George. Charles the Second, as we all know, slept here for a night, before he made, next morning, his escape from Shoreham. Harrison Ainsworth, the novelist, might often have been seen here, perhaps working up all the local colour he could into the novel founded on the incident. For a time he settled down in a semi-detached villa in the neighbourhood of Brighton. Louis Philippe was, at least in the little port of Newhaven, near Brighton, in the plain, unassuming character of a Mr. Smith. An old lady, an American friend of mine, from her apartments in the Rue de Rivoli, had, only a few days before, seen him emerge from the gardens of the Tuileries, call a cab, and drive off for good. There are still persons in the neighbourhood of Brighton who had commercial relations with the dethroned king.

A good many literary notes might be made on Brighton, unless one rigidly limited their scope. Brighton is a fashionable suburb of London, but it is not "the literary suburb" as Twickenham might claim to be in the last century, or South Kensington in our own. It has no such literary reputation as Edinburgh or Lakeland. But there is hardly a statesman or politician, poet, novelist, or artist that has not "run down" to Brighton. We invariably meet with touches of Brighton in fiction and biography. A friend of Tom Moore's writes to him to say that he has gone to Brighton for the sake of economy, and owns that it is a signal failure. Grenville talks of it in his memoir in his somewhat cynical fashion : "Place very full, bustling, gay, amusing. Plenty of occupation in visiting, gossiping, dawdling, riding, and driving ; a very idle life, and impossible to do anything. The Wilberforces come down. Lord Byron pays the expenses of a pugilist to come and visit him. Sir Walter Scott comes down ; so do Rogers, Tom Moore, Lord John Russell," and the list might be multiplied out of the memoirs.

It is curious to know that Samuel Rogers, when a boy, dined in a house, the site of the present

Pavilion, which he characterized as a respectable farmhouse. In the literature of the last century we have some notices. John Wilkes came here, and the people would willingly have given him a public welcome. He affected privacy, however, but they set the church-bells ringing, and the people give him many marks of enthusiastic approbation. Dr. Johnson came to Brighton to visit the Thrales. He did not take very kindly to the place. He thought the Thrales' house was at the "world's end." He wrote to his friend Dr. Taylor : "I have no great heart to go into the sea, and have yet been there but three times." He spoke of the country as "so truly desolate, that if one had a mind to hang oneself for desperation at being obliged to live there, it would be difficult to find a tree on which to fasten a rope." Fanny Burney (Madame d'Arblay) has an interesting notice, written about a hundred years ago (1782); "Mrs. and the three Miss Thrales and myself all arose at six o'clock in the morning, and by the pale blink of the moon we went to the seaside, where we had bespoke the bathing-woman to be ready for us, and into the ocean we plunged. It was cold, but pleasant. I have bathed so often as to lose my dread of the operation, which now gives me nothing but animation and vigour. We then returned home and dressed by candlelight, and as soon as we could get Dr. Johnson ready, we set out upon our journey in a coach and chair, and arrived in Argyle Street

at dinner-time." These are the *loci classici* about
Brighton in the literature of the last century. There
is no such courage now shown in bathing in the sea
by moonlight.

It may be said that Brighton is indebted to
literature for a large portion of its prosperity. Two
medical men, Dr. Russell and Dr. Pelham, wrote up
the use of sea-bathing and its singular efficacy in
some complaints. Indeed, Dr. Russell, in a greater
degree than the Prince Regent, was the founder of
the fortunes of Brighton. Among the crowds of
visitants many literary men might be enumerated,
who have run down here for the invigorating sea-
breezes, some of whom have made careful studies of
the place. Thomas Campbell, that true lyric poet,
was invited to give a course of lectures here, but, at
that time, he had given up lecturing. He seems
frequently to have come down to Brighton. With
him a great specific for health was " a short run to
the coast." His medical biographer says : " Those
short runs into the country or the sea-coast seldom
failed to produce relief, both mental and physical.
Instead of medicine I endeavoured to enforce the
necessity of regimen—with a literary task, something in which his taste and feelings were enlisted—
or a short run to the coast. This method, adopted
at intervals, was often attended with the happiest
results."

Dickens especially delighted in a Brighton

audience when giving any of his readings. " I may tell you that in round numbers we find one thousand stalls already taken here in Brighton. Last night I had a most charming audience for ' Copperfield,' with a delicacy of perception that really made the work delightful." He turned to good account one of those constant railway journeys to Brighton which we are all making. "Coming down in the railroad the other night (always a wonderfully suggestive place to me when I am alone) I was looking at the stars and revolving a little idea about them." This was his " Dream of a Star," which, curiously enough, he never included in his printed pieces. In his usual grotesque way he describes a Brighton storm : " It blew a perfect hurricane, breaking windows, knocking down shutters, carrying people off their legs, blowing fires out, and causing universal consternation. The air was for some hours darkened with a shower of black hats (second-hand), which are supposed to have blown off the heads of unwary passengers in remote parts of the town, and to have been industriously picked up by the fishermen."

Some further literary notes might be combined. White, of Selborne, has an allusion to the birds, and Yarrell to the fishes that are caught in the neighbourhood. In Lord Campbell's " Life of Lord Thurlow," in his " Chancellors," there is an account of Thurlow at Brighton. Thurlow told the Regent

that he should not call at the Pavilion until he kept
better company. That good writer and good man,
Vicesimus Knox, came down to preach in the camp
at Brighton. He gave great offence to some of his
military audience, because he protested against the
love of war. " In the evening," he writes, " I propose walking on the Steyne, while hoping to meet
my offended hearers in the military profession, but
I did not recognize any of those who were in the
church." Sidney Smith ran down, and cut his
witticisms on the Dome. One of the best bits of
description of Brighton is to be found in the
" Journals " of Fanny Kemble, where, as usual, an
earnest tone is apparent in her jest :—" There were
crowds of gay people parading up and down, looking as busy about nothing, and as full of themselves,
as if the great awful sea had not been close behind
them—the contrast of all that fashionable frivolity
with the grandeur of all natural objects seemed to me
incongruous and discordant. We walked on and
on till we had nothing but the broad open Downs
to contrast with the broad open sea, and I was
completely happy. I walked and ran along the
edge of the cliffs, gazing and pondering, and enjoying the solemn sound and the brilliant sight. . . . .
The sunshine was dazzling, and its light on the
detached masses of milky chalk made them appear
semi-transparent, like fragments of alabaster or
cornelian."

Let us look a little more closely into the personal surroundings of Frederick Robertson at Brighton. And, first of all, of its vicar, Mr. Wagner, with whom it was his lot to be brought into regrettable collision. The Wagner family have been most closely connected with the town of Brighton, and have been great benefactors of the place. Mr. Wagner was its vicar between forty and fifty years.

There was a connection between the Duke of Wellington, and the vicar, and the parish church that belongs to general history. In his youth the Duke of Wellington used to worship in the old time-worn church of St. Nicholas. The Duke of Wellington had asked the authorities of Eton College to recommend him a tutor for his eldest son, the last Duke, and his brother. Mr. Wagner, who had a good name at Eton, was selected, and was tutor to the young men for eight years. This included the time when they were at the University; when one, at least, of the brothers was not on friendly terms with the authorities of Christ Church, and when the Duke withdrew him, eager that his son should not be bothered by "a pack of parsons." When Dr. Carr, Vicar of Brighton and Dean of Hereford, was made Bishop of Chichester, the Crown, according to custom, claimed the patronage of the living of Brighton, and the Duke of Wellington appointed his sons' tutor to be vicar. In 1852, when the great Duke died, Mr. Wagner proposed the restoration of the parish church and monument to him, and headed the subscription list with a thousand pounds. A beautiful monument to the Duke stands in the chantry with the inscription, " In memory of the great Duke of Wellington this sacred building, in which in his youth he worshipped God, is erected."

Mr. Wagner's work in Brighton was not showy, but it was solid and useful, and such as perhaps no other man could have performed with equal efficiency. He was a wealthy man. He had married the only daughter of Joshua Watson, the model layman of the Church of England, one so like Robert Nelson, of *Fasts and Festivals* renown. He sold the old vicarage, in Nile Street, now a part of Prince Albert Street, and with the money purchased the site of the present vicarage, a house that might do for a bishop's palace or baronial abode; rather a white elephant to any future vicar who might have to live on his living. He used his wealth nobly. To him, to his sister, and to his son, the churches and charitable institutions of Brighton are largely indebted. He founded some of them. He gave them his best of time and thought; he guided them in their progress: he never spared himself any toil in their interest; he gave to them largely of his substance. His first work was to open St. Peter's church as a chapel-of-ease to the parish church, and now St. Peter's has become the parish

church, and St. Nicholas only one of the churches in
the parish. Many churches were built in his time,
and mainly through his influence ; the legal position
of each being that of chapel-of-ease to the mother
church. That noblest of hospitals on the south
coast, the Sussex County Hospital, found in him a
foster-father; also the eye infirmaries, and institutions
for the blind, and the deaf and dumb.

He was in many ways a very remarkable character.
He was a terse, earnest preacher, and many admired
the force, manliness, and sincerity of his teaching
and of his character. Prompt in decision, peremptory
in tone, determined in action, he established a kind
of influence which seems to have been as much
military as religious.   He was at war with vast
bodies of parishioners on church rates and general
politics. Of course he followed the great Duke's
politics, and was always first at the polling-booth.
He was a man who would fight fair and strike hard.
He never spared himself in purse or person.   When
very aged and infirm, he would bend his tottering
steps on a stormy night to visit some case in
his parish. The clergyman who now holds Robertson's former church, Trinity, said, " the good wishes
and kindly words this aged man more than once
expressed to me concerning the future of my
ministry remain in all their freshness, and have,
through his death, acquired a new and richer
value and importance."

It must be admitted that there was more of the stern disciplinarian about the old vicar than of the spirit of love. He was essentially autocratic, and could write letters to his inferior clergy which it was not by any means pleasant to them to receive. He was a man who could feel keen resentment, and also could make his resentment keenly felt. I remember an aged tradesman, one of the most respectable of his class, telling me that in a business controversy with the vicar he submitted to a very heavy loss rather than incur his ill word. The worst blow to his popularity was undoubtedly his treatment of Robertson, in which we think some measure of injustice was done him. We think that under all the circumstances Mr. Wagner hardly deserved the full measure of obloquy which he received, and Robertson exhibited less generosity and common sense than we should have accredited him with.

The figure of Mr. Wagner was a familiar and an imposing one in Brighton. The figure was a soldierly one, and indeed he was much given to manage things in martinet style. In some respects he seems to have taken the great Field-Marshal as his model. Many characteristic anecdotes are still related respecting him. On one occasion, when he was in church, at the time of divine service, two young officers entered and conducted themselves in a very unbecoming manner while the prayers were being said. Mr. Wagner observed this, and marched

down the aisle in hood and surplice, and to the
astonishment of the offenders took his place between
them.   Shortly afterwards the officers met him and
remonstrated with him on rendering them conspicuous and ridiculous.   By way of salving their
wounded honour they requested the vicar to make
them a formal apology.   They had, however, entirely
mistaken their man.   "Gentlemen," said the vicar,
" I know the Duke of Wellington.   I may say that
I know him very well.   It is you who owe me an
apology, and not I that owe you one.   Unless you
sit down immediately and write me an ample
apology for your improper behaviour, I shall immediately write to the Duke and complain that
you have acted in a way unbecoming officers and
gentlemen."   The vicar carried the point, and an
apology was duly made.   The vicar frequently
showed himself in this unamiable light of a casti-
gator.   He would frequently correct men for their
soul's health and the reformation of their manners.
It is said that he even stooped to physical castiga-
tion.   Once the church rates were refused.   Whereupon the vicar stopped the church clock, to the
indignation of some, and the amusement of others.
As the vicar was riding past on horseback, a small
boy—and Brighton has its *gamin* class—called out,
" Who stopped the clock ? "   The vicar dismounted
and administered personal correction, for which he
was in due course of law summoned and fined.

It may be said at once that the final controversy between the vicar and Mr. Robertson was certainly very unfortunate; but at the same time Mr. Wagner has not received justice in the matter. The few words which we have to say on this matter may be said here, as it is a matter which may be deposed from the undue position it has occupied in the narrative of Robertson's last days. Mr. Robertson had nominated a curate whom the vicar refused to accept. Legally, any curate of Mr. Robertson, was the curate of Mr. Wagner. The vicar gave the nomination, and was legally responsible for the stipend, although the private arrangement with the incumbent gave him security on this point. The clergyman to whom Mr. Wagner took such a violent dislike had served a curacy in the neighbourhood for many years, and, with his many friends, was well able to hold his own even against the autocratic vicar of Brighton. Altogether wrongly, Mr. Wagner had a fixed idea unfavourable to this gentleman, and it is impossible to move such individuals as the late Mr. Wagner from their fixed ideas. He was within his legal rights, and legal rights are what such men rejoice in. Mr. Robertson confronted him with as inflexible and equally military determination, and, as it seems to us, with some of the pride of the old Adam. The church might be shut up; he might die from the overwork, as, in fact, he did, rather than he would give way.

In this inflexibility we see very little to admire. Robertson's conduct seems to me to have been childish and self-willed. There were faults of temper on both sides, and exactly the same kind of fault. Both have shown so much because they have been spots on a dark surface. It is time that the wretched squabble should be entirely forgotten, and that we should only retain in memory the real work which both these good men did.

The good work which the Wagner family has wrought in Brighton has been immense. The vicar, as we have seen, built the noble vicarage, with its groves and lawns. The Vicar of Brighton has always been a kind of *bishop in partibus*. The preceding vicar had been bishop; the succeeding one has become archdeacon. Next to the vicarage is the fine residence of Mr. Arthur Wagner, with its interesting library and mediæval collections. Robertson was a near neighbour, and would take his share of the hospitalities which the Vicar of Brighton would vouchsafe to his clerical neighbours. He might be taciturn, curt, unpopular in his manner, but he might have been worse than that. He might have been one whose unconquerable volubility allowed no one to speak but himself. He might be one whose mind never rose above the level of ecclesiastical statistics, and was utterly destitute of the sympathy and spiritual affinities that could warm or encourage any mind brought

into contact with his own. He might have been
one who would refuse intercourse with his clergy,
and throw difficulties in the way of their taking
counsel with him. There might be a love of
popularity and of power, and an absence of that
stern conscientiousness which was the characteristic
mark of the elder Wagner. There might have been
worse vicars than old Wagner of Brighton.

The Wagners are great owners of house property
in Brighton, especially among the poor, and in these
days, when so much is said about this subject, it
may be mentioned that their method of dealing
with the poor is truly admirable. They have shown
their Christian munificence by the erection of
churches in Brighton, on whose architecture and
adornment immense sums have been lavished, and
where a very perfect working organization has been
created. They meet the wants of all classes, and
especially of the poor. The church of St. Paul's in
West Street ranks first in the good doings of the
Wagners. Many are those who have reason, like
the present writer, to turn with affection and gratitude towards this church. Its portals constantly
stand open: the silence, the sacred gloom, the music,
the stained windows, and the times of service are
full of rest and refreshment to those who turn aside
from the glare of the cliffs, and the tumult of the
streets, to meditate and to pray. The other Wagner
churches should be enumerated. The name chiefly

to be associated with them is that of Mr. Arthur Wagner, the incumbent of St. Paul's, and of the Church of the Annunciation connected with it. To the Brighton world his figure, at the date of our time, and at the present date, ranks as one of the most conspicuous in Brighton. Indeed, all England became familiar with his name at the time when that unhappy woman, Constance Kent, made her sad confession to him—which certainly under no circumstances would ever have been revealed in a law court. The immense church of St. Martin, in the valley running westward between the heights, has met the wants of a large new district that has been growing up since Robertson's time. The name of Wagner is part and parcel of the history of Brighton.

There was yet another very remarkable member of the Wagner family, whose ministry for some years was parallel with that of Robertson. This was George Wagner, the nephew of the vicar, and the incumbent of St. Stephen's, one of the dozen churches which the vicar built. There was a singular sweetness and attractiveness in the character of George Wagner. Like Robertson himself, he was intensely spiritually-minded and cultivated; the intellectual power being distinctly below Robertson's. He was brought up at Hurstmonceux Place, to which he has given a fresh association, which had passed only a year before from the hands of the

Hare family into those of his father. When Julius Hare came to the living of Hurstmonceux, George Wagner was taken from Eton to be placed under his tuition, and there he became acquainted with Sterling and a number of illustrious men who visited Hare. When he lived in Paris with his parents he saw much of M. Berryer, the great Legitimist orator, and Prince Charles de Broglie. From such antecedents it might have been expected that an intellectual and public career lay before him, but, forming an intimacy with James Vaughan, and deeply impressed by his teaching, after much travel, and the Cambridge course, he became a clergyman, and one of an eminent family and apostolic stamp.

Indeed that singular interest which gathered around such men as Henry Martyn and Henry Kirke White belongs in a very high degree to George Wagner. The saintliness and self-sacrifice of his life shone with an almost supernatural beauty. The late Dr. Blakesley, who spent much time with him at Marienbad and other German spas, speaks of the many hours daily which he devoted to the study of the New Testament. His first work lay in a sea-bound parish of the weald of Sussex, above the broad expanse of the Pevensey Level. His life at Dallington very much recalls that of George Herbert at Bemerton, with the quaint incidents recorded by Isaak Walton. He would take away the pillow from his own bed to take to a sick man, or would carry an old woman's pail for her up a difficult hill. He turned rooms in his vicarage into schoolrooms for boys and girls, and formed village classes to whom he taught Latin and mathematics. The parallel holds good with George Herbert in that delicate health, that daily dying, in which, nevertheless, so much spiritual energy and constant work were combined. He had a special power in addressing children, which is the highest and rarest of ministerial gifts, a heavenly art, in which he may have been assisted by his friend, Mr. Vaughan. We find him writing to his sister: " Vaughan [now Dean of Llandaff] has been staying some days with us. He was more delightful than ever; cheerful and full of Christian feeling. Since he left us he has been to Paris with Arthur Stanley, whom he persuaded to accompany him the day after the latter arrived at Hurstmonceux. . . . I have likewise been much tempted for some days, and have felt very deeply the difficulty of the Christian life. Pray for me that I may stand in the evil day. I fully believe that Satan's most fiery darts are aimed at ministers." This is so far in corroboration of Cæsar Malan's idea.

When the living of Dallington was given away to another man, George Wagner was displaced as curate-in-charge, and found his occupation gone. He filled up the *interregnum* in the best way. He had a much-needed rest—so far as such an earnest man would allow himself rest—for the next three years. He applied himself to geology and Hebrew. He attended sedulously to the Hurstmonceux household, and the poor of the parish. He deepened his intimacy with Mr. Maurice and A. J. Scott, of Manchester, and went up to town to hear the lectures delivered by the famous Archbishop Trench. He made a visit to Scotland, where he had some intimacy with Erskine of Linlathen, just the man whose mind might have powerfully influenced Robertson for good, if he had known him, and at Linlathen he met Thomas Carlyle, who exercised such a powerful influence upon Robertson, and none at all upon himself. Robertson had an intense receptivity, which responded eagerly to all impressions, while George Wagner, rooted and grounded in the principles he professed, could view with imperturbable calmness the sea of discussion resounding on every side.

In 1850 his uncle offered him the church and district of St. Stephen's. It was a small church and pre-eminently ugly, built from the materials of the Pavilion Chapel, and wrought up with very slight departure from architectural form and detail. Similarly, when St. Peter's, Eaton Square, a very ugly church, was happily burned down a number of years ago, the architect who had the chance of restoring it, flattered himself that he had reproduced the original structure, brick for brick. Robertson

had been in Brighton three years when Wagner
came, and Wagner outlived him two years. So to
speak, each man was consumed by the fire of his
work. He was "no orator as Brutus is," Brutus
in this case being Mr. Robertson, and his deafness
shut him off from much of social life. But his
ministry was singularly unique and effective. Five
hours a day he gave to parochial visitation. He
did a wonderful work in the sick-room, and that
which in a place like Brighton is of the highest
importance, in the many schools of the upper classes.
From Mr. Vaughan he derived his system of
children's services ; he devised various agencies for
the good of servants ; he instituted a service in
German for the good of German musicians, and he
originated and established the Brighton Home for
Female Penitents. George Wagner unconsciously
became a great power in Brighton. He was known
everywhere, and visitors, if they did not know him
personally, knew his church. He was one of the
English clergy—nor have we many—who keep up a
strong interest in the development and progress of
good causes on the Continent, and who find their
zeal for home work not lessened but quickened
thereby, as for instance in good works in Basle and
Dusseldorf. "I think," says Erskine of Linlathen
" he was one of the most lovable beings I ever met
with. In fact, I cannot say that I ever met with
any one like him. His beautiful simplicity gave

such a charm to all the rest of his character, and in that character there was a harmony undisturbed by a single jarring note."

His greatest work was at the Penitents' Home. The late Princess Alice, when she visited the Albion Hill Home, objected to the word "Penitent" being applied to this special class of people. "We are all penitents," said the Princess; "clap a label on my back; I, too, am a penitent." The designation, through the wish of the Princess, is now the Albion Hill Home. The interest which George Wagner took in the Penitents' Home, which he founded in Brighton, was of the most intense description, a work in which Robertson would fully sympathize. To learn how he could thoroughly work out his benevolent plans he sought the friendship of a lady, at this time unknown to the world, who became famous as Florence Nightingale.

This remarkable work of Mr. Wagner's, in which Robertson would so thoroughly have sympathized, was taken up by one of the most remarkable women of Brighton, who passed away in the spring of 1885—Mrs. Murray Vicars. Mr. Wagner sent the poor girls up to London at his own expense until the London institutions would receive no more. At this time Mrs. Murray Vicars was devising the plan of a home for "penitents" in the neighbourhood of Brighton. She was a Jewess, and, like other Jewesses who give up their religion from conviction, she underwent a storm of opposition and opprobrium. Indeed, this was her special cross in life, that this opposition should never wholly cease while life endured. "One of the unhappy girls of the class among whom the mission lay, was seized, when on a visit to Brighton, with cholera. Her companions were so stricken with horror and remorse, that they came in a body to Mrs. Vicars, and implored her to save them from their guilty life." Mrs. Vicars and Mr. Wagner combined their efforts, the one being superintendent, and the other secretary. One of the last letters of the Princess Alice was written to congratulate Mrs. Vicars on her work, and Mrs. Vicars could show me and her friends a most affecting correspondence :—

"*Neue Palace, Darmstadt,*

"*September* 21*st*, 1878.

"DEAR MRS. VICARS.—I have returned from visiting the Home, so convinced of your excellent management of it in every respect, that if you still feel my becoming patroness of the Home (and of the Ladies' Association for the care of Friendless Girls connected with it) can further the good and noble work, I am most willing to comply with your request. The spirit of true Christian loving sympathy in which the work was begun by you, and with which it is carried out, the cheerfulness you impart, the motherly solicitude you offer to those struggling to return to a better life, cannot fail to restore in a great measure that feeling of self-respect so necessary to those voluntarily seeking once more a virtuous life, and by so doing regaining the respect of their fellow-creatures. 'Inasmuch as ye have done it unto the least of these My brethren, ye have done it unto Me.' In this spirit may the Home, as well as the Association connected with it, continue its good work. My entire sympathy and good wishes will be ever with it.

"Ever yours truly,

"(Signed) ALICE."

The Albion Hill Home is now one of the most magnificent institutions of Brighton, and will always be associated with the memory of George Wagner. The penitential work might not seem best suited for a young unmarried priest, but Archdeacon Hare well said, "that dear George's pure and heavenly spirit was just the one which fitted him for such a work, and that with him the disadvantage of comparative youth and of being unmarried would be compensated for by his purity and likeness to that Heavenly Master, who came to seek and save the lost, and did not shrink from 'the woman that was a sinner.'" Thus he worked on in his narrow lodgings, his bedroom only separated by a folding-door from his one sitting-room, but its sides lined with books—books which he was prepared to sell, if necessary, for the poor penitent girls. It is difficult, in reading his biography, to understand if he were Low, High, or Broad in the common acceptation; his views seemed those of Erskine, Hare, and Scott, and his own subject, above all others, was that of the Atonement. The bronchial cough and clergyman's sore-throat forced him from time to time to leave Brighton. He went to the South of France and to Malta in search of health, and at Malta he was greatly cheered by a visit which his uncle, the Vicar of Brighton, paid him. He died, somewhat suddenly at last, at Valetta, and on the walls of the homely church of St. Stephen is a touching tribute to his memory and worth.

Any survey of Brighton at this time would be incomplete without some mention of two remarkable brothers, whose history is indelibly bound up with that of the town, and who have obtained their own place in religious literature. These are the celebrated brothers, Henry Venn Elliott and Edward Bishop Elliott. With these names should be mentioned that of their sister, Charlotte Elliott, whose hymns are widely known wherever the English language is spoken,[1] among thousands who have never heard of her brother's ponderous " Horæ Apocalypticæ." The father was one of the Clapham sect, and long resided at Clapham. For many years the elder Elliotts had a house in Brighton on

[1] " Just as I am, without one plea;" " My God, my Father, while I stray."

the west cliff, called Westfield Lodge. About 1812 there were only three houses further west before they came to the fields and lanes which then filled the broad space between Brighton and Hove, ground now covered with brilliant streets and stately squares. Thus, from first to last, the Elliotts were thoroughly Brightonians, and in many ways they elevated and improved the district where their lot was cast.

Henry Venn Elliott was a great power in Brighton. For thirty-eight years he ministered in the proprietary chapel which his father had purchased for him, which ultimately became a parish church. The original building is now replaced by one of the stateliest churches on the south coast. Elliott was just one of those men who become bishops and archbishops. At Cambridge he took an unrivalled degree, at least one that is not often paralleled—a high wrangler and Chancellor's medallist. Circumstances threw him into association with some of the most distinguished statesmen and nobles of the time. He had travelled abroad for years, in days when foreign travel was much more rare and difficult than at the present time. We believe that he never really derived a penny from his profession, all his limited means from this source being given away, with much more, in charity. Like Keble of Hursley, no promotion was ever offered to him. " The Lord kept me from honour," he used to say.

The only times almost when he left Brighton were
when serving the office of Select Preacher in Cambridge—which happened nine times—and when
his appearance in the pulpit of St. Mary's always
excited the deepest attention, and never failed to
throng the galleries with dense ranks of University
men.

It is interesting to notice the old-fashioned ways
to which Mr. Elliott adhered, especially in his earlier
years at Brighton. Thus we find him at times get-
ting up in the pulpit and reading out a homily.
We wonder when the clergyman of a fashionable
Brighton church, or indeed, of any church, was
last known to read out one of the homilies. On
another occasion he reads out "An adaptation of
Bishop Stillingfleet;" in the afternoon he reads Mr.
Spragge's sermon on the "Syro-Phœnician woman."
Some of the most celebrated men of the day occasionally assisted him. Thus one summer we have
Henry Melville, Dr. Maltby, Charles Simcox, Lionel
Pratt, Basil Wood, Robert Wilberforce, and J. H.
Newman, " Fellow and Tutor of Oriel." We are
unable to find any trace of any similar sort of
assistance being rendered to Robertson. Sometimes
Mr. Elliott was not altogether delighted with his
fellow-workers. " The Rev. —— preached a sermon altogether extempore, having found that when
he descended from the reading-desk his sermon-
case was empty. As might be expected, it was a

poor performance, but may the. Lord bless it." It is curious to meet with the recurring names of Newman and Dr. Pusey. A published fragment of his journal gives us a perfect gem about Dr. Pusey, which may well find place in any future biography of that great man :—

"I dined at two o'clock, after many kind invitations, with Dr. Pusey, and had four hours of close and interesting conversation with him. I asked him point-blank the question, 'Do you think you have increased the unity of the Church by your publications and your movements?' And he answered, just as I expected, 'No, not at present; but, perhaps, ultimately it may be so.' There was great kindness, for after three hours he walked a fourth with me. There is always, I think, a haziness and mistiness about his views. Towards the end I spoke to him fully and freely on what, I thought, would support an immortal soul in dying, namely, 'The Righteousness of Christ,' 'The Lord our Righteousness.'

"I met afterwards, at tea, a remarkably sweet person, with her husband, who are members of my congregation. They asked me the critical question, 'What is the precise difference between you and Dr. Pusey?' Taken offhand, I said, 'Dr. Pusey would get his religion from the Church, and I mine from the Bible.' I told Pusey this, and he did not dispute the fairness of it."

Pusey, however, might have rejoined that the Church was in existence before the Bible.

Like Mr. Robertson, Mr. Elliott dealt with many of the subjects of the day: "Grant to Maynooth," "Sunday Observance," "Railway Excursion Trains," "Missionary Work." On some of these subjects there would be a considerable divergence of opinion between the two; and it seems to be understood that, generally speaking, Robertson received only a scanty meed of sympathy from Mr. Elliott—and this was a matter which he felt very much.

The peculiar honour of Henry Venn Elliott was the good and benevolent work which he did for the Church of England in the founding and sustaining of the well-known Clergy Daughters' School, St. Mary's Hall, Brighton. This institution provides perpetually for the education of one hundred young ladies, the daughters of poor clergymen. The school—as the buildings are provided, and there are no profits to be made—is practically self-sustaining, from the payments made on behalf of the children. But Mr. Elliott was the great benefactor. Through him, land and house and a scanty endowment were furnished. Though a family man, and with many and large claims upon him, he was a lavish benefactor. In addition to his large published contributions, he was also a large anonymous giver. His time and best efforts and his warmest affections were devoted to the school. He taught the children much himself, and looked after their individual interests. It may be said generally that it has nobly answered his expectations. Perhaps at the outset there may have been too much strictness, but in every point of view the institution has been thoroughly improved. We have hardly ever heard any preaching more taking and pathetic than when this good man had been pleading on behalf of this institution, which he loved so well. It is curious to know that all sorts of carpings and criticisms were directed against him in the course of his generous and disinterested work, so much so that he used to tie up bundles of vexatious correspondence under the title of "Thorns and Prickles." Many instances of his generosity are recorded. He gave up being a member of the Athenæum Club, that the subscription thus saved might go to a charitable object.

One very fine feature about his character was his personal kindness in doing good. He was a rich man, and it was easy for him to write cheques. People thought that he must be saving largely, but all that he did not spend on his crowded and hospitable home was given away. Elliott gave that element of personal service, without which the costliest charity is nothing. It cannot be too much impressed upon Christian people that no amount of pecuniary liberality can exonerate them from the duty of personal service to Christ in His poor. Elliott's favourite occupation lay, to use his own phrase, "in taking pains to do good." Going into a poor woman's house, he found a number of pawn-tickets lying on the table. He quietly took them away, and sent back all her property redeemed. He would take up a poor child in his carriage, and send him back to his mother with a present of tea. When a servant seemed ill, and to herself the illness seemed very slight, he would go out himself in the night and bring back a doctor. He would go among the roughest men and stop a street-fight.

He and his brother, perhaps, more thoroughly belonged to Brighton than any other clergymen of the place. To use their constant phrase, "They dwelt among their own people." It is to be regretted that no memoir of E. B. Elliott ever has been or ever will be written.

One clergyman, very memorable among the Brighton clergy of his day, happily remains, with eye undimmed and natural force unabated, up to the present day—James Vaughan, who for between forty and fifty years has been the Incumbent of Christ Church, Montpellier Road. A first classman of Balliol, it seemed that this gifted man might enter any avenue of scholastic or social distinction; but with a rare simplicity and absorption of aim, he consecrated all his powers to the work of a parish priest. For many years it has been permitted to him to fill a position of singular power and usefulness, and though he has almost sought obscurity, and on no occasion tempted popular fame, yet "Vaughan of Brighton" has become a name throughout the country. His sermons have regularly been published in the "Brighton Pulpit," and though this circumstance has been a cause of annoyance to him, as a similar circumstance was to Henry Melville, and Robertson himself in one stage of his history, without doubt it has greatly enlarged the area of his usefulness. Mr. Vaughan was himself a leader of the evangelical school, toned down by catholicity and wide sympathies, but in the religious world, as it was at that time constituted, divided by a broad line of demarcation from Robertson. From all those party feelings Mr. Vaughan held aloof. He has been known to speak of Robertson enthusiastically, of his innate nobility of character. He believed that Robertson was one of those characters which more and more ripened and improved towards the last. With his usual passion for letter-writing, Mr. Robertson used to send letters on theological subjects to Mr. Vaughan. As those letters were marked confidential, they have been kept strictly private. Various of his letters were so marked, and their privacy has never been infringed. Surely it was in itself a hopeful sign that the leader of the Evangelicals should be on such terms with the leader of the Brighton Broad Church party. In his last illness Mr. Robertson summoned Mr. Vaughan to his dying-bed, but his friend was unfortunately away from home.

Mr. Vaughan in his time was one of the land-marks of the Church in Brighton—one of the pillars of all its highest and best interests. The writer trusts that he may be forgiven for acknow-ledging his own deep sense of obligation to Mr. Vaughan's teaching, a teaching singularly fertile in thought and rich with practical results.

A very remarkable man was the late Archdeacon Garbett, Archdeacon of Chichester. He was a close neighbour of the Brighton clergy, and he held the Brasenose living of Keymer-cum-Clayton, in close proximity to Brighton. He was successor in the archdeaconry to Cardinal Manning, who had vacated the archidiaconal office when he went over to Rome. The Manning family were not infrequent figures in the Brighton of that day. It had been thought a great triumph for the Protestant cause at Oxford when Garbett had been elected Professor of Poetry in opposition to the High Church party. In the ecclesiastical history of England during the present century he will hold an honoured place. In the whole evangelical party there were none perhaps so highly accomplished as himself. It is said that once, when examining an undergraduate at Oxford, he asked a question, the answer to which depended on some knowledge of Tasso. The examinee replied that he was unacquainted with Tasso. "Not

know Tasso?" ejaculated the Professor of Poetry,
—"not know Tasso?" his mind being apparently
unable to take in the existence of such abnormal
ignorance. Remarkable enough for his scholarship
and his poetry, he had also a great knowledge of
natural science. He was a great authority on all
questions connected with the telescope and the
microscope. This unusual combination of scholarship and science was almost unrivalled in the
diocese. Robertson possessed this combination,
but neither his scholarship nor science would hold
comparison with Mr. Garbett's. As both were
members of Brasenose, in all probability they
were acquaintances; indeed, some of the Garbetts
had a remarkable familiarity with the details of Mr.
Robertson's personal history. The present writer
has few more pleasing recollections than those of
this pious and gifted dignitary of the Church,
whose loss to the diocese has never been replaced.
In the brief but much-prized intercourse which he
had with him in the dim evening of his days, the
Archdeacon still retained the deepest interest
in all that passed around him. There was one
lovely inconsistency in the Archdeacon's character.
He was an admirable controversialist, and no
one in the seclusion of his study knew better
how to indite a stinging letter. But all he
cared for was the intellectual gratification of
exercising his gift. When once he met his opponent

face to face, there was nothing but beneficent welcome and the very milk of human kindness.

There was yet another archdeacon in the diocese, not so near to Brighton in point of residence as Mr. Garbett, but Archdeacon of Lewes, in which archdeaconry Brighton is situated—Julius Hare, of whom we speak in this volume elsewhere.

The Bishop of Chichester, at this time, was the excellent Bishop Gilbert. Chichester has been for many a year fortunate in its bishops. Bishop Shuttleworth, far less known in the present day than he deserves, was a writer of depth and acumen that recall the best thoughts of Bishop Butler. He was succeeded by Bishop Otter, who had done much admirable work for the diocese and the Church at large. His name will always be identified with the development of religious education in the county of Sussex. To him had succeeded Dr. Gilbert, for many years the head of Brasenose, and it was under his mild and gentle rule that Robertson officiated at Brighton. Dr. Gilbert was, I believe, a man of large means, which he employed generously, and gave many proofs of nobility of character. The line has been worthily continued to the present venerable bishop, who still administers it, under an increasing burden of years and sorrows, with a power and elasticity which many a younger man would be glad to possess.

Another very distinguished man at this time in Brighton was Joseph Sortain, the minister of Lady Huntingdon's chapel in North Street, the chapel which Lady Huntingdon built out of the sale of her jewels. As an orator, he was probably, in another line and in another style, the equal of Robertson. But, unlike Robertson, the sermons which he preached were mainly attractive in the preaching, and have failed to secure any permanent reputation. Yet this man was offered valuable preferment, if he would only take orders in the Church of England, and Empson, the editor of the *Edinburgh*, asked him to write review articles for him, which he did; and Thackeray was his correspondent in some of the deepest tones which he ever used. It is singular that in the "Life of Robertson" we have no mention of Sortain, and in the "Life of Sortain" we have no mention of Robertson. We regret that we have no outward evidence of a real sympathy and union. They would fundamentally agree in all important matters. There were circumstances in the outward history of each which were very similar. Each struggled with devoted energy against the weakness of a frail constitution, bent upon discharging their work to the last, and also bent upon keeping faith with the fame which they had won, striving to keep equal to the reputation they had gained, and in each effort recognizing that they had their strongest rivals in themselves.

There was one clergyman who will probably have a higher name than any of those whom we have mentioned in the history and literature of the Church of England. The late Canon Mozley lived for many years at Old Shoreham, in the neighbourhood of Brighton. He had not come to live there in Robertson's time, but the offices which he held at Magdalen College, Oxford, brought him into connection with that neighbourhood of Brighton where Magdalen College held property. So great is the interest belonging to this remarkable man, that I shall not think it necessary to make any apology for offering some reminiscences of him.

When he was at Old Shoreham, I was a neighbour of his at Worthing, within the distance of a few miles, and knowing some friends of his, we became acquaintances. I remember that my first call upon him was made one morning, quite early, and I quoted against myself an old saying—I think, Archbishop Usher's—"that he doubted whether a true scholar ever came out before twelve o'clock." He received me most benignantly, and, I may say, laid himself out to oblige and interest his guest. He showed me his grounds and garden, which was almost a little park, and took me to see the church and parish. At his kind invitation I stayed to lunch, and remained conversing with him till late in the afternoon. I may say that this was the manner of our intercourse. Every now and then, but at long intervals,

I thus spent a day with him. I believe his kindness
and hospitality would have made me welcome oftener,
but knowing how precious was his time, I used my
privilege sparingly, and always looked forward with
great delight to the occasion of a visit. I used to
make notes of his interesting and instructive conversation, but I am sorry to say that, though I have
made a search, I have been unable to find them.

As a rule, in the morning he was somewhat silent.
We either talked or read, as we liked. Occasionally
he would fetch me one of his books to illustrate
some point. I remember his bringing down one of
the Fathers to illustrate that there was a *Præparatio
Evangelica* in the heathen world, amid its purer
souls, for the coming of Christ. Curiously enough,
when I had been speaking about this time at one
of Mr. Kemp's delightful meetings at St. James'
Rectory, Frederick Denison Maurice had dwelt upon
the same subject. What little talking was done
was left chiefly to myself before our stroll and lunch.
In the afternoon he would go into monologue which
occasionally taxed all my poor powers of appreciation adequately to follow.

He spoke very freely of his experiences and his
literary plans for the time being. What immensely
impressed me was the intense earnestness, serious-
ness, and simplicity of his nature. He told me that
when he took the living of Old Shoreham he gave
up a valuable journalistic appointment, until at

least he could make himself quite sure that the claims of his country parish would allow him to continue such work. At this time he was thinking of publishing his Oxford University sermons. He took out some of his manuscripts, and read aloud part of his sermon on the dogma of Papal infallibility. As he read, his colour rose, his voice trembled, and the tears seemed to gather in his eyes. It was impossible not to be affected both by his manner and the splendid eloquence of the passage he read. I mention this because I believe his ordinary way of reading his sermons and lectures at Oxford was very dry and indifferent. Even his friends would hardly recognize this description of his speaking. My own idea is that he was a man of intense feeling, that he was afraid to trust himself to the expression of emotion, and adopted a dry manner as a kind of mental armour. He was intensely interested in the interests and prospects of religion. He seemed to take desponding views of the future of the Church. It so happened that I had taken charge for some little time of St. Peter's, Windmill Street, where Mr., now Bishop, Wilkinson was vicar, and to which his brother Arthur succeeded. He inquired very carefully about the details of the parish, and I was able to give him details which he liked to hear. I remember discussing the system of Comtism and its alliance with Radicalism. This was the only occasion on which he ever made any approach to talking politics, beyond my understanding that he was in general sympathy with Mr. Gladstone. He said that the leaders of this movement had doubtless large practical aims, which they veiled under much reserve. I mentioned this in the *Morning Star*—a periodical then approaching its last days. There was a stereotyped paragraph just above the leaders, written, I believe, by Mr. John Morley, the present M.P. for Newcastle, and then the editor, in which he avowed that his party was perfectly conscious of special aims, although they were not expressly enunciated. It was not difficult to surmise these aims, but hardly worth discussing them until brought within the range of practical politics.

I remember that one subject of discussion arose one day respecting the deutero-Isaiah theory. It rose in reference to Mr. Cheyne's first work on Isaiah, which was of a somewhat revolutionary character, which he has largely modified in subsequent editions. We agreed that great Hebrew scholars with much positiveness had maintained contradictory opinions. We then spoke of internal evidences. No doubt the style of the first thirty-nine chapters varied exceedingly from the fortieth to the sixty-sixth. I argued that the variation of style was no disproof of the identity of authorship. The difference was not greater than that between Milton's description of Eden and his description of Pandemonium, nor, to take another order of thought, between Mozart's mass music and his operatic music. I daresay the criticism was not worth much, but I noticed the eagerness with which he welcomed it as he always welcomed every point made in a discussion.

Similarly he said one day that Darwin's theory of development enabled us to understand better the Mosaic cosmogony. It was some remark like that of the Duke of Argyll that we might write down all the discoveries of science on the margin of the first chapter of Genesis. I said, " I would just like to ask you in what stage of the development, from the ascidian to the ape and from the ape to savage humanity, did God say, " Let us make man in our own image ? " He said at once this difficulty was insuperable.

He never made a single allusion to his published writings and his eminently successful literary career. A man more utterly unconscious of his great genius and great position could not be met with. A re-markable article had come out in the *Quarterly*, on the "Argument from Design." I taxed him with the authorship, which he at once admitted. He said that he had waited a long time, at least a twelvemonth, for its insertion. That was the diffi-culty with the *Quarterly*; it took so long to get anything in. He mentioned that he had written, or was writing, another article from it, on Cardinal

Newman's "Grammar of Assent." He again and again reverted to the subject of Bley's "Argument from Design." "It is impossible for people to get out of it, any way," he said. "Wherever we look we get arrangement—intelligent collocation." This phrase seemed to please him, and he repeated several times "intelligent collocation." He tried for a moment to imitate a boy who was stammering his way through the construction of a passage where the nominative had lost all sight of the verb, an illustration which he had employed in his article to illustrate the mental condition of some people. He was extremely anxious that this "Argument from Design" should be understood and appreciated by people generally. He addressed a long letter to the editor of one of the infidel journals, I think either Mr. Bradlaugh or Mr. Holyoake, in which he practically gave the pith of the article, and pressed it home with admirable force and lucidity. He seemed anxious to impress the minds of thoughtful working-men and others with this truth as a defence of Revelation, and bring them to a belief of the divine Personalty.

I have mentioned his slight references to Mr. Gladstone. He spoke of the pleasure which he had in breakfasting with him, such as all Mr. Gladstone's breakfast guests experience. One Sunday morning there arrived a letter from the Premier. When Mrs. Mozley saw the envelope, she exclaimed,

"Here is an offer of something from Mr. Gladstone." It proved to be the offer of the Professorship of Divinity at Oxford, with a canonry of Christ Church attached. It was surmised by several of his friends that the last occupant had been moved upwards in order to create a vacancy for Mr. Mozley. The living of Ewelme which accompanied the canonry was hardly acceptable to Mrs. Mozley, who loved her old home, her garden, and her little farm. Her wish to remain was met by the Premier, and this slight incident, which was made the occasion of a serious party move against him in the House, has become historical.

I remember his asking me, as having a fresher experience of Oxford men than myself, whether there was any hint which I could give him in his way of dealing with the young men, and this was said with an expression of anxiety for their good and of humility to his own powers. I ventured to say that in my time I thought the dons had stood too much aloof from the young men. Dean Stanley had been a great exception to this. He regularly invited the undergraduates who attended his classes to breakfast. Dean Stanley was a little uncertain, being sometimes conversationally disposed and at other times not. It was a great pleasure and privilege to listen to him. I think I spoke very gratefully of him, and frankly expressed my opinion that it was an example that might be well followed by other professors. I know that he did act on the principle, but whether to any great extent I am unable to say. Attendance on Dean Stanley's lectures was, generally speaking, voluntary; whereas all men seeking orders were obliged to attend the lectures of the Divinity Professor. Dr. Mozley greatly enlarged the scope of the chair by giving lectures to graduates, which made a profound impression.

At Oxford I only saw him twice. The first occasion was when he occupied the house used by the late Bishop Jacobson. It was a bright, cheerful luncheon party, but I cannot recall any of his talk. The last time I saw him was when he had removed to another side of Tom Quad. There was a great difference, and no wonder, for he had in the interval lost his wife. He received me with all his ancient kindness, but he seemed out of sorts and poorly, and for the only time in our acquaintance he did not ask me to stay with him. As usual there was no small talk, but he went at once to the heart of some great subject. He seemed to have an expression of trouble on his face, and he said to me very earnestly, "You seem to go about a great deal. Now, tell me, do you really find any belief in the supernatural?" I said that I certainly knew a number of places, and that in nearly every place I knew, I was sure that there was much heart religion and intense faith in the supernatural. "I am so thankful to hear you say that," he said; "so very, very thankful," and his face brightened up.

I did not think it right to call upon him again as I heard such poor reports of his health. . I should say that once or twice, with some trouble to himself, he had opportunities of doing me kindliness, and he took them at once. He impressed me as being eminently righteous, and one of those few men who are really great men.

CHAPTER V.

In the immense *cortège* which attended Robertson to his last home—a funeral the like of which Brighton has never seen before or since—there was one illustrious lady, sincerest of mourners. With a singularity that was in full unison with an eccentric but noble life, Lady Byron on this occasion refused to use her carriage. She was not worthy, she said, even to walk behind the hearse of one so gifted and so holy as Frederick Robertson. As she stood by the side of the open grave, she said to a friend, that from the very first day of her acquaintance with him she could not but painfully discover that he was sowing himself beyond his strength, and that his very calm was a hurricane. His memory was ever affectionately cherished by her to her latest day, and her regard for and interest in his children was also unabated to the last. We are able to lay before our readers the following stanzas written by Lady Byron on hearing (when at a distance) that the grave of Frederick W. Robertson was covered with flowers. They were printed, and privately circulated at the time :—

"I may not strew with Earth-born flowers the turf where
        thou art laid,
   But flowers there are which Love may rear, and such as
      cannot fade ;
   Transplanted here from Eden's soil, to give their grace to
      Time,
   When in a spirit, meek and pure, they find a genial
      clime.

"While offerings to thy tomb are brought, by faithful hands
        unknown,—
   Hands that have held the slender thread, or hewn the
      wave-washed stone,
   Be mine to cherish every germ, which in thy breast has
      been,
   And bind a wreath around thy brow, most real, though
      unseen !

"But what can shadow forth *thyself*,—the lone, the un-
        reveal'd ?
   A myth thou wert to all but God, thy bosom bravely
      seal'd;
   If parted clouds a moment show'd the blue depths of thy
      soul,
   'Twas but to prove them far beyond the skies where thun-
      ders roll."

Between the widow of the greatest poet of his age and the fervid young priest there had gradually

grown up an intense and famous friendship worthy
of comparison with the renowned friendships of
antiquity. Between her and the priest there existed
a keen sympathy on all subjects affecting the higher
life, and on all matters of practical beneficence.
They were drawn into close personal relations.
Robertson was her counsellor and friend in all her
private and public plans of good. He was the
depository of her most sacred confidences. He
attended the dying-bed of her daughter, and shared
her plans for her grandchildren. Hers was one of
the very few houses which he visited away from
Brighton, and on one occasion he writes: " Lady
Byron left a sick-bed ten days ago to come and see
me." Robertson was to have been her literary executor, and had been entrusted with the letters and
documents that would have thrown light on the great
and still unsolved mystery of her life, but in the
incalculable decrees of Providence the aged peeress
survived for many years the intrepid priest, her
chosen confidant and friend.

Lady Byron was a very remarkable woman, as
remarkable in her ways and history almost as her
husband, though without any spark of his magic ray
of genius. There are many indeed to whom her
name is a household word. Without doubt she was
one of the most striking female characters of the
present century. Lately we were looking at two
portraits of her; one taken in youth, the other in

extreme old age. The likeness of the one to the other was plain enough. We could understand how the beautiful girl became the beautiful old lady. The impress of personal beauty, of which so very little has been said, is unmistakable. The later portrait reminded us a little of that of the Mère Angelique of Port Royal. It showed strength of will and character, and great intellectual force. The forehead is somewhat square, and as a hostile Jesuit said of the great Jansenist lady, "People with square foreheads are generally obstinate" it must be owned that Lady Byron was often obstinate to very admirable purpose.

To the last Lady Byron was rather striking. It was a very remarkable head. The forehead was abnormally high—the head seemed half face, half forehead. The face was noticeable for its extreme pallor. The eyes were beautifully blue, with an expression wild and keen. Her favourite attitude was to stand on the drawing-room hearth; the little fist clenched somewhat imperiously, the tones of voice somewhat dogmatic. The attitude was always graceful. Her singular appearance was partly due to the state of her health. She suffered greatly from heart complaint, which caused her intense pain, and which could only be subdued by bleeding. Her health was always in a state of delicate balance. As is often the case with those who suffer from heart symptoms she survived till an extreme old age, and died of something else. As she stood on her hearth it was a great delight to her to lecture young people phrenologically. She was a great believer in the science, and from the depths of her phrenological convictions she was able to lecture young people on the untoward tendencies of their characters, and point out the sort of career for which their qualities best suited them.

A very few words respecting her previous history will here suffice. Anne Isabella, familiarly known as Annabella, Milbanke, as all the world knows, was the only daughter of Mr. Ralph Milbanke, married Lord Byron in her twenty-first year, and before her death became Baroness Wentworth in her own right. Byron certainly had not married her either for her fortune or for her rank. This should be remembered in justice to him, as the facts have often been very differently stated. Her fortune was very moderate, the Milbanke estates being entailed, and the poet would have been sixty-eight if he had lived to the time that his wife attained her peerage. Simple, refined, sincere, but perhaps somewhat stiff and formal, and far more intellectual than most women in the society of her day, she seems to have inspired the poet with a genuine respect and regard. "She is said to be an heiress," wrote Byron to Moore, "but of that I really know nothing certainly, and shall not inquire. But I know she has talents and excellent qualities, and you will not deny her judgment, after having refused six suitors and taken me." Lord Byron made her a bad husband. He was a bad man, and under any circumstances would have made a bad husband to any woman doomed to intrust her wifely happiness to him. So abnormally evil was his conduct that the wife soon had reason to suspect that her husband was mad. When she found that he had not even the terrible excuse of insanity her heart turned against him for ever. She did not at first disclose the full extent of her wrongs to her father, but when she did so, it was adjudged impossible by her friends that she and her husband should ever live together. This was the advice of her famous lawyer, Dr. Lushington, and even her husband's counsel, Sir Samuel Romilly, refused to undertake his defence, and returned all fees.

The late Earl of Balcarries (Lord Lindsay) once wrote a remarkable letter to the *Times*, in which he printed a letter which Lady Byron wrote to her friend, Lady Ann Barwood. It is a remarkable letter, clear, incisive, well-written, evidencing great intellectual force :—

" I am a very incompetent judge of the impression which the last canto of ' Childe Harold' may produce on the minds of indifferent readers. It contains the usual trace of a conscience restlessly awake, though his object has been too long to aggravate its burden, as if it could thus be oppressed into eternal stupor. I will hope, as you do, that it survives for his ultimate good. . . . . He is the absolute monarch of words, and uses them, as Napoleon did lives, for conquest, without more regard to their intrinsic value, considering them only as ciphers, which must derive all their import from the situation in which he places them, and the ends to which he adapts them with such consummate skill. Why, then, you will say, does he not employ them to give a better colour to his own character? Because he is too good an actor to over-act, or assume a moral garb which it would be easy to strip off. Nothing has contributed more to a misunderstanding of his real character than his affectation of being above mankind, when he exists almost in their voice. I trust you understand my wishes, which never were to injure Lord Byron in any way; for though he would not suffer me to remain his wife, he cannot prevent me from continuing his friend. It is not necessary to speak ill of his heart in general; it is sufficient that to me it is hard and impenetrable— that my own must have been broken before his could have been touched. I might appeal to all who ever heard me speak of him, and still more to my own heart, to witness that there has been no moment when I have remembered injury otherwise than affectionately and sorrowfully. It is not my duty to give way to hopeless and wholly unrequited affection; but so long as I live my chief struggle will probably be not to remember him too kindly."

Lady Byron in early life had the idea that she was capable of authorship, and had begun to form literary plans of some extent. It was probably from these literary tastes and the nameless charm of a high and somewhat severe character, rather than from mercenary motives, that the intimacy arose followed by the marriage. From all that remains of Lady Byron we see both the promise and performance of much literary power; but she has better served society by her long life of practical well-doing, by which we may believe that she has made some expiation for the moral evil wrought by her husband. Whatever moral safeguards her husband may have thrown down, they were always sedulously rebuilt, so far as lay in her power, by the good wife.

At the same time, a remarkable incident may be mentioned in illustration of the relations with Lord Byron. Lady Byron had accumulated a great mass of documentary evidence, papers and letters, which were supposed to constitute a case completely exculpatory of herself and condemnatory of Byron. She placed all this printed matter in the hands of a well-known individual, who was then resident at Brighton, and afterwards removed into the country. This gentleman went carefully through the papers, and was utterly astonished at the utter want of criminatory matter against Byron. He was not indifferent to the *éclat* or emolument of editing such memoirs. But he felt that this was a brief which he was unable to hold, and accordingly returned all the papers to Lady Byron. Robertson was to have been her literary executor, and whatever may have been his views about Lord Byron, he would have been able to render full justice to the many good points and the stainless career of the illustrious wife. After the death of Robertson, the papers were handed over to another clergyman, who was then the minister of the Presbyterian Hanover Place Chapel, but who is now beneficed in the Church of England. It is remarkable, although many years have elapsed, and the interest of the papers continues unabated, that this gentleman has not seen his way to make any literary use of them.

The public memorials to Lady Byron are very numerous. Many of our readers will remember that Mr. George Macdonald dedicates his story of "Elginbrod" to the beloved memory of Lady Byron, with "a love stronger than death." He strikingly says: "There are a few rich, who, rivalling the poor in their own peculiar excellencies, enter into the kingdom of heaven in spite of their riches, and there find that by means of their riches they are made rulers over many cities. She to whose memory this book is dedicated is—I will not say *was*—one of the noblest of such." "I would almost as soon discuss my father and mother as her," writes Mr. Macdonald in a private letter. "Thus much only would I say, that, knowing her, I think I may say intimately, for years, I counted her one of the noblest, as well as ablest of women, and that, so far from being cold-hearted, I believe she loved her husband to the last, whatever *the last* may be interpreted as being." The poet Campbell speaks thus of her :—

"I wish to be as ingenuous as possible in speaking. Her manner, I have no hesitation to say, is cool at the first interview, but is modestly and not insolently cool; she contracted it, I believe, from being exposed by her beauty and large fortune in youth to numbers of suitors, whom she could not have otherwise kept at a distance. But this manner could not have had influence with Lord Byron, for it vanishes on nearer acquaintance, and has no origin in coldness. All her friends liked her frankness the better for being preceded by this reserve. This manner, however, though not the slightest apology for Lord Byron, has been inimical to Lady Byron in her misfortunes. It endears her to her friends, but it piques the indifferent. Most odiously unjust, therefore, is Mr. Moore's assertion that she has had the advantage of Lord Byron in public opinion. She is, comparatively speaking, unknown to the world, for though she has many friends, that is, a friend in every one who knows her, yet her

pride and purity and misfortunes naturally contract
the circle of her acquaintances."

And with this coincides the talk about her in the
Noctes Ambrosianæ: " I don't know if you have seen
the last brochure. It has a charming head of Lady
Byron, who, it seems, sat on purpose—a most calm,
pensive, melancholy style of native beauty, and a
most touching contrast to the maids of Athens and
all the rest of them. In her old age she is represented
as being still striking and beautiful. At sixty-one
her form was slight, giving an impression of fragility;
her motions were both graceful and decided; her
eyes bright, and full of interest and quick observa-
tion. Her silvery-white hair seemed to lend a
grace to the transparent purity of her complexion,
and her small hands had a pearly whiteness. She
wore a plain widow's cap, of a transparent material,
and was dressed in some delicate shade of lavender,
which harmonized well with her complexion." She
suffered from ossification of the lungs, from which
she might die at any moment, or, on the other hand,
she might live on for years. All her affairs of life
and benevolence were always in exquisite order. To
the last she kept up an unfailing interest in all
matters of science, literature, and religion.

Many instances of her bounty are related. On
one occasion she lodged a hundred pounds in a bank
for benevolent purposes, and so arranged matters
that the names of the persons relieved should never

be known. For five-and-thirty years she tried every kind of means of doing good. Her methods anticipated some of the best designs of later days, and are still well deserving of being studied. While she lived at Brighton, in a house now pulled down, near the Pavilion, she had a permanent home at Hanger, near Ealing, and in 1836 she opened what was probably the first industrial school in the country. She had been at the expense of sending a master to Switzerland, to learn Dr. Fellenburgh's method. She took on lease five acres of land, and went to great expense in the matter of buildings and gardens. The boys spent half their time in study and half in garden and field work. The lads rented their allotments, kept regular accounts, received wages for all the labour they did, and were able to show a balance in their favour. Besides agriculture, some mechanical arts were taught. There were a hundred pupils, of whom fifty were day-boarders, who paid a little more than one-half of the price of their maintenance. She exerted herself in other parts of the country to promote similar schemes of usefulness. Many persons watched the working of her philanthropic experiments, and the Poor Law Commissioners pointed out their merits. The Ealing school continued till 1852, when the lessor reclaimed the land for building purposes. Before that date she had opened a still more extensive industrial scheme in Leicestershire. She built schools on her Leicestershire and also on her Warwickshire property. When a season of distress befell the Leicestershire stocking-weavers, she fed the children for months together. She co-operated with Miss Carpenter in her good work of the Bristol Reformatory for Girls. She sent out tribes of boys and girls accoutred for the business of the world. Her sympathies were strong with the Sicilian cause and with the anti-slavery cause in the United States. She had various residences. She had a summer residence on Hove Common. Once she resided at Burgess Hill, near Brighton. Wherever she lived she showed a fine enthusiasm of humanity.

Lady Noel Byron told one of her friends that "at a very early period of her life she had formed a plan of action, from which she had never deviated, viz. a series of practical exertions in behalf of her fellow-creatures as the best mode of serving God. She felt sufficient confidence in her powers, even at that time, to know that at some period or other she might be enabled to write a valuable work, but had deliberately surrendered this object for the sake of the other." This is the statement of Francis Trench, the brother of the Archbishop, who gives a letter of hers, which is replete with philanthropic views:—
"I have seen a slight notice of Liberia, some months ago, and was struck by the prospects it opened to both continents, but did not know where to gain any further information. As your kind confidence disposes me to speak with equal openness, I will

own that it appears to me most desirable to avoid connecting benevolent institutions with any establishment, not merely on account of the state of the Irish, but of the 'visible' Church, though, as you observe, it is not in consequence necessary to leave 'le sentiment religieux' uneducated. It is then always liable to be perverted to the worst purposes." Lady Byron goes on very sensibly to argue that the discontented both in England and Ireland should be made thoroughly acquainted with all the sympathy that exists and of the efforts that are made on their behalf.

Among other good works Lady Byron gave most effective assistance to Mary Carpenter, who was doing a great work for the destitute poor children of Bristol, a philanthropic movement which extended throughout the country. Lady Byron offered a prize of 200*l.* for the best essay on the duty of society towards destitute children. She carried on a constant co-operation with Miss Carpenter, who was greatly encouraged and sustained by her zealous co-operation. Lady Byron's great idea was that all reformatory schools should be rural schools, an idea which has been thoroughly carried out in the history of the movement. When Mary Carpenter had secured for her young folk the house which John Wesley had built for himself at Kingswood, with a garden walk where he used to meditate, Lady Byron gave liberal help, and handed over a quantity of furniture which

she had used in her Ealing school. When Mary
Carpenter proceeded to her second great work, that
of reformatory work among juvenile delinquents, she
again had Lady Byron's sympathy and assistance.
Lady Byron sent some "suggestions," which ladies
were invited to hear, and then form a committee.
The school at Kingswood extended into a second
school at the Red Lodge, near Park Street, Bristol,
the purchase of which was greatly helped forward by
Lady Byron. Lady Byron, however, acted unwisely
in telling Miss Carpenter some unkind things which
Harriet Martineau had said about her. Poor Miss
Carpenter endeavoured to set things right by a very
sympathetic and conciliatory letter, but the mighty
Harriet surprised her by a severe rebuke of her
arrogance. In 1857 we find Miss Carpenter staying
at Lady Byron's, with "talks of books and general
movements of philanthropy." Lady Byron rendered
the most generous and effective aid to all friendly
schemes. Her sick-room was a council-chamber,
where all kindly deeds were planned and plotted.
She purchased a house in Park Street, near the Red
Lodge, as a residence for Miss Carpenter. She also
purchased a cottage, where a number of girls should
be trained for domestic service. We find, from one
of Miss Carpenter's letters to Lady Byron, that she
had been paying some rent, and other acknowledg-
ments. In her will Lady Byron appointed Miss
Carpenter one of her three literary executors, and

bequeathed a legacy, which enabled her afterwards to purchase the Red Lodge property. Had Lady Byron lived, no doubt she would have furthered the other good works for which Miss Carpenter was famous, in the treatment of convicts, and the four voyages which she made to India in her old age, to improve the condition of the Hindoo women. She has a characteristic note on Lady Byron's death :—" The loss was deep and irreparable of my beloved Lady Byron. Her spirit helped mine much, and she had true sympathy in my work. Our friendship steadily grew ; it will be perfected, I feel sure, in the Father's house ! What a meeting has been hers ! Have her beloved ones yet been purified, and has she seen mine ? Faith answers ' Yes.' "

Mr. Gallenga, in his recent autobiography, has some mention of Lady Byron. He found her staying at a house which she had taken " to oblige a friend who could not have afforded to travel as he wished without letting his house, and could not easily have found another tenant." The next time he met her she was staying at Esher, " for there seemed to be about her a restlessness which allowed her to find no permanent abode, at least at or near London. She held forth incessantly, as if anxious to impress me with the conviction that her zeal for the cause of progress and humanity engrossed all her energies to the exclusion of any other thought." Lady Byron at this date, according to Mr. Gallenga, was forty-seven, and hardly looked forty. " Her complexion seemed to me rather dark for an English-woman, marble-like, quite colourless, but her features were faultless, and her expression was sedate, serene, with hardly a trace of grief long since buried." That day at Esher the purity of the air brought up the subject of Italian skies, and Mr. Gallenga, without thinking, quoted a line of her husband's book, but she showed no recollection either of " Childe Harold " or its author.

Anything relating to Byron's child Ada will not fail to be deeply interesting. The subject of the Byron family, especially the character of " Ada, sole daughter of my house and heart," had a very great attraction for the late Lord Beaconsfield. It is the main subject of his novel of " Venetia." It is a literary amusement to disentangle the threads of his delineations. Disraeli's method in his por-traitures is well understood. He makes a photo-graph of his characters, and instantly blurs the image. He distributes among different and even opposed characters the traits which belong to one of them only. In his dedication to Lord Lyndhurst he virtually avows his intention—very imperfectly fulfilled—of shadowing forth those two great spirits, Shelley and Byron. The fact that Ada, Lord Byron's daughter, did not know until she was grown up anything about her father's history and work, is made the central fact in the development of Disraeli's story. The character of the mother of the heroine is obviously meant for Lady Byron, and the imagination of the novelist is exuberant in depicting a reconciliation. The hero's mother and Lord Byron's mother are the same. Cadureis Abbey, with its cloisters and lakes, is Newstead, and the catastrophe at Spezia, where the author drowns Byron and Shelley at the same time, is a partial transcript of facts. Writing at a time when Lady Byron and her daughter were both living, Disraeli is even unusually careful to blur his figures.

Francis Trench has an interesting reminiscence of Lady Byron and her daughter: "I dined a few days ago with Lady Byron at Hanger Hill, not far from Ealing. I like her society very much, and consider her one of the cleverest and most bene-volent persons I ever met in my life. Her history, of course, must make her of peculiar interest to all who know her. Her daughter is now about sixteen, with a fine form of countenance, large expressive eyes, and dark curling hair. Her features bear a likeness to her father's, but require some observa-tion before it appears strongly. Then, I think, it does. At present her health is delicate, and she is obliged to use crutches. I had much pleasant, and to me profitable, talk with Lady Byron, and nothing could be more simple, and at the same time more forcible and original, than the tone of her conver-sation. She is deeply read in all useful subjects, and at the same time most practical in all details of action for the good of her fellow-creatures."

In early life the daughter Ada showed a remarkable aptitude for mathematics, a line of studies not very congenial, as a rule, to young ladies, although there has been a senior wrangler who said he had learned all his mathematics from his sister. Dr. King, a great friend of her mother's, gave her great assistance in her mathematical studies.

Some letters of Lady Lovelace's have found their way into one of the magazines,[1] which appear to be the index of a very remarkable character. They evidence how far she partook of both the intellectual nature of the father and the moral nature of the mother. Her correspondence was with Mr. Cross, the electrician, and shows some striking points of character as well as a remarkable aptitude for physical science. She gloried in being a Byron. She had the most passionate affection for her father's memory. "I play as much (on the harp), perhaps more than ever, and I really do get on gloriously. I believe no creature ever could will things like a Byron. And perhaps that is at the bottom of the genius-like tendencies in my family. We can throw our *whole life* and *existence* for the time being into whatever we *will* to do and accomplish." She observed once to Mr. Cross: "Our family are an alternal stratification of poetry and

[1] The *Argosy*, vol. vii.

mathematics." Here is a kind action of hers which reminds one of her mother's philanthropy: "My journey was very wretched—so cold, so late, so dreary. I could not help lending my cloak to a lady who was my companion, and who seemed to me more delicate and in need of it than myself."

She appears even then to have had very bad health. She says, "I think I may as well just give you a hint that I am subject at times to dreadful physical sufferings. If such should come over me at Broomfield, I may have to keep my room for a time. In that case, all I require is to be let alone. With all my wiry power and strength, I am prone at times to bodily sufferings of no common degree or kind. I do not regret the sufferings and peculiarities of my physical constitution. They have taught me, and continue to teach me, that which I think nothing else could have developed. It is a force and control put upon me by Providence, which I *must* obey. And the effects of this continual discipline are mighty. They *tame* in the best sense of that word, and they *fan* into existence a pure, bright, holy, unselfish flame within that sheds cheerfulness and light on many."

Here also she falls into some of her mother's religious vagueness: "Religion to me is science, and science is religion. In that deeply felt truth lies the secret of my intense devotion to the reading of God's natural works. It is reading Him, His

will, His intelligence; and this again is learning to
obey and to follow (to the best of our power) that
Will! For he who reads, who *interprets* the
Divinity, with a free and simple heart, then obeys
and submits in acts and feelings as by an impulse
and instinct. He cannot help doing so. At least
it appears so to me. And when I behold the
scientific and so-called philosophers full of selfish
feelings, and of a tendency to war against circumstances and Providence, I say to myself, *they* are
not true prophets, they are but half prophets, if
not absolutely false ones. They have read the great
page simply with the physical eye, and with none
of the Spirit *within*. The intellectual, the moral,
the religious seem to me all naturally bound up, and
interlinked together in one great and harmonious
whole. . . . That God is one, and thus all the works
and the feelings that He has called into existence
are one; this is a truth (a Biblical and Scriptural
truth too) not, in my opinion, developed to the
apprehension of most people in its really deep and
unfathomable meaning. There is too much tendency to making *separate* and *independent* bundles
of both the physical and moral facts of the universe,
whereas all and everything is naturally related and
interconnected. A volume I could write you on
this subject."

Lady Lovelace unhappily fell into extreme sceptical opinions. If she read the Bible, it was to

object to its statements, and her notes on many a tract were expressed in the language of direct contradiction. In her last and her best days, things were very different. We are told that Frederick Robertson absented himself for a time, and it transpired that during the period of his absence he was in close attendance on Lady Lovelace in Clarges Street, during her last illness—in which all her doubts passed away—an illness in which she was completely nursed by her mother, and carefully taught and guided by Robertson, her mother's pastor, and now her own.

After the death of Lady Lovelace, Lady Byron steadily devoted herself to the education of her daughter's children. The eldest, Lord Ockham, was a cause of much anxiety.

During the year 1855, Crabbe Robinson " was called upon to act as arbitrator in a case of the most honourable kind to all concerned. Lieutenant Arnold, son of Dr. Arnold, had been engaged by Lady Byron as tutor to her grandson. For reasons into which it is unnecessary to enter, the tutorship came to an end in a way which involved an unforeseen pecuniary settlement, and Lady Byron proposed to pay just double what Lieutenant Arnold thought it right to receive. The award of the arbitrator satisfied the conscience of the one and the generosity of the other.'' Another person who kindly acted as a sort of tutor and guardian to Lord

Ockham, and his brother Ralph King was Dr. King, who, we believe, was some connection of the King family. The lads were placed under his care during times of visits and holidays. With Dr. King Lady Byron maintained a constant correspondence, and when he died in 1865, five years after Lady Byron, Mrs. King had the whole of it burned, according to her husband's express wishes.

Lord Ockham was not a satisfactory subject. We may here transcribe a letter of Miss Mitford's to her friend, Mr. Field, of Boston :—

"Has anybody told you the terrible story of that boy, Lord Ockham, Lord Byron's grandson? I had it from Mr. Noel, Lady Byron's cousin-german and intimate friend. While his poor mother was dying her death of martyrdom from an inward cancer,—Mrs. Sartoris (Adelaide Kemble), who went to sing to her, saw her through the door, which was left open, crouching on a floor covered with mattresses, on her hands and knees, the only posture she could bear. —whilst she, with the patience of an angel, was enduring her long agony, her husband, engrossed by her, left this lad of seventeen to his sister and the governess. It was a dull life, and he ran away. Mr. Noel (my friend's brother, from whom he had the story) knew most of the youth, who had been for a long time staying at his house, and they begged him to undertake the search. Lord Ockham had sent a carpet-bag containing his gentleman's clothes to his father, Lord Lovelace, in London. He was therefore disguised. and from certain things he had said, Mr. Noel suspected that he intended to go to America. Accordingly he went first to Bristol then to Liverpool, leaving his description, a sort of written portrait of him, with the police at both places. At Liverpool he was found before long, and when Mr. Noel, summoned by the electric telegraph, reached that town, he found him dressed as a sailor-boy, at a low public-house, surrounded by seamen of both nations, and enjoying as much as possible their sailor yarns. He had given his money, 36*l*., to the landlord to keep; had desired him to inquire for a ship where he might be received as cabin-boy; and had entered into a shrewd bargain for his board, stipulating that he should have, over and above his ordinary rations, a pint of beer with his Sunday dinner.

"The landlord did not cheat him, but he postponed all engagements under the expectation—seeing that he was clearly a gentleman's son —that money would be offered for his recovery. The worst is that he (Lord Ockham) showed no regret for the sorrow and disgrace that he had brought upon his family at such a time. He has two tastes not often seen combined, the love of money and of low company. One wonders how he will turn out. He is now in Paris, after which he is to reenter in Green's ship (he had served in one before) for a twelvemonth, and to leave the service or remain in it, as he may decide then. This is perfectly true; Mr. Noel had it from his brother the very day before he wrote it to me. He says that Lady Lovelace's funeral was too ostentatious—escutcheons and silver coronets everywhere. Lord Lovelace's taste that, and not Lady Byron's, which is perfectly simple. You know that she was buried in the same vault with her father, whose coffin and the box containing his heart were in perfect preservation."

Lord Ockham afterwards showed himself as a man of thoroughly protestant tastes. He dropped all the social advantages of his position, and went to live as a poor man among the poor, making their lot his own.

Lady Byron has given her own explanation of the vagaries of her grandson. He was a man of wonderful physical and muscular strength, with hands like a blacksmith, and she says that he went into what is called " low society," as that required more vigorous animal life than could be found in his own station. He was then working as a mechanic on the iron-work of the *Great Eastern.* He was simply known by his fellow-workmen as Ockham. He was pointed out to a friend of mine one day when he was visiting the *Great Eastern.* He sang out his number cheerily, and passed by, smoking his cutty pipe. " The great difficulty with our nobility," said the old lady to Mrs. Stowe, " is apt to be that they do not *understand* the working classes, so as to feel for them properly ; and Ockham is now going through an experience which may yet fit him to do great good when he comes to the peerage. I am trying to influence him to do good among the workmen, and to interest himself in schools for their children. I think I have great influence over Ockham." It may be questioned, however, if Lady Byron really understood the rights of her grandson's story.

He lived in a small house in a row of small houses at Deptford, and, we believe, worked as a common labourer. He wished to marry a girl in the same row, employed at an inn ; but the young man's rank was really well known in the neighbourhood, and the young woman very sensibly refused to marry a man whose line of life was so different to her own. A very similar history to Lord Ockham's was that of the late Earl of Aberdeen. He preferred to go to sea as a common sailor, and was lost at sea when serving in the humble capacity of a mate—last seen with a Bible in his hand. No doubt there is a certain charm and freedom of life which is found among the poor, and perhaps a rich man, sojourning among them, might have the enjoyment of feeling himself a sort of Haroun Alraschid with an immense reserve of power. Or perhaps, as in the case of Lord Ockham, there might have been a touch of insanity, derived by the law of atavism from a progenitor. Lord Ockham died early, and was succeeded by his brother, Lord Wentworth.

A sister, married to Mr. Wilfrid Blunt, has displayed great personal daring and great literary ability.

We may speak still further of the relations between Frederick Robertson and his illustrious friend. On one occasion he mentions a visit which he made to Lady Byron at one of her country residences: "This morning I arrived on a visit to Lady Byron, and have been in the house all day, having had no time yet to go out and see the country, which I am told is interesting, with rich woods and fine commons. Lady Byron showed me a picture of Lady Lovelace, taken at seventeen. How different from what she was when I knew her—unquestionably handsome, and with an air of sad thoughtfulness which then characterized her. I have seen, too, to-day, the original MS. of "Beppo," from which the poem was printed. . . . The quietude of this place is refreshing after the inevitable life *en évidence* of Brighton, its hurry and its glare. I have been only a few hours away, and I feel as if I had got back to the home life of life, and am myself again, with no weight of weary duty hanging over me, and no necessity of addressing a crowd of critics who are supposed to be before me to be taught ! "

In one of his lectures there is an unmistakable reference to Lady Byron :—

" And yet, as there are some persons who cannot conceive of human elevation, except as connected with circumstantial condition, I must tell you an anecdote to satisfy even them. A lady, with whose friendship I am honoured, was travelling last summer in the lake district of Cumberland and Westmoreland. Being interested in education, she visited many of the national schools in that country For the most part the result was uninteresting enough. The heavy looks and stolid intellects, which characterize our English agricultural population, disappointed her. But in one place there was a striking difference. The children were sprightly, alert, and answered with intelligence all the questions proposed; traced rivers from their sources to the sea, explaining why the towns along their course were of such and such a character, and how the soil had

modified the habits and lives of the inhabitants—
with much of similar information. The schoolmaster
had been educated at one of our great training
seminaries. He was invited by the tourist to spend
an hour at the hotel; and when, after a long conversation, she expressed her surprise that one so
highly educated should bury himself in a retired,
unknown spot, with small stipend, teaching only a
few rustics, he replied, after some hesitation, " Why,
madam, when this situation was first offered me, I
was on the point of marriage; and I calculated
that it would be worth more to live on a small
salary, with domestic peace, in the midst of this
beautiful scenery, than on a much larger sum in a
less glorious spot."

We may transcribe a narrative from the life
of Byron, in connection with Lady Byron and
Robertson : [2]—

" On a certain Tuesday morning, of April, 1851,
an aged lady, having the appearance of an extreme
invalid, came to the London Bridge Station, and
seated herself in a first-class carriage of the next
train for Reigate—the place of her destination. At
a glance it was obvious that she could never have
been beautiful; must even in the spring of her
youth have been plain. But the signs of sickness
and sorrow in her countenance made her interesting

[2] " The Real Lord Byron," by J. Cordy Jeaffreson. Hurst
and Blackett.

to her fellow-travellers, and won their sympathy. She was, indeed, a woman of sorrows, and had made acquaintance with griefs unimagined by most of her sex. Of those griefs too much has been told elsewhere. She was Byron's sister, stricken with years and illness, and within a few months of the hour when trouble and unkindness ceased to vex her.

"A loiterer on the platform of the Reigate Station, waiting for the arrival of this train, would have seen among the persons about him a manservant in drab livery. On the arrival of the down train this footman bestirred himself. Taking a lady's calling-card from his pocket, he hastened to the first-class carriages, and went from carriage to carriage, holding out the card to the view of the occupants of the seats. At last he came to the carriage in which Mrs. Leigh was seated. On seeing the card with Lady Byron's name upon it, Mrs. Leigh declared herself the lady he was seeking. The man said a fly was in attendance, and in another minute Mrs. Leigh was driving to the White Hart Hotel of Reigate. On leaving the carriage at the door of the inn, she was shown to a private room, where Lady Byron and the Rev. Frederick Robertson, of Trinity Chapel, Brighton, were expecting her appearance. Lady Byron, an invalid, had come from Brighton with the clergyman for an interview with her sister-in-law. During the long years which had passed since their estrangement Augusta had often wished for friendly speech with her sister-in-law. It had come to Mrs. Leigh's knowledge that she was said by Lady Byron to have been the influence that prevented the poet from coming to just and kindly views respecting his wife. There were times when Lady Byron's chief sorrow was that she and her husband had not been reconciled before his death; times when her greatest complaint against Mrs. Leigh was that the reconcilement would have taken place had not she used her influence over her brother to perpetuate the estrangement. . . . Knowing she had not long to live, and holding the old simple notion that the words of the dying are strong to convince even the most suspicious and incredulous hearers, Mrs. Leigh journeyed to Reigate, hoping that the assurance of her lips (so soon to be still for ever) would relieve Lady Byron's mind from its misconceptions, more especially of the quite groundless notion that she had been the cause of her brother's persistence in unkindly feeling towards his wife. No good resulted from this curious meeting, which opened with Mrs. Leigh's assurance that in former time she had been loyal alike to her brother and his wife. To this assurance Lady Byron replied with a show of surprise that her sister-in-law had nothing more to say. Mr. Robertson looked as though he were puzzled,— as though he and Lady Byron were being trifled with. What more Lady Byron and Mr. Robertson expected to hear from Mrs. Leigh does not appear. That they had come to Reigate for some larger and more momentous communication was obvious from their words and looks; and it may well have distressed Mrs. Leigh, after her return to town, to know that Mr. Robertson suspected her of refraining at the last moment from saying what she ought to have said, and what she had come there to tell them. These expressions of dissatisfaction on the part of Lady Byron and the clergyman were followed by words between the ladies that did not make them better friends. Lady Byron directly charged Mrs. Leigh with aggravating Byron's bitterness to her, and encouraging him to remain in enmity towards her. Mrs. Leigh repelled the accusation warmly, and, in support of her assertions that she had consistently and invariably done her best to be a peace-maker, quoted certain words spoken by Hobhouse—words which agitated Lady Byron profoundly, causing her to start and change colour. Of course, no good came of all this. Lady Byron returned to Brighton with a determination never again to see or hold communication with her sister-in-law. And Mrs. Leigh went back to London in grief at Lady Byron's perplexing treatment of her. Mrs. Leigh would fain have seen Mr. Robertson again, to satisfy him, by the exhibition of letters, that she had spoken nothing but the truth to Lady Byron in his hearing. But as he was of opinion no good could come from the interview, or from his examination of the documents, the clergyman declined to see her again on the matter, or go further in the business.   It is nothing to Mrs. Leigh's discredit that Mr. Robertson regarded her with something more than suspicion, for his mind was wholly prepossessed by the representations of the other lady."

We may add a letter of Robertson's in reference to this subject, which was printed for the first time quite recently in the *Times :—*

> *" St. James's Palace, London,*
>
> *" May 21st, 1851.*

" MADAM,—I regret to say that I feel it impossible to accede to the proposal which you have made, viz. to favour me with an interview in which you might substantiate your assertion made to Lady Byron.

" In the meeting at Reigate Lady Byron expressed her conviction that your influence on Lord Byron's mind had been unfavourable to his coming to just conclusions respecting herself.

" This you denied strongly and distinctly ; and you quoted a speech of Sir John Hobhouse, one sentence of which appeared to shock and startle Lady Byron exceedingly.

" No one but myself was witness of this conversation.   I am a stranger to you, and my opinion can be of no importance.   I need scarcely say that the topics of that interview are sacred, and that they will never pass my lips. The proofs which you desire to give me could only be given in Lady Byron's presence, and she will never consent to another meeting. The last was final. My investigation of such proofs therefore would be inconclusive and useless; besides which, as it could not have any reference to my own personal judgment, I do not feel that I have any right to enter into an investigation so painful and delicate. If your own conscience is free and clear, and Lady Byron is no way injured by you, the sense of innocence in God's sight will make the opinion of any human being a matter of small importance. If, on the contrary, there was anything for the sorrowful acknowledgment of which that meeting was the last and final opportunity which you can ever have in this world, then, of course, no opinion of Sir John Hobhouse, written or expressed, nor of Lord Byron to himself, can reverse the solemn judgment upon the whole matter, which must be heard very, very soon, when you meet God face to face.

"I remain, Madam, your obedient servant,

"FRED. W. ROBERTSON.

"P.S.—I ought, perhaps, to add that I did not transmit your letter to Lady Byron, and therefore return it. She is resolved that the communication was ended with the last letter she wrote; and, indeed, the result of that interview has been a dangerous illness."

"I trust you will not look upon the plain words I have spoken as expressing harshness of feeling. I would gladly, now or hereafter, as a minister of Christ, do what might be in my power to alleviate sadness, but I am quite sure that it is not my duty to receive any evidence of the nature you propose."

It is to be regretted that a collection of Lady Byron's letters has never been published. We believe that the materials exist for a large volume. The present writer is acquainted with at least two persons who have sets of letters in their possession. Several have found their way into contemporary literature. Some of her letters are preserved in the Crabbe Robinson volumes. Under November 29, 1852, we read, "I went to Robertson's and had two hours of interesting chat with him on his position here in the pulpit; also about Lady Byron. He speaks of her as the noblest woman he ever knew." In the May of the following year he met both Lady Byron and Mrs. Beecher Stowe. "The last lady was the object of general curiosity. Lady Byron was also present, to whom Mrs. Jameson introduced me, and with whom was Dr. King. Lady Byron echoed my praise of Robertson, who has consented to take a curate." "September 13th (Brighton).— Dr. King called, and in the evening I called by desire on Lady Byron—a call which I enjoyed, and which may have consequences. Recollecting her history as the widow of the most famous, though not the greatest, poet of England, from all I have heard of her I consider her one of the best women of the day. 'She lives to do good,' says Dr. King, and I believe this to be true. She wanted my opinion as to the mode of doing justice to Robertson's memory. She spoke of him as having a better head on matters of business than any one else she ever knew. She said, 'I have consulted lawyers on matters of difficulty, but Robertson seemed better able to give me advice. He unravelled everything, and explained everything at once as no one else did.'" A few days later he writes, "I was much pleased with Lady Byron. She is a most generous and remarkable woman, and is most just and high-minded. She places Robertson, as I do, at the head of all the preachers I have ever known." In his last entry respecting him, Lady Byron tells Mr. Robinson a very interesting anecdote about her husband. Once Byron went to a dinner where he would meet Wordsworth. When he came back Lady Byron said to him, " Well, how did the young poet get on with the old one?" " To tell you the truth," said he, " I had but one feeling from the beginning of the visit to the end—*reverence.*"

A series of letters from Lady Byron to Mr. A. C. Robinson have been reprinted, which are replete with interest. They contain interesting references to Frederick Robertson, to her own husband, and various allusions to her own opinions and experiences.

Soon after Robertson's death she interested herself
with the idea of a forthcoming biography, a project
which was not carried into effect till twelve years
later.   Mr. Robinson had written a short memoir of
his friend in the *Christian Reformer*, which Lady
Byron had wished him to print on letter-paper for
circulation among friends.   She thought that the
good effects of such a paper would be "(1st) To
enlarge the views both of Churchmen and Dissenters,
and to expose the folly of making, as it were,
a brazen horizon to any Christian Church, instead of
a soft, melting, aërial boundary.   (2nd) To show,
by the example of one whose ministry was so
short, and under many unfavourable circumstances,
the *power* of such expansive charity to obliterate
sectarian distinctions."   Every one will agree with
the sympathizers of expanded charities, but those
who find it necessary clearly to define to themselves
what they do and what they do not believe, who
find themselves adopting with loyalty the language
of creeds and confessions, without claiming brazen
horizons, find themselves of sterner material than to
desire "a soft, melting, aërial boundary."   Lady
Byron appears to have been a great deal more
indefinite than her friend Robertson.   Her next
letter describes Dr. King, who was indeed some
remote connection of hers, but whose acquaintance
she had made oddly and accidentally through a
pauper saying to her that he was the poor man's

doctor. "This passed in '43 between him and Robertson. Robertson said to me, 'I want to know something about ragged schools.' I replied, 'You had better ask Dr. King; he knows more about them.' 'I?' said Dr. King. 'I take care to know nothing of ragged schools, lest they should make *me* ragged.' Robertson did not see through it. Perhaps I had been taught to understand such suicidal speeches by my cousin, Lord Melbourne. . . . There is something pathetic to me in seeing any one so unknown. Even the other medical friends of Robertson, when I knew that Dr. King felt a woman's tenderness, said on one occasion to him, 'But we know that you, Dr. King, are above all feeling.'"

Her next letters relate to a projected review which ultimately took form and ran a somewhat brief existence as the *National Review*. It was supposed by many that Mr. Maurice was connected with this review, but Mr. Maurice once assured the present writer that this was not the case. Mr. Robinson is credited by his friends with having had a great deal to do with starting and supporting the review. Lady Byron writes to him about the choice of an editor. She would like an American, one Freeman Clark of Boston, who she thinks "better fitted for a leader than any other of the religious 'Freethinkers.' . . . He so far adopts Comte's theory as to speak of religion itself under three successive aspects, historically—1. Thesis; 2. Antithesis; 3. Synthesis. I made his acquaintance in England, and he inspired confidence at once by his brave independence." She next writes to him about J. J. Taylor, with a very interesting reference to her daughter Ada. "Though almost a stranger to him I have a peculiar reason for sympathizing. A book of his was a treasure to my daughter on her death-bed. I must confess to intolerance of opinion as to these two points—*eternal* evil in any form and (involved in it) *eternal* suffering." In three other letters she discusses the *Review* recurring to other subjects especially near to her heart at the time. "From what you said I think you agreed with me, that a latitudinarian Christianity ought to be the character of the periodical, but the depth of the roots should correspond with the width of the branches of that tree of knowledge. . . . 'Grounded in Christ' has, to me, a most practical significance and value." She wants "a new literary combination for distinct special objects—a review in which every separate article should be *convergent*. If instead of the problem to make a circle pass through three given points, it were required to find the centre from which to describe a circle through any three articles in the *Edinburgh* or *Westminster Reviews*, who could accomplish it? Much force is lost for want of this one-mindedness amongst the contributors. It would not exclude variety or freedom in the unlimited discussion of means towards the ends unequivocally recognized. If St. Paul had edited a review, he might have admitted Peter as well as Luke or Barnabas."

She recurs to other subjects. She writes about her friend, Mary Carpenter: " I, too, have anxiety about a friend—Mary Carpenter—whose life is of public importance; she, more than any of the English Reformers, unless Nash and Wright, has found the art of drawing out the good of human nature and proving its existence. She makes these discoveries by the light of love. I hope she may recover from to-day's report." She goes on to speak about her schools. "The *desideratum* is, well-qualified masters and mistresses. If you hear of such by chance, pray let me know. The regular schoolmaster is an extinguisher. Heart, and familiarity with the class to be educated are all-important. At home and abroad, the evidence. is conclusive on that point, for I have for many years attended to such experiments in various parts of Europe." She will not discuss the politics of Russell or Palmerston, for which she has no responsibility, " but much in deciding whether the ' village politician,' Jackson or Thompson, shall be leader in the school and public-house." This remotely reminds us of a remarkable passage in one of the letters of Lord Chancellor Hatherley. The Ministry of which he was such a conspicuous

member had been defeated in the House of
Commons, and he had to resign the Great Seal.
This, he says in a letter to a friend, does not give
him the least concern, but what causes him the
greatest concern is the bad conduct of a man whom
he has been employing as a village schoolmaster.

Lady Byron seems to have been a believer in
what is called "Spiritualism." She writes, "I have
a mind to say something more about the 'manifes-
tations.' I omit 'spiritual' designedly, as on that
word the question is begged. It appears to me
that no one who has accepted the *resurrection* as an
historical fact can refuse assent to the accumulated
evidences of these *re-appearances*." In fact, Lady
Byron came to look on these appearances as satisfactory evidences of the Resurrection of Christ—
which otherwise rests on "testimony in a remote
age, and by no means completely satisfactory."
Still, "having rested tranquilly in that faith from a
very early age I could not be troubled by Middleton
or Strauss."

It must be also said about Lady Byron that she
was extremely positive in all her opinions. She
fully endorsed—at least it has been so represented
to us—the doctrine of her own personal infallibility.
She assumed as an axiom in all discussion that she
was in the right, and any one who contradicted her
must be in the wrong. "Orthodoxy," said Bishop
Warburton, "is my doxy. Heterodoxy is my

opponent's doxy." Some of her opinions indeed, whether derived from Robertson or not, are hardly fraught with orthodoxy. She had the opinion that the Church as a Church ought to have no opinions, that is to say not any Creed. She objected, in general, to all creeds. As in Tennyson's " Palace of Art," where the soul thinks that it has much good laid up for many years, she seems to say,—

> " I sit as God, holding no form of creed,
> But contemplating all?"

Robertson's teaching, however good, seems to have had not very much definite meaning for her.

I am only repeating the statements and summing-up the impressions of various of her Brighton friends. There was a strong vein of eccentricity in her character. She would lie in bed late. She would dress untidily. She would take violent and unreasonable prejudices. She was capable of a very strong tinge of bitterness. She would show great and lavish kindness, and the kindness, without any reason would be capriciously withdrawn. Indeed one of her medical friends who had watched her very narrowly has declared that in his judgment her mental balance was impaired, and believed that strong prejudice and suspicion, combined with the mental disturbance of which she suspected her husband in their first married days, were the chief causes of her charges against him. Such words as these are not pleasing to write, but they are useful if they help to clear away the most awful of the aspersions with which the fame of a great English classic has been obscured.

Indeed, Lady Byron never fully possessed the gift of order. She led a nomadic life and a desultory state of things prevailed generally. It was not an unusual thing for the boys' tutor to resign, or for the whole of her domestics to quit their situations in a body. There was one gift which she shared with Robertson. She could write exquisite little notes, in exquisite caligraphy, always putting some point briefly, in an effective way, with kindliness and grace. There are various people who cherish such little notes from Lady Byron and from Robertson. Other matters should, however, be mentioned. But, with whatever shortcomings, she eminently possessed the gift of "largeness of heart," and while she could give the kindliest attention to a child, she took a vivid interest in the largest interests of humanity. Indeed, it was said of her —though perhaps the remark has been made of various other good women—that she was doing more good than any one else in England. It was not only the quantity, but the excellent quality, of her benevolence that made her famous. While her favourite charity was the extension of education to the poor, she would at the same time assist, so far as her strength went, every good cause and every deserving person. She would, it may be mentioned, give very large help to some deserving and distressed author. Her agents have stated that all her business was most methodically arranged, and nothing ever disturbed the smoothness of her arrangements. Although she seemed to hold life by the frailest tenure, she lasted long. Dr. King writes in 1854: " Lady Byron is now quite recovered. She is always feeble, and obliged to husband her strength and calculate her powers ; but her mind is ever intact, pure and lofty. It seems to pour forth its streams of benevolence and judgment even from the sick-bed; a perennial fountain. Her state of mind has always given me confidence in her severest illnesses. Yet her power of bearing fatigue occasionally, as during the illness and death of her daughter, is as wonderful." Six years later, May 16, 1860, she died, one of the famousest of Englishwomen through her connection with the great poet, and to those brought within the range of her personal influence the object of an affection and veneration such as the great poet himself could never claim.

CHAPTER VI.

THE NEIGHBOURHOOD OF BRIGHTON.

It is interesting to gather up what we find of Robertson's *villegiatura*, his visits to, and residences in, the neighbourhood of Brighton. The sea cuts every neighbourhood in half, and thus materially limits the area of county scenery and society. Brighton is all sufficient for itself. It shows us to a considerable degree the highest outcome of modern civilization. It exhibits all that modern luxury has to show, all the wealth, improvements, manifold resources of our time. In almost violent contrast we meet in the neighbourhood of Brighton with some of the most primitive, old-world villages that are to be found anywhere in the country. They seem to reproduce for us almost exactly what England used to be in the days of the Stuarts. In the soft and striking outlines of the Downs you find a surpassing loveliness of curve and form. In order to appreciate their beauty they should be visited, not from Brighton, but from the London side. On this side there is a boldness of escarped declivity, a beauty of rounded combe, which hardly belong to the Downs as you approach them from the sea. Hidden away in the folds of the hills are villages, lovely as they are embowered in woods, old moated manorial halls, quaint churches with curious towers, remnants of vast primeval forests, sheets of water of moderate size—one of them is exactly the same space as the Serpentine—old historic towns, such as Lewes, where the county record becomes national history. The favourite walk of all is to the Dyke Hill—it was Robertson's favourite walk—where we behold the curious convolution of the Devil's Dyke, and look down on the tower, embosomed in foliage, of Poynings Church and the rectory, with its wide grounds and water dell. There resided here in Robertson's time, and indeed to this present date, a clergyman who is the poet of his region, who has sung its groves, and birds, and scenery, a poet whose natural tones would not be disclaimed by Cowper or Wordsworth. Robertson must repeatedly have visited the parish. Thomas Agar Holland, who with his father before him has occupied the living some threescore years, was the grandson of Lord Chancellor Erskine, and one whose youthful muse received a guerdon of praise from Sir Walter Scott. In those former days Robertson was an incessant walker. He would walk any man "off his legs," as the saying goes. He not only walked; he ran, he leaped, he bounded. He walked as fast and as incessantly as Charles

Dickens, and, like Dickens, his mind was in a state of incessant activity all the time. There was not a bird of the air or a flower by the wayside that was not known to him. His knowledge of birds would have matched that of the collector of the Natural History Museum in his favourite Dyke road. The people about Brighton exactly match the inhabitants of Attica, as described by Thucydides. There are the men of the seaboard, the men of the hills, or, as we should say, the Downs, and the men of the plain, or rather the weald. Robertson, in his incessant walks, must have examined thoroughly the whole region, and could turn out a map as clearly and cleverly as any Prussian Uhlan. We will speak of some of the localities which he must have visited, and which must be fresh in the minds of all Brightonians. It was in this region that Mantell laid the foundation of his geological achievements.

As the London traveller comes to Brighton, before he enters the suburb of Brighton, Preston, where the tickets are collected, he passes three stations: Hayward's Heath, Burgess Hill, Hassock's Gate. Perhaps the traveller may have a gleam of curiosity in his disposition, and may ask, Who was Hayward? Who was Burgess? Who was Hassock? It is supposed by some that Hayward was a celebrated highwayman, but another interpretation gives a different meaning. Near it is Balcombe, with its lovely lake and embosoming woods. Burgess was the name of an honest farmer who lived on the incline, an elevation or ridge of land which is now populous with villas embowered with gardens, chiefly the retreats of the Brighton business people. It was formerly in the parish of Keymer, one of the rich livings of Robertson's college of Brasenose; but the daughter parish has outgrown the mother parish fourfold. One season, at least, Lady Byron had a house here, and Robertson would not fail to come over to see his old friend. "Hassock," we believe, is not the name of a person, but the word indicates wood-land. Hassock's Gate, as it was then called—but now the railway company, London, Brighton, and South Coast Railway, has abbreviated the name into Hassocks, and what may be called a railway population has sprung up by the side of the bran-new station—was then chiefly known as the railway-station for Hurstpierpoint. Here, at least, on one occasion Mr. Robertson went over to deliver a lecture to the Hurstpierpoint people. His friend, Mr. Towers, was for ten years curate of Hurstpier-point, and on his account the lecture was delivered. I have heard some details of these lectures from several people who are still living. The aged rector remembers something of his conversation with him, and one striking expression that he used, "that everything in nature was a sacrament," a thought that frequently occurs in some of his writings. Some ladies remember Robertson speaking of this lecture,

and pronouncing that his Hurstpierpoint auditory
was " very bucolic."

The neighbouring villas and vicarages and country
seats would probably furnish a quota to listen to the
most celebrated clergyman in Brighton. But the
mass of the people would consist of small shop-
keepers and peasants. We can well understand how
Robertson pronounced them bucolic. The Sussex
peasants are patient and honest, but they are stupid,
and they are unmusical. Unlike the northern folk
of Lancashire and Yorkshire, they have no understanding of anthems, chanting, and intonings. They
seem wonderfully devoid of imagination or sympathy. Their vocabulary is very scanty, not exceeding a few hundred words. His subject was "The
Progress of the Working Classes," and it was at
least satisfactory to him that so many of the working
classes should be present at the big room of the
village inn to meet him. The notes of the lecture
have been preserved and printed. Sorely puzzled
must have been the bucolic mind when he spoke of
"Falaise" and Guizot, and explained that the
individual must be sunk in society in general, and
exploded the thoroughly British and thoroughly
Sussex idea that an Englishman is equal to two
Frenchmen. To one of Robertson's right way of
looking at things, the obvious incapacity of his
audience to comprehend one-half of what he said
would not signify so much. If he could only in

the least degree stimulate the sluggish intellect; if he could impart any germ of thought that might hereafter fructify, he would think that his labour was not in vain, but that he had done a good evening's work.

There was one circumstance that could not fail to be satisfactory to him, and that was the lovely drive or walk from Hassocks to Hurstpierpoint. He would just get a glimpse of the castellated entrance to the Clayton tunnel, the longest on the Brighton line, and one of the longest on the English railway system—the tunnel which Thackeray mentions in the "Newcomes," and which was in the scene of one of the most fearful accidents in railway history. All along in front of him would be the lovely waving line of the South Downs, with their highest points of Ditchling Beacon and Wolstonbury Beacon, and far away to the west the tree-crowned height of Chanctonbury Ring. In one of his letters he gave an account of a visit to Hurst, but this was evidently not on the occasion of his lecture, as he came and went back on the same afternoon. He was very much struck with the beautiful atmospheric effects which are often witnessed in the region of the Downs. On this occasion he had lost his train, and had to wait an hour and a half at the station, like Lord Tennyson, who "waited for the train at Coventry." Robertson passed the time in reading one of Professor Ulmann's works. An essay might be written on the different ways in which people spend their time when they have to wait for hours at railway-stations : " It was rather fine to see the black and lead-coloured clouds drifting over the steep sides of the Downs, sometimes so dark and solemn in their travel that I felt a kind of awe creeping over me—some sweeping quite low, and only topping the hills, others sailing more slowly far above, and with tracts of clouds between these. . . . Coming home the heavens cleared brightly towards the setting sun, while all the rest was denser and more leaden by the contrast. Orange flakes and lines were shot across a clear sea-green sky, passing into blue, but made green where the yellow mingled with the blue, without any red to keep the two from blending. But it was the wildness of the whole, and the recklessness with which the whole air seemed animated that gave the day its peculiar character and power of exciting interest. I sat and read, and watched effect after effect, until the air and I seemed friends."

Robertson's remark to Prebendary Borrer, which I have quoted, of the sacramental character of natural objects, is illustrated by a passage from his "Lectures on the Corinthians:" "Bread, Wine, Water, Cloud; it matters naught what the material is, God's Presence is everything; God's Power, God's Life—wherever these exist, there, *there* is a sacrament. What then is the lesson which we learn ? Is

it that God's Life and Love and Grace, are limited
to certain materials, such as the Rock, the Bread, or
the Wine? Is it that we are doing an awful act only
when we baptize? or is it not much rather that all
here is sacramental, that we live in a fearful and
divine world; that every simple meal, that every
gushing stream, every rolling river, and every drifting cloud is the symbol of God, and a sacrament to
every *open* heart? And the power of recognizing
and feeling this, makes all the difference between the
religious and the irreligious spirit."

One day he went out to Lindfield. Going out
he would traverse the district now known as St.
John's Common, in the business part of Burgess
Hill. In his time it was a veritable common, with
very few cottages interspersed. The parish church
was Clayton, miles away, under the South Downs.
It is a mark of the development of the country that
since his time there has arisen quite a township, fast
developing into a town. At Lindfield, on the other
hand, there has been very little change. There is
the wide open English green, and the wayside pond,
almost approaching the dignity of a lough, and the
long straggling single village street, the old house,
and the old inn, that are the delight of archæolo-
gists, and the plain parish church of an unre-
storing era. Here Robertson's family had been
spending some time in *villegiatura*. "They all
came in from Lindfield yesterday. I went out to

fetch them, and spent some hours in the village of
Lindfield itself, where I strongly felt the beauty
and power of English country scenery and life to
calm, if not to purify, the hearts of those whose
lives are habitually subjected to such influences."

These parishes, under the Downs, have a very
quaint and peculiar character. As a rule they are
long and narrow, running some five miles out into
the Weald, but coming as near to each other as
they can under the Downs. Perhaps the Downs
gave them some sense of shelter and security.
From the heights they might, in unsettled times,
watch the incursions of any foe, and take steps
among themselves for co-operation and self-defence.
Eastward from Hassocks station—such a lovely
little station in Robertson's time, but which has
now given way to one of the big structures which
the London, Brighton, and South Coast Railway
loves so much—in quick succession come Clayton,
Ditchling, Westmeston, Street, Plumpton, and so
on till you come to Lewes. Each looks up, close to
the Downs, with those lovely curves which travellers say we can only see in such perfection in the
islands of the Pacific. Gilbert White passionately
loved this region, and even preferred it to his own
Selborne. Hard by each church lies the old
vicarage, with belt of woodland and portion of
glebe and sunny gardens—the whole making up
a kind of sacred Τέμενος. One dear old clergy-

man, in such a village, said once to me: "For sixty years I have been rector of this parish; it is only a man of a quiet mind that could have stayed long in this quiet spot." In such villages, and in a few seaboard villages, you see the old genuine Sussex life. When you come to the vicinity of the railway you find the old inhabitants quickly suppressed and outnumbered. The trim villas are occupied by the trading and professional people, who day by day go up to Brighton; but when you have passed Hayward's Heath Junction the Brightonians drop off, and the Londoners occupy the villas.

Another place which he visited, and of which we have a detailed account, is Lewes, the old historic capital of Sussex. He was chaplain to the High Sheriff, and had to preach the Assize sermon. Lewes at the present time still seems to retain a remarkable likeness to the Lewes of the time of Simon de Montfort and the Barons' Wars. Nearly six hundred years ago it was described as forming an irregular group of narrow streets and timbered houses. Only from the north of the town to Fletching, where the barons were, there extended a dense forest, peopled by herds of swine and deer— a region now disafforested. Here he preached the Assize sermon, so far out of the routine of assize sermons, that the judges were fairly astonished. In this sermon he told them that truth was the first thing necessary, and the second thing necessary, and the third thing necessary. In turn the presiding criminal judge fairly astonished Robertson by the wonderful force and acumen by which he unravelled difficult criminal cases. Sir John Jervis seemed to have an art of solving mysteries akin to the genius of Goboriau.

One day we find Robertson writing :—

"To-day I walked to Lewes with H—— over the Downs and home by the road. The walk to Lewes was a stiff one, for the hills were wet from the scarcely-melted snow, and on the north sides they were hard with frost, so that we slipped about considerably. We did it, however, all the way at a racing pace—there and back in three hours and a half. I took a hot bath in my own room directly on my arrival, and felt considerably refreshed, the brain clearer, and at this moment all my nature sinking into a natural and healthy weariness such as has not come to me for a long time."

There was yet another place which he visited at times, which to many is the most venerable of Sussex shrines. This was Hurstmonceux, where dwelt his Archdeacon, Julius Hare. There are many who make a pilgrimage to Hurstmonceux, to that noble castle ruin; above all to the rectory, the house which was "all library," and the famous terrace identified with the gracious form and beautiful countenance of Julius Hare.

The road from Brighton by rail or road, as far as rail can be used, is dreary; but to one who, like Robertson, could find his way through woods and over downs, replete with interest. Julius Hare was better known to his county than in his parish, in England than in his county, and on the Continent than in England. His quiet retired rectory has now become more widely known than any other English shrine, from its associations with John Sterling and the Maurices, from the description of its frequent visitant Arthur Stanley, from its place in that lovely and instructive work, the " Memorials of a Quiet Life," and we should add Mr. G. W. Dasent's autobiographic novel, " The Half of a Life-time." In Robertson's time things were very different to what they had once been. Sterling had been dead for many years, and was becoming a tradition. Sterling, in one of his last letters, writing to his child, says of some gum-cistuses in the garden : " I think I like them chiefly because I re-member a large bush of the kind, close to the greenhouse, through which one passed into Mr. Hare's library. The ground used to be all white with the fallen flowers. I have so often stood near it, talking to him, and looking away over the Pevensey Level to the huge old Roman castle, and the sea and Beachy Head beyond. The thought of the happy hours I have so spent in talking with him is and always will be very pleasant. . . . I know that if we met to-morrow, or to-morrow come a hundred years, it would be as of old, like brothers."

In Robertson's time Priscilla Maurice had become the wife of Julius Hare. Mrs. Augustus Hare had removed to the Limes close by, and afterwards to other residences. The health of the great archdeacon had given away before the incursions of the disease which carried him off two years after Robertson's death. In 1851 had come to Brighton, to the diocese, and to the country generally, the great shock of the defection of Cardinal Manning. The nomination of Dr. Hampden to the see of Hereford and the Gorham decision had been too much for him, and forced him to follow in the steps of John Henry Newman. In these days Archdeacon Hare still gathered many friends around him. Dean Plumptre speaks of him :—

> " For round him gather'd such a band of friends
>   As the world knows but few, the noblest names
>   In the great host of truth's advancing ranks."

The poet has lines which were in all probability not intended for Robertson—doubtless Stanley was meant—but which would suit Robertson at least equally well :—

> " The bold young Luther of our later days,
>   With power to clothe high thoughts in glorious words,
>   To bid the buried past come back to life,
>   To bring earth's holiest scenes in vision bright
>   Before our wistful eyes."

Robertson would have again and again to listen to the marvellous charges of this archdeacon, which, side by side with the charges of his friend Bishop Thirlwall, constituted by far the most valuable part of this kind of ecclesiastical literature. We happen to know that Robertson was a visitor at Hurst-monceux Rectory. It would be interesting to construct a kind of imaginary dialogue between Frederick Robertson and Julius Hare.

We can imagine how the elder man would instruct the younger one in that deep philosophy of Coleridge, which he had so thoroughly absorbed into his own nature and writings, or would have told him that after all that modern scholarship and exegesis had done that there was none who had so profoundly penetrated into the spirit of St. Paul as old Luther. The opportunities of intercourse between the overworked town clergyman and the learned recluse of Hurstmonceux would have been few and far between, but it is pleasure, even though only for a few occasions, to have their names in combination.

Among Mr. Robertson's last letters there is an extremely interesting and vivid account of a visit which he made to Earnley. This is a village about six miles south-west of Chichester, on the seaboard. He spent the day at a good farmer's who showed him hospitality and put him up for a night. His intention was to shoot, but the streams were frozen and he was only able to bring down two snipe and two plovers. He walked alone for hours on the thick snow, and by the half-frozen streams, and then he turned his attention to the farmer and the farm. The farm-house was well built with cellars, which were turned into a dairy. Robertson's orderly eye detected the excellence of the farming, where there were no unbroken hedges and fences. The farmer could offer no foreign wines; they were not fit for farmers in those hard times, but Robertson appreciated the home-made orange wine. "Beer and home-made wines costing sixpence a bottle, and cherry wine, almost indistinguishable from cherry brandy, but saving very many shillings per gallon: these were the beverages of that hospitable home." The farmer told him a dreadful story of the inundation of the sea over his land. "The farm is liable to overflowing floods, which is considered in the terms of the lease—low in consequence. He told me of his dismay in seeing the tide once come pouring over the barrier, which it at last swept away and flooded the whole farm, regular billows going over his sown land up to the house. It went down, and, though the barriers were gone, did not rise the next tide beyond its accustomed height. For three years after such a flood the land is injured, and all the grass poisoned." The farmer was an interesting man with his own ideas about things. He had read one winter all through Milner's "Church History."

" ' I do not like,' said the farmer, ' to know nothing, and the clergyman to know all.' He made his labourers go to church, but for his own part he declined to turn to the East." "O sancta simplicitas." He approved of Sir Robert Peel's Free Trade policy, but was opposed to his views on the currency, and of course wanted a repeal of the malt tax. But Robertson soon fell from the cheerful into the moody vein. . . . . "I shall never forget those strange days; the sweep of desolate plain, the glaring snow, the bleak sunshine without wind, the frozen streams, the rushes without the usual life of birds springing from them, which one expects, the sea roar, the lifelessness of all, the stillness which was not relief, and the sounds which were not expressive, all combined to image that ' death in life, the days that are no more.' "

When a visitor at Grasmere wished to see Wordsworth's library, a servant showed him the room where he kept his books, but his study was in the open air. The best poets and orators have found their keenest inspirations in the open air. In a literal sense theirs has been a true peripatetic philosophy. From Demosthenes, haranguing the sea-foam, to Macaulay, roving along the London streets, " muttering half aloud the sentences destined one day to astonish and delight the world," the orator has loved to think out his thoughts and their expression in freedom and seclusion. And not least

such a sacred orator as Robertson.   Many a
difficult subject, many a tangled problem would
have been fought out in those long solitary rambles.
How often would the eye, braced and gladdened by
the visible beauties of nature, have been turned
inward upon itself!   How frequent the pause for
meditation, how frequent the uplifted prayer for
grace and guidance!   Sometimes we seem to recognize the freshness of the sea and the downs in his
bright rapid utterances, and we love to think of
him away from the crowded haunts of town in
solitary communion with nature and with God.

CHAPTER VII.

THE AUTOBIOGRAPHICAL ELEMENT IN ROBERTSON'S WRITINGS.

THERE is a strong autobiographical element in the works of Robertson. Of all literature, autobiography, when it is genuine, is the most valuable and the most entrancing, and gives the finest lessons both of history and of biography. If Robertson had written an autobiography, it would have been as faithful as the Confessions of Augustine or the Confessions of Rousseau. In his letters, so far as they have been published, and it is to be wished that the selection had been larger, the autobiographical element is of course to be more largely traced. Robertson himself could not but have been sensible of the extreme value and interest of his correspondence. His father told an American visitor that his son had designed publishing a collection of these letters. A fresh collection would have given a marvellous portraiture of the growth of a marvellous mind, and a brilliant sketch of the growth of contemporary life and thought. On the more obvious merits of the best letter-writers he would have engrafted the earnestness and mental analysis of Cowper and Eugenie de Guerin. It would have been as thoughtful a correspondence, but infinitely more lively, than the recent letters of Maurice and George Eliot. He would have fully bared in his own case, "the abysmal depths of personality." Indeed he has very largely done this in his published letters. There is at times something almost Byronic in his morbid sensitiveness, and the intensity of his feelings and affection. There is almost a tone of sublime egotism in his constant personal references. We shall not, however, so much dwell on the letters, which we may assume to be in the hands of most of our readers, as endeavour to eliminate the much less distinctive autobiographic element which may be detected in the addresses and sermons.

He speaks of the effect which poetry had on his own life, how it shaped its thought and character. "We can recollect how a couplet from the frontispiece of a hymn-book struck deeper roots into our being, and has borne more manifest fruits than all the formal training we ever got. Or we can trace, as unerringly as an Indian on the trail, the several influences of each poet through our lives : the sense of unjust destiny which was created by Byron ; the taint of Moore's voluptuousness ; the hearty, healthful life of Scott ; the calming power of Wordsworth ;

the masculine vigour of Dryden. It is only in after years that the real taste for the very highest poetry is acquired." We are reminded by these reminiscences of the formative principles of his mental history of the exquisite *Prelude* of Wordsworth, on the whole perhaps his favourite author, and whom he closely resembles in his intense sense and appreciation of nature, and the serene purity of his life and thought.

Here are two autobiographical reminiscences of his Oxford life, which we find in his lectures :—

"At Blenheim, the seat of the Duke of Marlborough, there is a Madonna, into which the old Catholic painter has tried to cast the religious conceptions of the Middle Ages, virgin purity and infinite repose. The look is upwards, the predominant colour of the picture blue, which we know has in itself a strange power to lull and soothe. It is impossible to gaze on this picture without being conscious of a calming influence. During that period of the year in which the friends of the young men of Oxford come to visit their brothers and sons, and Blenheim becomes a place of favourite resort, I have stood aside, near that picture, to watch its effects on the different gazers, and I have seen group after group of young undergraduates and ladies, full of life and noisy spirits, unconsciously stilled before it; the countenance relaxing into calmness, and the voice sinking to a whisper. The painter had spoken his message, and human beings, ages after, feel what he meant to say."

" I remember myself one of the most public exhibitions of this change in public feeling. It was my lot, during a short university career, to witness a transition and a reaction, or revulsion, of public feeling, with respect to two great men whom I have already mentioned and contrasted. The first of these was one who was every inch a man— Arnold of Rugby. You will all recollect how in his earlier life Arnold was covered with suspicion and obloquy ; how the wise men of his day charged him with latitudinarianism, and I know not with how many other heresies. But *the* public opinion altered, and he came to Oxford and read lectures on modern history. Such a scene had not been seen in Oxford before. The lecture-room was too small ; all adjourned to the Oxford Theatre, and all that was most brilliant, all that was most wise and most distinguished, gathered together there. He walked up to the rostrum with a quiet step and manly dignity. Those who had loved him when all the world despised him, felt that at last the hour of their triumph had come. But there was something deeper than any personal triumph they could enjoy, and those who saw him then will not soon forget the lesson read to them by his calm, dignified, simple step, a lesson teaching them the utter worthlessness of unpopularity or of popularity as a test of manhood's worth. The second occasion was when, in the same theatre, Wordsworth came forward to receive his honorary degree. Scarcely had his name been pronounced, than from three thousand voices at once there broke forth a burst of applause, echoed and taken up again and again when it seemed about to die away, and that, thrice repeated, a cry in which—

> 'Old England's heart and voice unite;
> Whether she hail the wine-cup or the fight,
> Or bid each hand be strong, or bid each heart be light.'"

When he is speaking of the enthusiastic reception of Wordsworth in the Sheldonian Theatre, he says, doubtless speaking of himself : " There were young eyes there, filled with an emotion of which they had no need to be ashamed ; there were hearts beating with the proud feeling of triumph that at last the world had recognized the merit of the man they had loved so long and recognized as their teacher. . . . Two young men went home together, part of the way in silence, and one only gave expression to the other when he quoted those well-known, trite and often quoted lines—lines full of deepest truth :—

> ' The self-approving hour whole worlds outweighs
> Of stupid starers. and of loud hurrahs ;
> And more true joy Marcellus exiled feels
> Than Cæsar with a senate at his heels.' "

Here are some reminiscences of his travels :—

"I wish I could describe one scene which is passing before my memory this moment, when I found myself alone in a solitary valley of the Alps, without a guide, and a thunderstorm coming on.   I wish I could explain how every circumstance combined to produce the same feeling, and ministered to unity of expression : the slow wild wreathing of the vapours round the peaks, concealing their summits, and imparting in semblance their own motion, till each dark mountain-form seemed to be mysterious and alive ; the eagle-like plunge of the Lämmergeier, the bearded vulture of the Alps, the rising of the flock of choughs, which I had surprised at their feast on carrion, with their red beaks and legs, and their wild shrill cries, startling the solitude and silence, till the blue lightning streamed at last, and the shattering thunder crashed as if the mountains must give way ; and then came the feelings, which in their fulness man can feel but once in life, mingled sensations of awe, and triumph, and defiance, of anger, pride, rapture, contempt of pain, humbleness, and intense repose, as if all the strife and struggle of the elements were only muttering the unrest of man's bosom ; so that in all such scenes there is a feeling of relief, and he is tempted to cry out exultingly : There ! there ! all this was in my heart, and it was never said out till now."

Another interesting reminiscence of his wanderings is this: "I have visited the finest museums in Europe, and I have spent many a long day in watching the habits of birds in the woods, hidden and unseen by them." One day he said to one of his friends, "There is not a bird on the wing but I know him."

His intense appreciation of the Brighton scenery often comes out. "It is a sociable habit, which I have noted more on the south coast than elsewhere, that people, though really neighbours, go and stay in each others' houses for a time." He goes and spends a few days with a neighbour who has a house exactly opposite the sea. "Until this visit I never estimated the advantages which the residences of *streets opposite the sea* have. The exceeding beauty, freshness, and the appearance of the sea and sky in early mornings, so different from the commonplace look of midday, have struck me very much. . . . I think I never felt the freshness of the world, and the truth that every morning is a new day—an universe unbroken and fresh for effort and discovery—so much as two mornings ago by the seaside." He then gives an account of sea and mist and cloudland indicating an intense poetical appreciation, and at the same time a wonderful power in the analysis of the emotion felt. On another occasion he speaks of a walk which he had taken along the beach and home by the Dyke

Road.   He had a very quick eye for birds, and he noticed hundreds of seagulls hunting up and down a field, and with them a huge flock of Norwegian or hooded crows, "and the distant hills were exceedingly distinct and clear, in that way which is often a prelude to rain; but I have observed that wind has sometimes the same effect."   Again, as he was walking down Regency Square one autumn afternoon, he was powerfully impressed by the appearance of the sky.   The letter might almost form a part of one of Mr. Ruskin's chapters on cloud beauty.   The sea and the clouds had almost a magnetic influence upon Robertson. "Looking at sea and clouds you hardly estimate distances.   The vault seems very measurable, and it does not occur to you that clouds which appear only a few yards in length are really acres and acres of vapour.   This combination of forms, however, forced me to realize the immensity of space, and a deeper sense of grandeur and loveliness came to me than I have felt for many weeks."   We may make one other citation: "I went out this afternoon to get some fresh air and cool a little feverishness.   After a walk I bent my steps to the spot most congenial to my feelings at that time, the churchyard at Hove.   It was quite dark, but the moon soon rose and shed a quiet light upon the old church and the white tombstones.   I went in, and was pleased to hear not a single human sound far or near. The moon was rising, like glowing copper, through the smoke at Brighton. Above these were a few dense clouds, edged with light, sailing across a marvellous blue, which softened towards the zenith into a paler and more pearly cobalt, with clear innocent stars here and there looking down so chaste and pure. I heard nothing but the sea; it found for me the expression I could not put in words."

"Nay, even round this Brighton of ours, treeless and prosaic as people call it, there are materials enough for poetry, for the heart that is not petrified in conventional maxims about beauty.

"Enough in its free downs, which are ever changing their distance and their shape as the lights and cloud. Shadows sail over them, and over the graceful forms of whose endless variety of slopes the eye wanders unarrested by abruptness, with an entrancing feeling of fulness and a restful satisfaction to the pure sense of form. And enough upon our own sea-shore and in our rare sunsets. A man might have watched with delight, beyond all words, last night the long, deep purple lines of cloud, edged with intolerable radiance, passing into orange, yellow, pale green, and leaden blue, and reflected below in warm, purple shadows, and cold, green lights upon the sea, and then the dying of it all away. And then he might have remembered those lines of Shakespeare, and, often quoted as they are, would have interpreted the sunset, and the sunset what the poet meant by the exclamation which follows the disappearance of a similiar aërial vision :—

> ' We are such stuff
> As dreams are made of, and our narrow life
> Is rounded with a sleep.' "

Here again he describes the prosaic side of Brighton.

" Brighton is not a manufacturing town, neither is it a commercial town. Brighton is a place of enjoyment for strangers. Something like one-third or one-fourth will be found not to be residents, but extraneous to the population. Every Saturday London pours out thousands to take advantage of the sea air. Let any man go to the railway-station, and he will be astonished to see the mass of human beings flocking into the town. . . . At Brighton and Cheltenham there is a peculiar difficulty, and the difficulty arises partly from this—that the inhabitants are wealthy. It is not the purchases of the rich themselves that form the great staple in the occupation of those hours, but it is the servants of the rich classes. I made it my business to make inquiries of the police, and the information given to me by them was of a most appalling character, because it told a sad tale of the result of that which is done in perfect ignorance. When the female servant is sent out at night, the mistress knows not the consequences, nor the sin and misery which often comes from female servants going out at late hours to purchase. . . . All the returns of your libraries show how few works of information are read—how many of fiction. More than that, the police tell us that the cigar-shop reaps a terrible harvest out of the wages of the young men ; that the billiard-table is at work ; that the public-houses, and houses worse than they, are full. Better far that the hours of business should even be extended than that extra hours should be gained for licentiousness, or for mere idleness, which is the grave of a living mind."

" I do not wonder at the success of Tractarianism among the Belgravians. Chanted services and innocent gentlemen with lilies of the valley in their dresses must afford something of the same cooling and sedative effect which I have felt in the burning South of France in going from a garden, on the walk of which innumerable lizards basked, and the sun's rays beat down intolerably, at once into the coolness of an artificial cave." With a single touch he brings back the Riviera. Then again he writes on a midsummer night in Brighton : " It is now nearly midnight—the only enjoyable time for writing, thought, or contemplation during the intense heat. By the side of a wall with a southern aspect the heat is of a tropical sultriness, the sun-beams striking off almost as in the focus of a convex glass, and you look along the stones expecting to

see the lizards basking in numbers as in the South
of Europe." As a matter of fact, Robertson's
travels in the South of France did not extend
beyond Lyons.

Robertson had seen a great deal of the fashionable society of watering-places. With the exception
of the brief interludes of Oxford and Winchester,
he had lived all his days in such places. By the
world generally he would himself be regarded as a
man of fashion. He himself keenly appreciated the
social and intellectual side of such society. But he
had a thorough suspicion and dislike of the essential characteristics of these places. This comes out
in his sermons and also in his letters : " If you wish
to know what hollowness and heartlessness are, you
must seek for them in the world of light, elegant,
superficial fashion, where frivolity has turned the
heart into a rock-bed of selfishness. Say what men
will of the heartlessness of trade, it is nothing
compared with the heartlessness of fashion. Say
what they will of the atheism of science, it is
nothing to the atheism of that round of pleasure in
which many a heart lives—dead while it lives."

In contrast with the fashionable people, he was
often delighted to find himself in contact with the
vigorous homely sense of the poor.

"It was only yesterday that I conversed with an
intelligent working-man in this town, and the man
expressed in very striking language the bitter in-

dignation which was felt by his class towards those who were, as he said, in a bigoted way endeavouring to rob them of their Sabbath. I trust that I convinced him—I tried at all events with all my heart to convince him that it was not bigotry in those who tried to take from the working-men their Sabbath; but I am not sure that I convinced the man that there was not great ignorance on the part of these persons with regard to the necessities of the poor."

Here is an instance of his warm sympathy with the humblest :—

"I have been interrupted by a visit of a lady of my congregation. She told me the delight, the tears of gratitude which she had witnessed in a poor girl to whom in passing I gave a kind look on going out of church on Sunday. What a lesson! How cheaply happiness can be given! What opportunities we meet of doing an angel's work! I remember doing it, full of sad feelings, passing on and thinking no more about it; and it gave an hour's sunshine to a human life, and lightened the load of life to a human heart for a time."

We gather up a few autobiographic sentences almost at random :—

"I recollect Weitbrecht, who recently died at Calcutta; and well do I remember the description he gave of the difficulties encountered by the Gospel missionaries in the East. What a picture he drew of the almost unconquerable depression which was produced by the mere thought of going back to India; to struggle with the darkening effects of universal idolatry—with the secret sense of incredulity in Christian truth, giving rise to the ever-recurring doubt, 'Can the Gospel light be only for us few, while countless myriads of the human race shall walk in the shadow of death?'"

Here is an evident reference to his own people at Trinity Chapel: "A man worships in a certain congregation, is taught by a certain minister, does not subscribe to certain societies; whereupon by that which arrogates to itself the title of the 'religious world,' he is at once pronounced an unbeliever, and not a Christian. This spirit besets our age, it is rife in this town, and demands the earnest protest of lip and life from every true man."

Here is a sentence dealing with one of the vexed questions of minor morals: "If for the sake of ensuring personal politeness and attention the rich man puts a gratuity into the hand of a servant of some company which has forbidden him to receive it, he gains the attention, he ensures the politeness, but he gains it at the sacrifice and expense of a man and a Christian brother.

"Who of us cannot recollect a period of his history when all his time was devoted to the cause of Christ; when all his money was given to the service of God; and when we were tempted to look down upon those who were less ardent than ourselves, as if they were not Christians?" Those words were doubtless true enough for Robertson, but we are afraid that there are not many of us who could look back on such a period. This, too, is surely autobiographical: "It is strange if a man has not found out long before he has reached the age of thirty that everything here is empty and disappointing. The nobler his heart, and the more unquenchable his hunger for the high and good, the sooner will he find that out. Bubble after bubble bursts; each bubble tinted with the celestial colours of the rainbow, and each leaving to the hand which crushes it, a cold, damp drop of disappointment." "As to religious books, I could count upon my fingers in two minutes all I ever read—but they are mine." "In a literary point of view I find Sir Walter Scott the most healthful restorative of any. There was no morbid spot in that strong, manly heart and nature." "Pray, let me have Faraday's letter back again. It did me more good than blisters, morphine, quinine, steel, or anything. Sound, genuine, healthy, scientific truth, instead of the sickly craving after mysteries and preternaturalism that masks the idler classes now." "When I have not *perfect* union with humanity I find in trees and clouds, and forms and colours of things inanimate more that is congenial, more that I can inform with my own being, more that speaks to me than in my own species. There is something in the mere posture of looking up which gives a sense of grandeur; and that I suppose is the reason why all nations have localized heaven there, and peopled the sky with Deity." . . . "I would rather live solitary on the most desolate crag, shivering, with all the warm wraps of falsehood stripped off, gazing after unfound truths—where bird doth not find bush, nor insect wing flit over the herbless granite, than sit comfortably on more inhabited spots, where others are warm in a faith which is true to them, but which is false to me."

Here are some remarks which are eminently autobiographic : "I now vindicate myself from the appearance of presumption. When the wisest and holiest have held opposite views, it seems immodest to speak with unfaltering certainty and decisive tone. Hesitation, guarded statements, caution it would seem, would be far more in place. Now to speak decidedly is not necessarily to speak presumptuously. There are questions involving great research, and questions relating to truths beyond our ken, where guarded and uncertain tones are only a duty. There are others where the decision has become conviction, a kind of intuition, the result of years of thought, which has been the day to a man's darkness, which has interpreted him to himself, made all clear where all was perplexed before, been the key to the riddle of truths that seemed contradictory, become part of his very being, and for which more than once he has held himself cheerfully prepared to sacrifice all that is commonly held dear. . . . To pretend to speak with hesitation of such convictions would be not modesty but affectation."

There are very interesting touches in this volume, the last printed, but chronologically the earliest. " Often have I felt when fevered by earthly excitement, and ruffled by earthly difficulties, as I looked up to the expanse of heaven above in the pure still moonshine, that it was an emblem of God's unchanging calmness rebuking the tumult within, and saying to the storm ' Peace, be still.' " So again he says : " There comes a solemn feeling at moonlight, by the sea or by Schaffhausen. The spirits of the universe moving on ! Mighty pulse ! " In this volume, so to speak, we are admitted into the preacher's study or the artist's studio. We get glimpses of his notes and preparations. Here is a somewhat curious expression in which perhaps the pride of the descendant of Highland chieftains speaks out: " I speak as the mouthpiece of a society composed of English clergy and of English nobles when I say : ' Let us raise our poor brethren to our own level.' " This was written in a plea for national education in a day when national education had no existence in the sense in which it exists now, and is another evidence of the prescient mind of Robértson, who rose far above the level of his contemporaries in this as in other things. He has an interesting argument that reverence, veneration, and awe are a class of feelings neither good nor bad, and may go along with religion or may not. Indeed, I have heard the late Dora Greenwell paradoxically argue, that the religious temperament is essentially irreligious. One of his notes is preserved: "Show this from Tyrolese chamois-hunter—and all the nonsense that travellers talk of the devoutness of mountain people." He laid great stress on *visiting*, and his practice in Brighton corresponded with his teaching: "Go to seek, do not wait till affliction offers itself. This is the peculiar spirit of Christian philanthropy. It is illustrated by the example of the Sœurs de la Charité, of Howard, and of Ashley. . . . All God's pleasures are simple ones : health, the rapture of a May morning ; sunshine, the stream blue and green ; kind words, benevolent acts, the glow of good humour." Then there are various sermons which he preached connected with Brighton, showing how thoroughly he identified himself with the life and interests of the place : a sermon which he preached at the time of an election ; a sermon on the Thanksgiving Day for the cessation of the cholera ; a sermon for the Brighton Female Orphanage.

Here he speaks of his work :—

"There is no minister of the Church of England who can pretend to a power of infallible interpretation. I give you the result of patient study and much thought. Let those who are tempted to despise flippantly first qualify themselves for an opinion by similar prayerful study.”

“ I waive the question of personal affection and private influence. In the public ministry of a church, week by week, a congregation listens to one man’s teaching; year by year a solemn connection is thus formed; for so thoughts are infused, perforce absorbed. They grow in silence, vegetate, and bear fruit in the life and practice of the congregation; and a minister may even trace his modes of thinking in his people’s conversation—not as mere phrases learnt by rote, but as living seed which has germinated in them. A very solemn thing ! for what is so solemn as to have that part of a man which is his real self—his thoughts and faiths—grow into others and become part of their being ? Well, that will be his rejoicing in the judgment day ; for that harvest he will put in his claim. . . . My Christian brethren, may that mutual rejoicing be yours and mine in the day of Jesus Christ ! ”

With a touching reminiscence of one of the sisters he had lost, he wrote : “ Two lines in the frontispiece of a little hymn-book, which I have not seen since five years old, seem branded with letters of fire on my memory :—

> “ ‘ Oh ! if she would but come again,
> I think I’d call her so no more.’

“ I envy you the society of the eagles. I would

give anything for leisure to think quietly, and get out of the jar of human life, and the perpetual necessity of talking, which consumes an amount of energy which should be thrown on action that few suspect or dream of.

"I have already known some ministerial trials, and I foresee more—much hardness and much disappointment; but I may tell you from experience that you would take nothing that earth has to offer in exchange for the joy of serving Christ as an accredited ambassador. . . . Whatever eyes have scanned my deficiencies, I can answer for it that none have scanned them so severely as my own.

"I will tell you of a want I am beginning to experience very distinctly. I perceive more than ever the necessity of devotional reading: I mean the works of eminently holy persons, whose tone was not merely uprightness of character and high-mindedness, but commands—a strong sense of personal and everliving communion with God.

"We know what a relief it is to see the honest affectionate face of a menial servant or some poor dependent, regretting that your suffering may be infinitely above his comprehension. It may be a secret which you cannot impart to him, or it may be a mental distress which his mind is too uneducated to appreciate; yet still his sympathy in your dark hour is worth a world. What you suffer he knows not, but he knows you do suffer, and it pains

him to think of it; there is balm to you in that.
This is the power of sympathy.

"Have you ever seen those marble statues in some public squares or gardens, which art has so fashioned into a perennial fountain that through the lips or through the hands the clear water flows in a perpetual stream, on and on for ever; and the marble stands there passive, cold, making no effort to arrest the gliding water? It is so that Time flows through the hands of men—swift, never pausing, till it has run itself out; and there is the man petrified into a marble sleep, not feeling what it is which is passing away for ever.

"I remember that half-painful, half-sublime sensation in the first voyage I took out of sight of land when I was a boy, when the old landmarks and horizon were gone, and I felt as if I had no home. It was a pain to find the world so large. The mind got familiarized to that feeling, and a joyful sense of freedom came. So I think it is with spiritual truth. It is a strangely desolate feeling to perceive that 'Truth' and the 'Gospel' that we have known were but a small home form in the great universe; but at last I think we begin to see sun, moon, and stars as before, with a latitude and longitude as certain and far grander than before."

The autobiographic element in Robertson's sermons—we mean personal references to his own life and work—is thin, but exceedingly interesting.

We may group some passages together. Some of these are found in his sermons on behalf of charitable institutions. One of the most perfect of his sermons is the one entitled, " The Human Race typified by the Man of Sorrows." This gives its title to the last volume of sermons which has been published, a volume which for its biographical interest is more valuable than any of its predecessors.[1]

" It is a minister's duty from time to time to visit those of his own district who may chance to be removed within those walls as in-patients—and he has opportunities of observing that the poor are treated with a gentleness, a human consideration, an attention as scrupulous as if costly rewards were theirs to give."   It is no doubt their duty to go after their people into the wards of a hospital or even of a gaol, but the chaplain of a prison told me lately that he had hardly ever known a clergyman come to the prison to look after some convicted parishioner.   Of course the answer would be that hospitals and prisons have their own clerical staff to look after the inmates. This makes, however, the more conspicuous such kindness as Robertson's in seeking out his poor in the hospitals. Again, in preaching for the Humane Society, he strongly urged upon his

[1] " The Human Race," and other sermons, preached at Cheltenham, Oxford, and Brighton, by the late Rev. Frederick W. Robertson, M.A. Second edition. C. Kegan Paul, 1881.

people an acquisition of the knowledge that leads to the saving of life. He anticipated the doctrine of our modern ambulance classes. "Such cases occur unexpectedly. No medical aid is near. Friends are alarmed. The vulgar means resorted to from superstition and ignorance are almost incredible. But gradually the knowledge is spread through the country of what to do in cases of emergency. Many here would be prepared to act if a need arose. I have been present at such a case, and have seen life saved by arresting the rough treatment of ignorance acting traditionally."

Sometimes we trace in his sermons the surrounding influences of the place, of the sea-side, and the passing events of the day. "The shallow fishing-boat glides safely over the reefs where the noble bark strands; it is the very might and majesty of her career that bury the sharp rock deeper in her bosom." So he reminds his people that recently the tragic death of eleven fishermen had enlisted the sympathy and charities of thousands. Sailors and soldiers, he tells us from his knowledge of them, are people that do not doubt. Here again shines out his personal feeling: "There are those who think it a surer and a safer Protestantism to use popular watchwords. Be it so. But with God's blessing *that will not I.* The majesty of truth needs other bulwarks than vulgar and cowardly vituperation. . . . I pray you, Christian brethren, do not join those fierce associations which think only of uprooting errors. There is a spirit in them which is more of earth than heaven, short-sighted too and self-destructive. They do not make converts to Christ, but only controversialists and adherents to a party. They compass sea and land. It matters little whether fierce Romanism or fierce Protestantism wins the day; but it does matter whether or not in the conflict we lose some precious Christian truth as well as the very spirit of Christianity."

So spoke Robertson of his views of baptism, and all his sermons have been wrought out with toil and thought which confer on them their permanent value. And we would fain believe that there are many preachers and multitudes of sermons to which such language is applicable. It was the saying of the late Earl Cairns, Lord Chancellor, that he never heard a sermon from which he might not gather something; and of another Chancellor, that if he had failed to gather something, it was his own fault. To most people nothing is more prosaic and commonplace than a sermon. It flows so easily, and seems to exact little thought in the composer and little thought in the listener. But in the preacher's own mind that sermon may have involved all that was most momentous in his own history. It involved the studies, the perplexities, the questionings of years. It may have been composed with tears, with prayers, with exultant hopes. It may virtually contain the confessions of his own blunders, failures, inconsistencies, and sins and struggles into a better hope. It may be associated in his mind with loss, sorrow, care, and with providential goodness of God. It may be associated in his mind with wanderings in the fields at eventide, with morning and evening vigils, with the sense that with each sermon he has given away so much of life, and force, and being. There is the mysterious sense that so much of his own life has been ordered that his innermost being should vibrate to each spiritual impulse, and that the events of his life's history should serve for the good of others. And so St. Paul says, that whether comforted or afflicted, the sufferings or comfort were for the consolation or salvation of others ; " that we may be able to comfort them which are in any trouble by the comfort wherewith we ourselves are comforted of God."

We append a passage from one of his lectures on " The Thorn in the Flesh," which seems to us to have a strong autobiographic character. We the rather do so as, in the published volume of the " Lectures on the Corinthians," the subject of the " Thorn " is passed over very rapidly. We subjoin full notes.

" Thus every man has his thorn. It is wondrously instructive, as we pass through the crowded town, to see each face except the very young, careworn, and having lines of suffering, and we are tempted to ask, Where are the happy ones? We may know a man, be intimately acquainted with him, and think his trials cannot be many.

"His domestic circle is peaceful; his burdens must be light; but do we not now and then catch a start of anguish passing across his brow, the causes of which are known only to God and himself? God alone knows what is the thorn which caused his anguish.

"2. It is something evil—a messenger of Satan to buffet him. We must not allow our understanding to be so perverted as to think that because pain can be blessed to us, it is in itself a blessed thing. In the ages of monkery—squalor and filth and wretchedness were sometimes considered as the normal state of man; and men coveted the pang rather than tried to get rid of it. Some argue that because it is written, 'the poor shall never cease out of the land,' that it is wrong to strive to put a stop to poverty; that because the curse of physical suffering fell upon one portion of our race, that to seek for any anodyne for pain is to thwart the will of God. The Bible calls pain an evil; it may be sent by God to do us good; but it is still an abnormal state, to be got rid of as soon as possible. No sophistry can make the ache in itself a joy. We cannot rejoice in tribulation itself, though we may rejoice in God through tribulation. We may pray that the thorn may pass away, or that God's grace may be sufficient for us.

" A thorn causes perpetual, unvarying, incessant pain ; to forget it is impossible ; interfering with all places and enjoyments, there is still the old rankling throb ; so that the child fancies that every person maliciously strikes him on the place where is the thorn. And some sorrows are like these. For example, some disgraceful lineage, some blot on our blood, or our birth, with which we have nothing to do, but which the world accounts our shame ; it rises to our recollection just when we are about to come to fame and happiness. Some domestic incongruity, some family unhappiness, the man may forget it at his labour in his shop—in the field ; but the time comes when we must go home, and there is the thorn awaiting him.

" Some diseased habit of mind that comes in solitude, in the midst of society we may forget it ; but alone, the thorn is there, and we carry everywhere with us the *ever-present possibility of that pang.*

" 2. The spiritual uses of this experience :—

" To make us humble, and to teach us our dependence, lest I should be exalted above measure, &c. To guard us against spiritual pride. It is strange that this pride is felt for those things over which we have the least control, and to which we have the least right. What hast thou that thou hast not

received, and how boasteth thou then as though
thou didst not receive it ?   In the school the vain
boy, and he of whom his schoolfellows are vain, is
not he who has amassed knowledge through hard toil,
but he whose brilliant genius is often an excuse for
idleness.   He is not a vain man who has acquired
learning by hard labour, but he whose brilliant,
irritable talent has made him erratic.   Hereditary
rank, over which we have had no control, which
only entails upon us greater responsibilities, and
demands that we should be more noble and honourable than other men—this is often the cause of
pride.

" He is not often proud of wealth who has toiled
from boyhood to old age to earn it, but he who has
realized a fortune by some sudden rash and acci-
dental speculation.   The hard worker is seldom
proud; he has known so much of his ignorance, his
weakness, his powerlessness, that his heart cannot
be proud.   He is the proud man whose fine feelings,
whose delicate sensibilities make him as the porce-
lain to the ordinary pottery of mortals, whose aspirations and whose wild dreams make him too grand
to have to do with the soil of this low earth ; and
when this pride finds its way into the church, those
are not spiritually proud who do good works, but
who substitute their fine feelings, what they call
their true gospel, their mysterious election in the
place of good works.

" Sharp, bitter penury will guard a man from
extravagance; but wild reverie and reckless speculation will bring to experience the meanness of
debt.

" There is no better humiliation than constant
physical pain—the feeling of the possible pang,
the hour of thrilling agony, that will make us cry
with the psalmist, 'I am weary of my groaning,'
&c.

" Such is the constellation of our planet. In the
temperate zone we have peculiar trials to our
•physical frame; the wind cold from the north and
east; in the warmer climate the mean serpent
and the constant fever. Everywhere is the thorn
in the flesh.

" This thorn might have been a *tendency* to sin;
and the Apostle could be brought ever to rejoice in
this if it were only a tendency without passing into
actual sin. There are more than one person in this
congregation who feels, as I am speaking, that he
has a thorn of this kind. It may be indolence, and
he may be haunted by dangerous reverie. He may
have thoughts known only to himself. My Christian brother, none know but God how you have
struggled with these thoughts; how you have battled
with them on your knees till they have seemed to
rise up against you as a living, acting, personal
enemy. Like the bullet that has gone deep into
the spinal cord, that no skill of the surgeon can

extract, it remains there to thrill the nerves to living agony. Such may the thorn in the flesh become, unless God give grace in our daily need.

"2. To teach us spiritual dependence :—

"Liberty is one thing—independence another. A man is politically free whose right energies are not cramped by the selfish, unjust claims of another; a man is politically independent who has cut himself free from all ties that bind him to his brother-man. This is national anarchy. Liberty bows to the law, I ought; independence to the accursed law, I will. And there are those in our day who would strive to set the child independent of his parent and the parent of the child, the poor of the rich and the rich of the poor, the master of the workman and the workman of his master, whose whole aim is to bring about this accursed independence.

"He is spiritually free who is not enslaved by his lusts, or by the thunders of his church, who is not compelled by the rules of society to believe what his conscience tells him he should not believe. Christian freedom is not independence. As a member of a church, he is not independent of those with whom he is connected in what is called the communion of saints. He is not independent of his brethren. Look at some of the inspired injunctions. Look not every man on his own things, &c. Bear one another's burdens, and so, &c. All things are lawful for me, but all things are not expedient.

" There is no independence on earth : we all depend on the breath of God. As well might the clouds that surround the setting sun, tinged with gold and vermilion, boast that they shine by their own light—the coming night would soon show them to be a dim, dark, dense bank of vapour. When we know ourselves aught we shall feel that we have nothing of our own that is good ; that we are strengthless, powerless, and must depend entirely on all-sufficient grace."

CHAPTER VIII.

IT has often been my privilege to meet persons who had some knowledge of Mr. Robertson. Their number is necessarily growing less and less. In every case I have been greatly impressed with the intense personal influence which he seems to have exercised over their minds. Some of them can reproduce in an extraordinary way his very accent, manner, and intonation. These old acquaintances of Robertson were of all classes of society, the most gifted and influential down to the humblest tradesmen. For the mere ways of conversation, the give and take of society talk, Robertson had not very much aptitude. His quality of pure wit was so admirable that it did not fail to elicit admiration and delight. But it was not till he came into closer intercourse, and touched on the deeper subjects, that his interest was aroused. Until such a point was reached this attention would often flag. The recent worthy Town Clerk of Brighton,

Mr. Freeman, has informed me that he would sometimes come to his office, lean against the door, become deeply absorbed in thought, and quite forget all that he had come about.

The late Mr. Bowdidge, of Brighton, was intimately acquainted with Robertson. Between the two there existed the closest intimacy and affection. The present writer had some instructive conversations with him, and Mr. Bowdidge also lent him some documents that he had. "He died in my arms," said Mr. Bowdidge to me on one occasion; "I would go through fire and water to serve him." Mr. Bowdidge said that he primarily moved in the matter of raising a testimonial fund, and raised 1400*l.* for the family. Between the two men, so different in all their belongings and modes of life, there existed a steady reciprocal affection which was only severed by death.

Mr. Bowdidge said that he had put on a sound financial basis the condition of the chapel, which he found in an unsatisfactory state. There was a large rent due to Mrs. Anderson, which was of course a heavy burden. Before his time there had been an unsettled state of things, and many stray small amounts which should have gone to augment the chapel revenues never came to hand. It was customary to pay for a sitting even for a single service. Mr. Bowdidge remembered receiving such a payment from Lord Shaftesbury. The receipts of the chapel under his fostering care came to nearly 1100*l.* a year, but the heavy expenses did not leave much margin. It was a system which Robertson himself abominated, but at that time no other system was possible.

Mr. Bowdidge lived, I believe, in those days close to the chapel. Robertson made it a house of call, or rather, I should say, a home. Sometimes he would go there between the services, instead of returning to his own house at some little distance. A little light lunch was all that he would take. On one occasion he reached the house of his friend Bowdidge very late on a Saturday night, returning from a shooting visit in Ireland at his friend's, Mrs. Fitzpatrick. I imagine that his family was away from Brighton at the time. He had travelled in a grey suit, and there was some little difficulty in rigging him out clerically for the next morning, but the kindly churchwarden undertook that as one of the duties of his office, and accomplished it successfully. On his way down he had occupied himself in preparing his sermons. He had had no note-book with him, and had scribbled down the divisions on the margin of a *Times* newspaper. Bowdidge thought that upon the whole this was the finest sermon of his that he ever heard. Bowdidge was never able to trace the sermon, either in the copy of the *Times* or in any transcript which Robertson might have made afterwards.

Robertson used to receive a number of anonymous letters. Some of them were extremely impertinent, and even commented on his personal appearance. There was one set which he handed over to his churchwarden. Mr. Bowdidge immediately recognized the handwriting of the offensive letters as that of a lady of rank, who was supposed to be a great friend of Robertson's. There was not the slightest imputation against Robertson on the score of personal vanity. On one occasion Mr. Bowdidge was with him when he had his photograph taken. Something was said about further copies, and Robertson threw down the negative, and stamped on it and crushed it.

Robertson pointed out to him in his last days a number of sermons, about twenty-three, which were fit for publication, and which he hoped would go for a provision to his family. After his death Bowdidge sealed up all his papers. He found various parcels of money lying about, which might amount to sixty pounds. He could bear his testimony that he was a man always most liberal towards the poor.

Bowdidge himself felt sure that the people of Brighton did not understand Robertson until after his death. People used to go and wonder at him, but he "did not bring them to their knees."

This Mr. Bowdidge was in his way an admirable man. He was one of the characters of Brighton.

He had much to tell of the history of Brighton and his own connection therewith; notably of being unjustly fined for leaving a cart unattended in the street, a matter which, at the expense of several hundred pounds, he carried to some of the highest courts in the kingdom. He has earned his modest place among the local celebrities. To the very last it was one of his greatest delights to speak of Robertson, and to impart any recollections of him to those who would seek information from him.

One day I called on an old shoemaker, living in a humble tenement in Nile Street, who had enjoyed some intimacy with Robertson. I found him a hale old man, aged eighty-two, and like many shoemakers, a decided philosophical Radical in his way of thinking. He pointed out a chair to me, and said that Mr. Robertson had often sat in that chair. What he especially liked in Robertson was the undoubted vein of Radicalism. He and a friend used to go about hearing different preachers and seeing how they liked them. One morning the friend came to him and said that he had heard that there was a wonderful preacher come to Trinity Chapel. It happened to be a very cold day, and he allowed his friend to go by himself. Later in the day his friend came back and said that he was the most wonderful preacher he had ever heard in his life. Accordingly he went to hear Robertson. He was at that time lecturing on the first book of Samuel. "Didn't he let into them. He showed them what kings were. Kings meant standing armies and taxation. That's what they meant." I asked my friend if he was not a Radical. "Yes, he was. He had always voted straight, and hoped to do so still. He was for the sacred cause of progress. He had heard Robertson lecture to working-men, and always liked him best on the platform.

"Robertson was a man, he was. I have always felt that I have seen a man once in my life. He was a most upright man, with a noble, beautiful face."

When his wife found that he was so pleased with Robertson's afternoon addresses, she advised him to go in the morning as well. This he immediately began to do, and in fact never missed them.

I had heard on good authority the following account of the commencement of their acquaintance. Robertson had noticed the man; always early, always standing, always eagerly intent. Robertson ascertained that there was a single vacant sitting in the gallery, and sent his churchwarden to say that he was greatly pleased with his attendance and attention, and he hoped that he would accept the seat from himself. The shoemaker sent back word that, as he could not afford to pay for a seat, he had rather not occupy one. My shoemaker grew a little restive when I recalled this incident. He said he preferred standing. There were other people in the gallery who were not able to stand.

"I daresay, sir, that you are under the idea that you know Robertson's sermons. You have read them, of course?" I assented. "Well, you don't know them for all that. No man could know them unless he heard them. The printed reports can tell you nothing of his manner. And the printed reports often omit whole passages. They do not give some of his most striking words. His words absolutely haunted you for days and days. Just compare him with a man like Sortain. Sortain would be twenty minutes in finding fine pegs to hang his words on."

I spoke of the doctrine of the sermons, the doctrine of the Atonement. Here my friend became very stern and determined. He poured out a passage of Robertson's about "heathen shambles." He stated the doctrine, as he supposed Robertson had denounced it, with almost rabid violence. I said that Robertson's statement of the doctrine was not the doctrine, but a caricature of the doctrine. "But was it not so held by some people, so held by extreme Calvinists?" Well, I admitted that some passages might be quoted from their writings of the kind, but still, I thought, only in a modified way. We had a long theological argument. My friend, fortified by his reminiscences of Robertson, held his own with vigour and pertinacity.

My shoemaker kindly insisted on reading aloud the conclusion of one of Robertson's lectures; a passage to my mind of the highest order of eloquence. He evidently aimed at reproducing the manner and intonation of Robertson, and, so far as I am able to judge, with considerable success. I have met with several persons who tried to do this, and the effect was always impressive.

Robertson told his humble friend, when he came to see him, that he was not able to do much visiting, and that he was afraid that his life would be a failure. This was a statement which he repeatedly made, and of which we may humbly hope that he is now disabused.

Another person with whom I have spoken was a very worthy second-hand bookseller well known in Brighton. The bookseller was himself a Baptist, and he came into connection with Robertson through the working-men's movement. Robertson treated him not only as a tradesman, but as a friend. He not only came to the bookseller's shop, but the bookseller visited him at the house. Naturally enough he gave special attention to the library. The library did not impress him as being a very considerable one, but it struck him as being extremely well chosen. Robertson did not appear to him to be so much a general reader as a special reader. That is to say, he worked hard on special lines. On one occasion he bought Fownes'

" Chemistry," and he told the vendor that in about six months' time he would be able to pass an examination in it. Robertson used to speak to him of the great isolation in which he was left by the Brighton clergy. Although a Dissenter our bookseller often used to go and hear Robertson. "There was always a great fashionable crowd. You really forgot that you were in a church, and found yourself ready to applaud." He could repeat by heart many portions of sermons which he had heard, and some of which are not to be found in the printed series. One of these was on the "Vain Man and the Proud Man." "For the proud man one might have some respect, but for the vain man—none." He was struck with a sermon about the "Cretians—always slow bellies." "That St. Paul should ever even have mentioned them. We must consider their case in a spirit like St. Paul's."

One of these tradesmen—indeed several—nearly cried when speaking to me about Robertson. There was never any man, said the old Brighton tradesman, whom he had loved so much. Robertson had taught him all the religion he had. All the truth which he had ever gained he had learned from him. He remembered having a talk with one of his servants. She said that what her master was in the pulpit that he always was in his own house. Mrs. Robertson was always very kind. He remembered that there was a poor crippled lad for whom she used to find books and money. It happened, quite by accident, that he went to hear Robertson. He was told that he was a new clergyman come to Brighton, who was very well worth hearing. At that time he was only an apprentice. He had no money, and was unable to pay for a sitting. So he always used to be first at the doors on Sunday morning as soon as they were opened. Many of those who heard Robertson once would never hear any one else. I have met repeatedly with persons who have told me that they never missed a single sermon. Others have sorrowfully said that they missed one, two, or three, and how deeply they regretted the omission. One of these was my friend, Mr. Morris Fuller, the well-known ecclesiastical writer, who, in the preface to his Dartmoor sermons, says : "The readers of Mr. F. W. Robertson's (of Brighton) sermons will probably notice thoughts and even turns of expression with which they are familiar. This may be accounted for from the fact that the author attended Mr. Robertson's ministry nearly the whole time that Mr. Robertson held the incumbency of Trinity Chapel, Brighton ; during which period he made very copious notes of his discourses : indeed some of the sermons in this volume are but the expansion of notes then taken, filled out perhaps with a more decided Church teaching than was Mr. Robertson's custom to give. They are ineffaceably imprinted on the 'mindful tablets of his memory' from the thrilling effect they produced in the oral delivery."

One more has told me that he had in his little parlour behind the shop Robertson's portrait on the wall. Whenever he was tempted to do any trick of trade, or behave unhandsome, he would hurry into the back parlour and look at the portrait. "And then, sir, I felt that I could not do it, that it was impossible for me to do it." "I would lay down my life for that man, sir," "I would go through fire and water for him," were expressions that I have heard. One of his greatest friends said to me once: "We wondered at him. We did not understand him till after his death."

I remember meeting with another of his tradesmen, who was full of love and admiration for Robertson. He had had so many conversations, and Robertson allowed his children to associate a great deal with his own. He had some fields near the Dyke Road, where the children used to play together, and a little carriage in which they might drive out together. "I never met with a man like him. He was a man, sir, who said what he meant, and meant what he said."

No one was more impressed by his teaching than the late eminent publisher, Mr. H. L. King, who commenced life in Brighton in a small way as a bookseller. Afterwards he had one of the principal shops and libraries in the town, and became the well-known banker and publisher in Cornhill. His wife is the authoress of the "Disciples," and some other remarkable poems. He became the publisher of the "Sermons" and the other "Remains." These were published from notes and shorthand reports made by several of his hearers, and by one lady especially, whose notes have furnished the larger part of the printed volumes of sermons. I may here say that I have seen a letter of Mr. Robertson's addressed to this lady, in which he thanks her for the transcript of his sermons, and does not mention that he had the slightest objection to the course which she had pursued. I the rather mention this because something different might be implied from some expressions which Mr. Robertson has himself used, and from the language in the biography. His own letter leaves no doubt on the subject, and his family have every reason to be grateful for the preservation and publication of the reports. Unfortunately a terrible misfortune happened, unfortunate alike for this lady, for Mr. King, and for the public at large. A large mass of Robertson's sermons, enough to fill about two printed volumes, was mislaid on the platform of a railway-station, and despite every search, and a reward of some hundred pounds offered, up to this point it has never been recovered. It may be hoped that this will yet prove a case of *treasure trove.*

Not many months ago there passed away a very

genial man of letters, possessing a sweet vein of poetry of his own, and one who, if his life had been spared, might have accomplished much more than had been done within the years vouchsafed. This was the late Mr. William Sawyer, whose name will be recalled with much affection by many in Brighton and London. Besides other literary property he was the proprietor or editor of a facetious journal called *Funny Folks;* but I suppose that more serious and religious conversation has hardly ever taken place than I have had with Mr. Sawyer at his office. A vein of the deepest earnestness underlay the humour and poetry of his mind. So much impressed was he with Mr. Robertson, that he had formed a collection of newspaper cuttings, engravings, notes and abstracts of sermons, with an examination of which I have been favoured. He had graphic recollections of one or two visits with which he was favoured by Robertson in his youth. He belonged to the class of clever, earnest young men, in whom Robertson took a special interest, and I suppose to this circumstance William Sawyer was indebted for the visits. Robertson had intended the visit for a ministerial one, but the conversation was almost entirely literary. The young clergyman was an ardent reader of contemporary literature, and this was ground on which the young *littérateur* could meet him on an equal footing. Sawyer had some personal knowledge of Douglas Jerrold, Thackeray, and other men of letters.

The two men talked together for an hour on literary topics. Then Robertson rose to go, saying that he had come to talk with him on very different matters, but that he must now go, and defer other subjects to another time. But the time for religious talk in this case never came.

I might add much respecting the feeling of intense reverence and affection with which those spoke of Robertson who were brought into closest intimacy with him, who knew him best, and were most capable of understanding and appreciating him. Here again I have met with hardly any personal influence that seemed so potent as his, or with such an absolute sway over the minds of others. The recollections of his friends respecting him are all vivid and kindly. He seemed to have that kind of influence which Virgil had over the mind of Dante. It is less with the intellectual side than with the moral side of his character that they are attracted. His nature was one that longed for love, and he received an amount of sympathy and affection which he himself hardly understood at the time.

CHAPTER IX.

THE LATER YEARS AT BRIGHTON.

WITHIN a year or two after his first coming to Brighton the state of Robertson's health had given alarm to his friends. One day in May, 1848, Crabbe Robinson entertained him at one of his memorable breakfasts, and afterwards called on his great medical friend, Dr. Bratt, who expressed himself in alarming terms respecting his view of Robertson's health. In the summer of that year Robertson made an excursion to the English lakes, and Crabbe Robinson gave him an introduction to Mr. Quillinan and the Wordsworths. Crabbe Robinson met him in the autumn of the same year in Brighton, and they had some long walks together. Robinson and other friends strongly urged him to give up Trinity Chapel and go out to Madeira. He had, however, consulted Dr. Watson—the Cicero of English physicians—who had pronounced that his lungs were not affected, but nothing was said of more terrible evils that might be lurking in ambush. Robertson was quite unwilling to go while there was work to be done, and while he still felt himself capable of doing that work. Crabbe Robinson plainly told him, no doubt, as a powerful argument in favour of his going away, that his sermons were not equal in power to those which he used to preach, an opinion, however, which Robinson practically retracted in a later portion of his diary.

His work thickened upon him, in the way that work always makes work. Unfortunately he undertook the heavier work just at the time when his health and the ultimate efficiency of his work demanded greater rest and leisure. With the exception of his October holiday, generally spent with the Fitzpatricks in Ireland, he took less and less change. The long walks and excursions into the neighbourhood were abbreviated. His step lost much of its elasticity, and his aspect of its joyousness. The indications which we have of his work show immense industry and intellectual fertility. Whatever he did he did it with all his might. Thoroughness was stamped on the whole of his work. For instance we are greatly impressed with what we are permitted to see of his confirmation labours. This is a kind of work which in times past has been done in a very slipshod way in many parishes, and in many parishes also has been looked upon as the most important, difficult, and arduous of all parish ministrations. Never was work of this kind done more

completely and devotedly than by Mr. Robertson.
By public addresses, by classes, by personal inter-
views, by correspondence, he sought to turn this
great practical special season of good to the best
account.   He especially recognized that it was the
dull and slow, the " unidea'd " girls with whom
he had to deal, and with whom he dealt most carefully.   He was especially winning with young
people.   We have seen various letters of his to
young ladies of his classes and congregation, to
whom he writes always with earnestness, sometimes
with brightness, and sometimes with much solemnity.
In one of his unpublished letters he says : " God
bless you, go where you will.   Those buoyant spirits
He has given you will, with His blessing, enable you
to float triumphantly over much of the rock reef of
life on which duller and heavier vessels strand themselves.   To Him I commend you earnestly."   To
another he writes in a deeply affecting and earnest
strain on the great verities of a woman's life, un-
folding themselves especially at such an epoch as a
confirmation.   Among the many young ladies whom
he greatly impressed were some who distinguished
themselves in after life by their intellectual power.
It was a constant habit with some of them to take
regular notes of his sermons.   One of them writes
to me: "Being then at an impressionable age, twenty-
one to twenty-seven, I naturally regarded him with
affectionate reverence, and took, in my own fashion,

regular notes of the powerful sermons he delivered. But beyond a kind of recognition of me as a Sunday-school teacher, and a few precious notes he sent on receiving some small tokens of remembrance on a recovery from illness—on his return after an absence—I had little personal intercourse. His father, Captain Robertson, was pleased with some verses which I wrote on his lamented death, and had them bound up with his copies of the sermons."

It is a common complaint with the clergy that they feel " Mondayish." The most active day of the week to the world ought for them to have something of a Sabbath rest and repose. Robertson's nerves were wretchedly out of sorts after the Sunday's work. It is a curious fact that he could not bear to have his hair cut on a Monday. He could not bear the sound of a piano in the adjacent houses. Once he came to a friend almost at midnight and asked, " Could he have no redress against those who were playing the piano ? " His tortured nerves seemed at the mercy of the least incident that might arise. Now we may be quite sure that the Master does not exact work of this kind from His servants that would lead to such results as these. He never exacts work, so exhausting to nerve and brain, that the very power of work must inevitably be taken away. The disability to work is the terrible punishment exacted for the violations of natural law. In these modern days the rock-ahead with most of us—

on which poor Robertson eventually split—is overwork; often arising from what old John Wesley
called "the lust of finishing." Life is a long game
and not a short game, and every attention should
be given to the conditions of the race.

He never seems to have had the art of managing
himself wisely. Doubtless he would have admitted
as a principle the inflexibility of the laws of health
and disease. He would have taught the sanctity
of the body. He would have indicated the duty of
taking due care and tendence of the cottage of the
soul. We need not suppose that he neglected the
appreciation or application of these truths. But,
like other good men, he had probably adopted the
deliberate idea that it was better to wear out than
rust out. From the first he had a presentiment that
the time was short. His days were numbered, and
he had better make the most of them. His work
must be done, and, at all costs, in the best way
possible. The Sunday effort became a tremendous
strain upon his system. For three or four days he
expressed himself as being good for nothing. These
were the days on which he permitted himself
relaxation. He would see his friends. He would
play with his children. He would read novels. On
the Thursday he would brace himself anew, and
prepare for the work that was to be done on the
next Sunday. When he was working he would
frequently wear a wet towel round his head. It

should be said that, while he did not professedly begin his work until the Thursday, it was his habit to choose his text for the next Sunday as soon as Sunday evening had brought the end of the previous week's work. There must have been a good deal of unconscious cerebration on the subject. This sort of work is very insidious. Many clergymen know what it is to have sermonizing on the brain. The only effectual safeguard is the thorough change of a prolonged holiday, but there is reason to fear in Robertson's case that, unless in one or two summers, the change was not sufficiently prolonged or thorough.

He felt the incessant pressure of his pulpit work exceedingly.

" The thought of drudging on here at the same work unvaried, two sermons a Sunday, inspiration by clockwork for several years, is simply the conception of an impossibility. ' Would to God I were not a mere pepper-cruet to give a relish to the palate of the Brightonians!'" Robertson seems almost to have delighted in crowding sermon upon sermon; engagement on engagement. He was burning the candle at both ends. He did not find that his strength was in quiet—in sitting still; in doing the Master's work steadily and equably until the Master Himself should give him release. One of the best of our modern poets[1] speaks of " the

[1] S. J. Stone, Preface to " Knight of Intercession."

joyful service of God, in courage and with a quiet mind, which should mark the life of the redeemed." There was the service of God and the courage, but the quiet mind was wanting. Seasons of deep depression often succeeded his seasons of energy and elatedness. " I have missed life," he was heard to say audibly to himself, as he stood one day sadly on the Brighton beach. We find him sorrowfully asking, " How long will sermonizing continue? With all my heart I hope not to the end of life, unless life is very nearly done ; for it is a kind of mean martyrdom by a lingering death." At all times the strain of constant hebdomadal preaching is hard upon a clergyman ; the strain, under Robertson's circumstances, must have been tremendous. Whether a clergyman's mind is highly wrought, and he is beyond himself, or whether he is spiritually and intellectually at zero, or has sunk below himself, he has to make these periodical appearances in the pulpit. The remedy is no doubt mainly in the hands of the clergy themselves. A more frequent interchange of pulpits, the substitution of Bible readings for much of the preaching, and the reading aloud of sermons by eminent divines, frankly telling the congregation that this is being done, would appear to be the best remedies against a prolonged and prejudicial strain.

It would have been a good thing for Robertson if he could have effected an exchange of duty, or in any way have altered the character of his work. But the idea does not seem to have occurred to him for a moment. To clergymen a change of position is often of the greatest importance and benefit, not only to themselves, but also to their people. So strongly did John Wesley feel this that in his connection no minister is allowed to stay more than two, or at the outside three, years at the same place. Within such a time an ordinary man has preached himself out. So to speak, by the end of two or three years the hearers know every creek and inlet of the preacher's mind, and can almost tell beforehand what he is going to say. It is one of the most remarkable attestations of the greatness of Robertson that his strength and originality in the pulpit to the last remained unabated. This was achieved at a tremendous cost, at nothing less than the cost of his life, but such was the result. Paley honestly avowed that one great reason for giving up one living and taking another was that he had arrived at the end of his sermons. A clergyman on entering upon a new charge feels that he has some positive resources to fall back upon. Some clergymen can go to the old tub or drawer, and steadily work their way through the old stock. Even in the case of extemporaneous preachers there are large bodies of matter, more or less in a wrought condition, ready to use, and which, so to speak, form a kind of available floating balance. A clergyman at

such a time is able to take a new departure, to
revise his ways of acting and thinking, to gather up
new views from his stock of experience, and to
sketch out the chart and campaign of the days that
may be yet left. But none of these things happened to Robertson.

Something may be said of Robertson in his
pastoral relations. His great gift was that of a
preacher—a gift which in these days is thought
very little of—especially by those who do not happen to possess it. The great gift which is thought
most of by those who desire the expansion and
development of the Church is a sort of business
talent for parochial work. A man may give the
best of his time to the study of sacred theology,
he may cultivate every gift for touching the hearts
and minds of men, but any one who can glibly
get through a short sermon, go very much to tea-
parties, get up schemes and committee meetings, is
considered more useful and attractive, and better
fitted for the work of a parish priest. It is said
indeed that the Apostles should leave the serving
of tables, and give themselves to preaching and
prayer; but the present way of looking at things
is decidedly in favour of serving of tables. Robertson knew very well that his great work lay
in the pulpit, and he discharged it manfully often
under circumstances of great difficulty and dis-
couragement.

It does not seem that his pastoral work was extensive. It was done under discouraging circumstances. He complained to those whom he visited that his work was a failure, and that he was isolated among his brethren. Indeed the Brighton clergy have at no time been celebrated for the closeness of their intimacies. "In Brighton you very seldom see two clergymen walking together," was the remark of a woman of the world who had watched the place closely for many years. As time went on he felt an increased longing for pastoral work. In his last days, when his congregation offered him a curate, he wrote : "One inducement towards accepting their offer is that it would enable me to take a district, and try to work it with a view to physical as well as spiritual improvement of the poor, acknowledging Christ as the Saviour of the body—a truth ingenuously ignored." And again : "I am anxious on my own account for assistance to enable me to devote myself less exclusively to pulpit work, and to become more pastoral." He did what he could in his Sunday-school work, which must have been to him an exhausting drudgery.

His congregation consisted of two elements—the steady and the fluctuating. There would be many demands upon his time by the regular members of his congregation, especially in times of sickness and calamity. He took his share in social life, which indeed he would regard as a portion of his sacred duties. It was noticed of him that he would always seek out those who seemed neglected or depreciated, and seek to set them pleasantly at their ease, and bring out what was in them. Wrapped up in his old military cloak, which he might have worn and in which he might have died in Afghanistan, he would wander in the congeries of streets that lie behind the magnificent sea-front of Brighton, and visit the sick and solitary whose cases had been brought to his notice. Often in his midnight wanderings he would meet with some poor, sinful child of sorrow and shame, whom he would endeavour to win back to the innocence she had lost, and he would express himself with righteous indignation against those who, with the profession of Christianity, would not suffer the hem of their garment to be polluted by any approach of the outcasts whom they should seek to save.

The Training College for Girls is now one of the most prosperous institutions in the diocese of Chichester, and one of the imposing edifices of modern Brighton. It is now in the hands of a clergyman who for some years was Robertson's successor at Trinity Chapel. Robertson was connected with it in the day of small things, long before it was removed to its present position. He undertook some work there at the personal request of the Bishop. He acted, we believe, both as chaplain and teacher. His subject was wholly or in the main ecclesiastical history. Fearing that the suspicion with which he was regarded might injure the institution, he offered to resign. It is to be regretted that nothing has been discovered in the records of the college respecting his official connection with it. He was often engaged day after day in his teaching work here. It would be an immense advantage for the future young schoolmistresses to be brought under the teaching and influence of a clergyman who combined the highest order of originality with the highest amount of intellectual culture.

In 1850, on February 17, he commenced his notes on Genesis, which lasted till the May of the following year. There is an interesting notice in the "Life" of this course of lectures, which is hardly sustained by the publication of the notes. These really give us nothing of the treatment of the conflicting claims of science and history with the sacred narrative; of the results of German criticism; of his discussion of the subject of "Inspiration," which had been promised, which no doubt occurred in the course of these unprinted lectures.[2] The book contains various passages which are almost the *ipsissima verba* that we find in the sermons. These were to him, perhaps, what Quintilian calls the *lumina* and *sententiæ* of composition. Every now and then we meet with a phrase which

[2] The arrangement is curious. Lecture xxx. was delivered May 18, 1851, and Lecture xxxi. in 1849.

we can well imagine came with an electric thrill to his audience. Here, too, we have some autobiographic touches. We may cite the first and concluding sentences of the first lecture :—

"We began two years ago the practice of giving the Sunday morning to a sermon and the afternoon to a lecture. And the difference between the two was that in the morning we took for our subject some single text, and endeavoured to exhaust it; but in the afternoon a chapter, and endeavoured to expound the general truths which were contained therein. The sermon was hortatory and practical; the lecture was didactic. The first appealed rather to the heart and to the conscience; the second rather to the intellect and analytic faculty.

"There is something solemn in a commencement, because it reminds us of a close. Twice have I begun, and twice have I finished a book here. Twice have I reminded you that many present at the beginning of my lectures would never live to hear their termination. Again and again has that prediction been fulfilled. The young, the vigorous, the beautiful have been taken away, and many of us who expected our summons are listening still. But do not forget that there are those among us now who will not hear this course of lectures close. Brother men, as we look back into those far distant reaches of the past, and speak of cities and people long ago perished, should we not be reminded that life is but a span? May God grant me courage, perseverance, boldness, inward strength to ascertain the truth and teach it! May God give my hearers the heart to attend with teachableness and with the love that covereth all things, even a multitude of sins. Again, one of our members since last Sunday has heard this voice in the coolness of the evening. He told me not three hours before of his anticipation of that voice, and that he was expecting a gradual extinction of his sight. Within three hours the summons came, and he was in a state of entire unconsciousness. Since then his voice has been heard once in the monosyllable, "Pray," once in thanks for some service rendered to him; twice has he grasped my hand convulsively, with a deep look of gratitude, as I knelt beside his bed in prayer.

"Brother men, believe that God is present with us now, and that He is as much with us at Brighton as He was at Peniel."

With this may be compared a noble passage, with which he concludes a sermon on charity: " Earth has not a spectacle more glorious or more fair to show than this—love tolerating intolerance; charity covering as with a veil even the sin of the lack of charity." His Bible-classes took up a great deal of his time, and Robertson was not a man who would spare himself trouble in preparation. And he often never came out more finely than when some subject had been suddenly suggested to him by some member of his class, when he would pour forth a strain of unpremeditated eloquence, or fling a flood of illustration on a difficult subject. His Bible-classes were often held in the vestry, and often also at his own private residence.

We obtain occasional glimpses of his life and work. A correspondent writes to me: " I believe I only met him twice in my life, and had only one long walk and talk with him coming back from Mr. Maurice's house in Queen Square, and parting somewhere in Grosvenor Place. This was, I think, in 1852. At the same time I always looked upon him as a friend, and felt his death as such, so free and intimate had our connection been. I need hardly say that a more *taking* man never lived. Voice and manner had each an inexpressible charm, and there was a frankness, loftiness, chivalrousness of tone and purpose that reminded one of a Sidney or a Bayard."

Mr. Malcolm Ludlow tells me that he distinctly recollects Robertson; speaking of some evening at a great house where Mr. Maurice had also been invited: this was Lord Carlisle's. Of his reaching the door exactly at the same time, and seeing Mr. Maurice get out of a hack-cab, whilst the grand carriages were drawn up in front, and of the thought coming across him, how different was God's judgment from man's, since that little insignificant man was greater in God's sight than all those grand personages.

We may say, since there are passages in Mr. Stopford Brook's biography of him that would convey an opposite impression, that Robertson distinctly looked up to Maurice, who on his part had for him the deepest admiration and regard.

Mr. Crabbe Robinson has a note of a certain talk at the Athenæum Club about Robertson, a few months after his death. " Sir James Stephen spoke highly of Robertson; Maurice praised him." And more significant was the unintended praise of another, who said " Robertson made me sad; his words seemed a message from God to myself."

Robertson's remark on Maurice was characteristic enough, but at the same time it was hardly one which we could endorse. It is very difficult to speak of the comparative value of souls. Probably there was no one of a greater name or greater influence that night at the great house, but there might have been humble souls even among the great ones equally acceptable in His sight.

Brighton is the place essentially of society. Visitors come down to be gay, and the large resident society are emphatically given to amusement. Every now and then he met good people from whom he heard good conversation. He was struck with the excellence of the best biography of the century, Stanley's " Life of Arnold." Every one spoke of

Arnold ; no one stopped to observe how well Stanley had done it." Lord Lansdowne was the first who made to him any remark on the biographer. Crabbe Robinson, the friend of Wordsworth and Goethe, as we have seen, kept up a faithful but somewhat fitful correspondence with him. One house to which he resorted very constantly was the home of the daughters of Horace Smith. That bright, genial wit had closed a honoured life some years before at Tunbridge Wells; but his children's home at Brighton was the resort of its most intellectual society. He met Mrs. Jamieson, to whom he gave his opinion of the theology of the worship of the Virgin. In the home of one of the best worthies of Brighton, Sir Lawrence Peel, he was most intimate, and also in that of Sir Robert's sister, Lady Henley. No one saw with a clearer vision than Robertson into the dangers of society, and he rigorously limited his share of it, but what he saw was of the best, and he did his best in it.

One of his greatest friends, perhaps the greatest, was Dr. Acworth, whose contributions to the well-known " Life " have imparted to it a special value. He had known Dr. Acworth intimately at Cheltenham, and it was a great pleasure to him to receive his old friend at his house in Brighton. Dr. Acworth had been a physician in high practice and great repute at Cheltenham. A change came over his medical views. He became convinced of the truth of Hahnemann's system, and with fearless conscientiousness and intrepidity he renounced allopathy, and so surrendered the large professional income which he was making at Cheltenham. He was unable to convert Robertson to his homœopathic view, but his self-sacrifice and fidelity to truth were just the points which Robertson could most admire and appreciate. Indeed between the two men there were many points of similarity of character. The true knightly element was common to both, the high-souled nature, the fearlessness, the tenderness. Indeed the analysis and description of Robertson's character, which Dr. Acworth in several ways contributed to the "Life," in the opinion of those best able to judge, might, *mutandis mutatis*, have stood for Dr. Acworth himself. Dr. Acworth, after Robertson's time, established himself as a homœopathic physician in Brighton, where he maintained his high character, and won back the old success upon the new ground. Like many of the Brighton physicians he had a country-house in the neighbourhood of Brighton for the purposes of *villegiatura*. This was at Hayward's Heath, where many of Robertson's friends came to sojourn with "the beloved physician." It was at Dr. Acworth's house at Cheltenham, on the occasion of his last visit there, that Robertson made the personal acquaintance of Tennyson.

It goes without saying how good he was to his

children. He would take his little son with him on some of his social calls. One day a Brighton clergyman heard Robertson talking with his boy. The boy, boy-like, claimed to be as " brave as a lion." The father took him up, and spoke of the natural bravery of a lion—of which, however, naturalists have some doubts—and assured him that he could not be brave in the sense in which a lion was brave. Again, when he found that the child had really got the right on his side in a matter, with generous fatherly impulse in the fullest way he brought out the child's rightness. The common saying is that no man is a hero to his *valet de chambre*. But those who were brought into closest contact with Robertson— those of his own household—spoke of him with the utmost affection and reverence. With tradesfolk and poor people he made great friends, putting them on an absolute equality with himself. He minded not high things, but condescended to men of low estate. Such were his " ways in Christ." He was generous to his full strength, and probably beyond his strength, in giving to the needy.

In 1851 he published a translation of Lessing's short treatise on "The Education of the Human Race." Few treatises have excited more attention than this treatise of Lessing's. Its leading thought was expanded by Bishop Temple, and preached in the first instance as a University sermon at St. Mary's, Oxford, and afterwards made its appearance in " Essays and Reviews," as the commencing essay. Dr. Temple subsequently withdrew his essay from the work. Robertson intended that this translation, with that of some other fragments which he had in mind, should be pioneers to a work on " Inspiration." He also published an analysis of " In Memoriam," in which we confess to some degree of disappointment. But those of Lord Tennyson's countless readers who may attempt to work out any analysis of their own will do justice to Mr. Robertson's attempt, and confess that they have a very faint hope of surpassing, or even equalling it.

What is called the " Sabbath Question " led to a controversy of extreme discomfort to him. The question of the authority and observance of the Lord's Day is one that will always be viewed differently by different minds, and by the same people at different times. The argument on one side is that the Sabbath belongs to the ceremonial law, and is abrogated; the other argument is that it belongs to the moral law; that it was a law of the creation—a law before the ceremonial law, and is of eternal obligation. The physical necessity for a day of rest, when man, the machine of machines, may be said to be adjusted and set going for his weekly toil, may be said to be admitted. The extreme opinions have found their practical exhibition in what is known as the Scottish Sunday and the

Continental Sunday. It is impossible to reconcile opposite opinions, which are held with equal honesty and equal pertinacity. The only right mode for each side is to respect the opinion of the other. It was the lot of Robertson to pass from one opinion to another, and he condemned with unqualified bitterness opinions which he once held. He had once said, in an unpublished Cheltenham sermon, " If this be the true state of things, and if Sabbath services be God's chief method for keeping religion alive in the soul, what is to become of that large class of men on whom virtually no Sabbath dawns, and who are found to spend the day in the service of the rich, in our public offices, and in the course of public travelling. It dries up the spirit of the rich . . . . . with all his other opportunities, to be without his Sabbath ; but take away the Sabbath from the poor man, and you have closed up the last, the only channel by which the dews from heaven might come down upon his hard, dry path.

" Brethren, in connection with this subject I am asked to bring before you a topic of local interest. It is that an Act will soon be passed to enable the Great Western Railway Company to bring their line within 500 yards of this church, and place their terminus in the heart of the town, near the parish church. There are petitions to both parties of the legislature lying at the libraries not to grant to the company the extension powers they ask without securing to this town and the servants of the company the repose of the Sabbath day. It is not a petition which would so interfere with man's liberty as to dictate *how* they shall spend the Lord's Day, but it is a petition to prevent their interfering with the salvation of others. It asks the legislature to interpose the strong arm of its protection to prevent the unhallowed thirst of gain from so intruding on the poor man's Sabbath hours as to make this world to him a dry and thirsty land," &c.

We now turn to the following expression of his later views. We fear that there is a good deal of pettishness and inaccurate thinking in such a passage as the following :—

" There is a tendency now to be very indignant about a poor man's spending Sunday afternoon in a tea-garden, whilst there is little zeal against the real damning sins of social life. Why do they not preach a crusade against noblemen driving in the park? Or why do they speak of God sending a judgment on this nation for a Crystal Palace, while they quietly ignore the fact, or are too polite to take notice of it, that four-fifths of our male population are living in a state of concubinage till they are married? Why do they hold up hands of pious indignation when a train runs by, while more than one religious person in this town drives regularly to church on fine days as well as wet? Why do they say it is a crime to sacrifice a single policeman to the comfort of the community by making him work on the Sabbath, when their own servants are 'sacrificed'—if it be sacrifice—in making their beds, cleaning their rooms, boiling their luxurious hot potatoes, &c., &c., none of which are either works of necessity or works of mercy—the only works, they say, which are excepted from the rule? Why do they not grapple with the slander and the gossip and the pride of society and the crimes of the upper classes? Why are they touched to the quick only when desecration of the Sabbath puts on a *vulgar* form?"

Now it is easily seen that this language is very strained and inconsequential, unlike Robertson, and argues want of health, both of mind and body. If "Sabbath-breaking" is wrong, the *tu quoque* argument that other things are wrong also does not affect the question. It must be said in fairness to the "Sabbatarian" preachers that they have heartily denounced, both in high and low, every form of the evil of which they complain, and they have not been slow in denouncing slander, gossip, and pride. If any works of necessity are to be allowed we should think cleanliness in the way of bed-making and cleaning, and food in the shape of "luxurious hot potatoes"—certainly a very humble form of luxury—might be permitted. The assertion that four-fifths of the population live a sinful life is, we are assured, an enormous exaggeration, and so is the implied assertion that the clergy " wink " at such forms of sin. Our impression is that Robertson must have been in an ill state both of mind and body when he penned such a paragraph.

In this matter, as in others, we see an unhappy sensitiveness. "It is very difficult to discuss this question of the Sabbath," he writes : " heat, vehemency, acrimony are substituted for argument. When you calmly ask to investigate the subject, they apply epithets and call them reasons—they stigmatize you as a breaker of the Sabbath, pronounce you 'dangerous,' with sundry warnings against you in private, and frequent hints in public." We have seen that Robertson can hardly be said to have had all the "calmness" on his side. It is possible that a certain amount of heat, vehemence, and acrimony existed in Robertson's own imagination. But I am sorry to say, from facts that have come within my own knowledge, that even good men, acknowledged lights in the religious world, did not scruple to apply to the great preacher the term " infidel," and would call his chapel the infidel chapel. Often he appears to have felt most acutely the loneliness of his life. There was in him a craving for sympathy, which he richly enjoyed when accorded, but often grievously felt the want of. This is the trial of so many human lives. The only remedy for the lonely is to throw themselves on the sympathy of Christ. So many suffer from the very intensity of their affections.

Robertson speaks most touchingly on the matter: "It is the trembling spirit of humanity in them. They want not aid, nor even countenance: but only sympathy. And the trial comes to them not in the shape of fierce struggle, but of chill and utter loneliness, when they are called upon to perform a duty on which the world looks coldly, or to embrace a truth which has not found lodgment yet in the breasts of others." Would it not have been best for him to have given up this feverish yearning for human sympathy, and to have thrown himself simply upon the sympathy of Christ?

Other disagreeables happened to him which he would not fail to feel. A complaint was made of his teaching to the Bishop, and he wrote out a copy of one of his sermons for the Bishop's inspection, and good Dr. Gilbert was unable to discern anything erroneous in the teaching. Then he had showers of anonymous letters. These he would not treat with absolute contempt, but carefully considered what they might have to say. One day he showed a whole set of such letters to his churchwarden, Mr. Bowdidge, some of them remonstrating with him rather coarsely on his personal appearance. Mr. Bowdidge identified the handwriting as that of a lady of rank, who was supposed to be one of his best friends. We find him writing thus:

"My DEAR YOUNG (Sir being, at your request, consigned to the official care of Mr. John Ketch),—

Thank you very much for your letter, which was encouraging, as all sympathy and approval are to a man baited or worried on all sides as I am. Your belief, however, in growing influence at Brighton, is the result of a friendly and vivid imagination: for I hear nothing in reference to myself but one confused buzz of all imaginable and unimaginable slanders. What there is in me to make the antipathy and opposition so virulent I cannot guess, and it sometimes puzzles me—since I am not aware that in society I am given to take the lead in conversation, or to lay down the law, which might exasperate. However, there must be something *personally* very offensive in myself or in my manner, or something else; for mere disagreement with my views would not account for the violence of the abuse which I provoke, and some of the lies are ceasing to be merely white ones. . . .

" The trifling persecution one is subject to in these emasculated days from emasculated religionists reminds one of the days when truth could only be sustained at a real cost, in comparison of which the buzz of a whole Brighton is but as the hum of gnats. Yet the incessant sting of gnats even is a semi-maddening thing in the hot, dusty noontide of work, when the freshness and hope of its morning are gone, and the soothing cool of its evening is not yet come. Sometimes (much in the same way as a fly may understand the gestation of an elephant) I think of Elijah under his juniper-tree and wish his wish.   But it is

> ' The good die first,
> And they whose hearts are dry as summer's dust
> Burn to the socket.'

" With this piece of sentimentalism to conclude,

"Yours very gratefully,

"————."

Robertson's health broke up.   The fact is that he lived persistently at too high a pressure.   Few clergymen throughout the six years at Brighton did as much work as he would crowd into his week. The physical strain was great, both in the preaching and what was often his inordinate exercise.   The mental and spiritual strain can never be efficiently gauged, but it must have been painfully great.   The distinguished Brighton physician who attended him has given me a history of his case.   It was the heart and not the brain that was principally at fault. There was an incompetency in one of the valves. The brain symptoms, of which we read in the biography, were occasioned by that.   The treatment was to palliate the symptoms, but it could not touch the seat of the disease.   The grand, noble heart had in every way been overworked.   From the first Dr. Allen took an unfavourable view of his illness. There was no good augury to be drawn from any circumstance in his case.   But he never himself realized that the end was so near.

In the time of his trouble about the vicar and Mr. Towers he came to see a friend who had a cottage in the country amid the Sussex downs. The friend writes :—" He walked to church with us, for he was come to be sponsor for my boy, and in the evening asked that he might have tea upon the grass. I well remember that evening. We sat on the edge of the lawn in front of a great walnut-tree ; all of us clustered round him till twilight deepened into night. We were almost silent listeners, while he talked on for hours remittingly. It was almost the only time I ever heard one of his wonderful monologues, ranging over many subjects, bringing light into the darkest recesses of each, and linking them, all diverse as they were, to one another with a power which could only have arisen out of the possession of great principles arranged in his own mind in harmonious connection with one another. . . . In that soft summer air we might have sat there the whole night—for he held us under his spell—had not the appearance of the wearied servant reminded us that it was twelve o'clock. I never saw again this lightening of the intellect. It seem to be the last effort of his expiring power. The next morning he began to read family prayers, and broke down, asking me to finish. Then he sat under the trees or in an easy-chair for hours, with eyes closed, more often suffering pain. On the Sunday he prepared to accompany us to church ; it was Communion Sun-

day, and he said he should like much to go. As we
walked together, he suddenly stopped and said, ' I
cannot go; I am in such extreme pain that I cannot
answer for myself.' My wife wished that we should
stay with him, but he would not permit it, saying
that he should be better by-and-by. . . . He said
once that the sense of his being able to talk or be
silent, to do exactly what he liked, was very con-
soling to him. . . . Before he left he spoke earnestly
with my wife of a change he was then contemplating,
approved it heartily, and in answer to an expression
of sorrow that it must separate us from his public
ministry, replied, ' My work is done!' and once
again he said to me, ' If I have been able to do any
true work for you, be very sure some one else will
come to you to carry it on.' On the way to Brighton
he was roused up by seeing in a field some birds
which he remarked he had never observed in Sussex
before. I could not even see them, they were so far
away, but his sight, keen even then, distinguished
them so clearly as to mark their peculiarities." [3]

Mr. Julian Charles Young, in his " Last Leaves," [4]
&c., has some very interesting things to tell about
Robertson. Robertson was essentially a peripatetic,
and his friend also belonged to the sect of the walking philosopher. Whenever Mr. Young went from

[3] Appendix G. to the " Life."
[4] An interesting work, only too little known. Edinburgh:
Edmonstone and Douglas. 1874.

Hastings to Brighton he always counted on the pleasure of a walk with Robertson. The condition was made that they should strike up-hill through the back streets, so as to avoid the interruptions and salutations of the crowds on the cliffs. As he passed through the frequented streets hats were doffed to him every instant, for all knew him, rich and poor, and while this was going on Robertson seemed constrained and reticent. As soon, however, as he gained the turf of the hills, he would fling out his arms, expand his chest, and seemed to exult with the sense of liberty and life, Young was generally the listener, while his friend poured forth the fire and music of his mind, all frivolity being banished, and the elevation of lofty thoughts sustained.

The last walk happened only a few days before the full development of the fatal illness. Let Mr. Young tell the story : " We had been having a singularly animated disquisition of three hours on ' things about this world and things about the next,' and I was in the act of accompanying him to the training-school in West Street, where he had to deliver a lecture, when, as I was telling him a story of painful and pathetic interest, in illustration of a certain theory he had advanced, he exclaimed with convulsive interest, ' How shocking !' and fainted in my arms. I carried him with considerable difficulty into an adjoining little shop—a cobbler's—and, as it had only just been taken possession of by a new tenant, and was destitute of furniture, I laid him on the flooring, consigned him to the care of the good man of the house, and ran over the way to a chemist's shop for some salts and sal volatile. On my return he lay still unconscious, and it was, I should think, a quarter of an hour before he came to. When he recovered consciousness he was in a state of complete enervation. It was, however, in vain that I urged the propriety of his going to his house with me in a fly. He expressed such determined repugnance to indulging in such effeminacy, as he called it, that I was compelled to yield to his wishes and slowly escort him home on foot. On the road he leant so heavily on my arm, and dragged his legs along with such difficulty, that I feared every moment that he would fall. On arriving at home I persuaded him, with infinite difficulty, to put up his feet on a chair, while he reclined on another. I had repeatedly expostulated with him on his disregard of his bodily health, urging on him the need of letting his over-wrought and over-cropped brain lie fallow for some time; for the meagreness of his appetite, the wakefulness of his nights, and the nervous pallor of his tongue, I thought were ugly symptoms. But to all my admonitions I received the same answer, ' Yes, you only tell me what my medical advisers confirm. I have a voice within which whispers to me that, young as I am, my day is far spent, and that my night will soon come. Let me, then, work while it is day, and if I am to die let me die in harness.' 'Surely,' said I, 'if you wish to do God's work and serve your fellow-men, you would wish not to curtail your power of usefulness by imprudence, but rather to prolong it by ordinary precaution. I wish I could frighten you!' With a sad and significant smile, he then confessed that though he had often suffered from distressing sensations at the back of the head, he had never conceived them to be of any moment."

Robertson promised his friend that he would come and spend a few days with him at Fairlight, near Hastings. On June 25th he writes:—

"I hope to be with you. May I bring my little boy, who will be satisfied with a shake-down in a garret or granary? But as Mrs. Robertson and Ida are going on a visit to Mr. Lamb, he would be left alone if he were not allowed to come with me."

Two days later he writes: "I am grieved to be so apparently capricious, but I am not yet fit for civilized society, and must wait some days before I can come to Fairlight. Allen has asked for a consultation. Taylor was the man I fixed on. The case is a very simple and trifling one, but I grieve to say I must postpone—I hope for not more than a week—my visit. [The Church] certainly is the most quarrelsome of all professions in the matter of a blue or green window, prevenient moonshine, or a bishop's night-cap, and most cowardly when it comes to a matter of right or wrong—of what they saw and what they did not see. Unless clergy of the type I am alluding to are forced to serve in the army for five years previous to ordination to make them men ' let alone ' gentlemen, I think the Church, as an Establishment, had better be snuffed out."

On June 30th, 1853, about three weeks before his death, he writes :—

" I am grieved to see by your note how much you are disappointed, and fear you may think that I have treated you capriciously or cavalierly. The fact is that both Taylor and Allen emphatically forbade my going away, or travelling by train even as far as Hurst. Allen this morning told me that he said to T., ' I do not think Mr. R. should go on the visit he intends,' and T. answered abruptly, something like, ' Pooh ! he must not.' On Monday and Tuesday, I was in about the state the Seneca was, after his veins had been opened in the hot-bath half an hour. Yesterday and to-day I am forbidden to receive visitors. . . . I am become an old man, or rather an old woman, fit only to toddle a few yards backwards and forwards in the sunshine. Never mind; I mean to be a compound of a Hercules and an Apollo before many weeks are over."

We take his last letter, written to Julian Young :—

"*Brighton, July 8th,* 1853.

"My dear Young.—You were kind enough to ask me for a bulletin in a week. Here it is, briefly :—

" Hot milk as soon as I awake, to prevent fainting, An hour's siesta. Up. Interesting contest between F. W. R. and a fainting fit. Faint says, 'I have you.' 'Not yet,' says F. W. R., looking like a ghostly turnip, and falls into a cold bath, a splash whereof robs Faint of his prey. Manful attempts at drying. Operation just concluded ; back comes the white demon. F. W. R. falls on the bed, reflecting strangely on supported vertebral column, and congratulating himself on his profound knowledge of anatomy. Ten minutes elapse. F. W. R. fortifies himself with two spoonfuls of citrate of ammonia, on the strength of which he goes on triumphantly till the barbarous operation of shaving comes, in the middle of which Faint shouts, with a provoking little squeak, ' He ! he ! he !' So much for anatomy, and down goes F. W. R.

" All day long sofa or bed, languor, pain, uselessness ; luxuries in the shape of ice, claret, *recherché* soups sent from all quarters, reminding F. W. R. unpleasantly of the contrast between the life of Him who would fain have ' satisfied His morning hunger upon wild figs and His death-thirst upon vinegar,' and the invalidism of His modern ministers, bepetted, befondled, with the fat things of earth at command. The only consolation is that I am too feeble to make any use of them.

"Citrate of iron through the day. Night comes. Blisters behind the ears to allay suffering in brain. Morphia to deaden pain and to give some chance of rest. Pleasant night following pleasant day; i.e. if the day were pleasant. There is a facetious sketch of my highly useful life. I am very glad that I did not go to you. Many a day I cannot walk across the room, or even hold up my head.

"But, Young, I am learning two lessons, or rather having them forced upon me, nothingness and dependence. As I told you before—whether humbly or not, God knows—another thing I learn, and I learn it with all my heart—gratitude for countless attentions and tendernesses. I am tired. I can write no more. As it is I can only write with a pencil, reclining. With pen and ink I do but splutter. My kindest remembrances to Mrs. Young.

"Ever yours,

"FRED. W. ROBERTSON."

There was one faithful friend who was always deeply attached to Mr. Robertson, and who had the happiness of being able to render to him some signal services. He had placed the business arrangements of Trinity Chapel on a sound basis, and so far had assisted Robertson in his difficult fight with the world. He it was who in his last illness carried

Robertson upstairs, and Robertson died in his arms.
For many very interesting particulars I am indebted
to Mr. Bowdidge. "My work is over," he said.
"Let God do His Will on me." In those days of
meekness and distress Robertson's heart yearned for
sympathy and communion with his brethren. It
would be something to exchange thoughts and
experience, and obtain some measure of strength
and refreshing from those who might stand by him
in those deep waters by which he seemed to be
overwhelmed. It is remarkable that in those last
hours, whether by accident or intention, he reverted
to those who held most strongly to the Evangelical
opinions which he had seen reason to denounce.
There was no clergyman in Brighton whose character, both on the intellectual and religious side, stood
higher in Brighton than that of James Vaughan, formerly the curate of the parish church, and now the
incumbent of Christ Church. Whatever might be
variations of opinion, the two men thoroughly appreciated and loved one another. He summoned Mr.
Vaughan to his sick-bed. Unfortunately Mr.
Vaughan was away from Brighton at the time, and
they never met as had been Robertson's desire.
St. Margaret's Chapel, Brighton, has always preserved an intense and peculiar type of Evangelicalism. It may be said that its clergy have been
of a line of vigorous and devout men, who have
preserved an organic unity of teaching, and have

been able to raise among their people immense sums for philanthropical and religious purposes. The incumbent at this time was a Mr. Du Pré, who, having experienced at one season of his life the *res angusta domi*, eventually came to a condition of great affluence, but amid all circumstances was eminent among those are eminent for piety and goodness. The incumbent of Margaret Chapel visited what proved to be the dying-bed of Robertson, and was a source of help and consolation to him. Into the particulars of that conversation, of those *novissima verba*, I am of course unable to enter. But I have been informed by one who speaks with authority on the subject, and who would be most anxious to speak with perfect accuracy, that Robertson's difficulties on the subject of the Atonement passed away. One phrase that Robertson used was constantly remembered and repeated: "I see it all. It is Christ, and only Christ."

When it was known that Robertson was really dead, it is not too much to say that a wail of grief and surprise rose from the gay city of the waters. He was cut off in the midst of his days, when his work and usefulness were at their height, and when it might not be unfairly anticipated that many years of fame and use lay before him. His funeral knell must have had a reproachful sound to the hearts of many, not least to those who for those six years had hard, unkindly thoughts and words respecting him, but who had never brought themselves within the range of his preaching, or sought to comprehend the teaching which they condemned. A wave of sorrowful emotion passed over the whole community. Such a public funeral had never been witnessed in Brighton, never before or since; an exhibition of profound public sorrow and pity, one so rare and so creditable in such a community as Brighton.

Robertson left no will. His modest possessions, administered to by the widow, were estimated as under one thousand five hundred pounds. It was felt by many of his friends that if he had sowed to them in spiritual things, it was right that they should give to him of their earthly things, and so precious had been his teaching to them, that, after all they could do, they would still be his debtors. A large sum was raised, dictated by this feeling, for the use of his children, to which Lady Byron, with customary munificence, gave very largely. His children have taken positions in the world in no wise inferior to what they would have occupied had his life been spared. They have found that the heritage of a good man is a priceless inheritance, and that they are " beloved for the father's sake."

"Sleep sweetly, tender heart, in peace:
  Sleep, holy spirit, blessed soul,
While the stars burn, the moons increase,
  And the great ages onward roll.

"Sleep till the end, true soul and sweet,
  Nothing comes to thee new or strange.
Sleep full of rest from head to feet;
  Lie still, dry dust, secure of change."

CHAPTER X.

ON THE RELIGIOUS TEACHING OF ROBERTSON.

WE now approach the important subject of the nature and effect of Robertson's distinctive views of religion. Many of the views which appear to have startled some of his contemporaries are now among the accepted commonplaces of the churches. There was something also in that teaching which excited criticism and alarm in Brighton during his ministry, and not, we think, without a measure of justice. Robertson cannot be said to have founded any school, or to have left behind him any body of disciples. It is customary to speak of him as belonging to the band of those who are popularly called Broad Churchmen, of whom Archdeacon Hare, Maurice, and Kingsley are the most eminent examples—men who in their day impelled a wave of Liberalism through the region of English theology, the effects of which are still very perceptible. Nothing, however, is clearer than that Robertson acted in entire independence of these illustrious men. One was his master, even Christ.

It is this genuine independence of all party ties which constitutes to a large degree the merit and the manliness of Robertson. He refused to label himself by any party name of High, Low, or Broad. He sought for and reverenced truth wherever he might find her. It may be hoped that some day a fourth party may rise in the Church of England, the leading characteristic of which will be that it belongs to no party at all. It is in this tolerance and many-sidedness of Robertson that members of various schools of thought find their affinity to him. Circle touches circle, though only in a single point, and there is hardly any circle of opinion but finds its affinity with Robertson. For many years of his life he had been intimately associated with the Low Church. In his later years he seemed to find his natural position with the Broad Church. At one time of his life it seemed probable that he was moving somewhat in the High Church direction. The story is told that he was offered church promotion if he would join their standard. He seems to have believed this himself, but it is hardly probable that any such offer could ever have been seriously made. On one public occasion he said, "If there are any persons here holding High Church views, I implore them to believe that, although I am not a High Churchman myself—far from it—I can yet sympathize with them in all their manliness and high-mindedness, and recognize much in them that is pure and aspiring." Some of his sermons, more especially those on the Glory of the Virgin Mother, would more especially recommend themselves to the catholic-minded. But there was one party in the Church towards which he felt an immoderate and rancorous hostility. This was the Evangelical party, to which he had once heartily belonged, but which he came to dislike with that peculiar energy of hatred common to those who have belonged to one camp, and, for some reason or other, have then gone over to the opposite. Nevertheless there is reason to believe that in his latest days he returned to the simplicity of his earliest beliefs.

There are several defects which to the Anglican mind must detract greatly from the value of his sermons. These very defects have, no doubt, greatly contributed to his popularity. They have caused his sermons to be read by those who would refuse to read any other sermons. They have met and created sympathies in a class of minds into which the average pulpiteer has no possible means of gaining admission. He has too much self-consciousness. He never seems quite able to forget himself in his message. He carries into his sermons his sense of isolation, his idea that personal injustice and persecution formed his unjust lot, his protest against whatever chafed and irritated him in life. Of course these things never became the substance of his sermons; but it seems to us impossible not to detect them in an unhealthy proportion. Robertson believed the revealed truth he taught, but his belief did not bring to him as it did to multitudes of humble Christians, peace and joy. Much truth also that he taught was held in a tentative and hesitating way. In the midst of very confident language he will use expressions which will throw uncertainty and negation over whole tracts of religious teaching. The result was that some of his hearers questioned whether the fervour he exhibited could always be reconciled with the opinions he held. " These are my opinions," he said on one occasion to a friend, who reported the saying to the present writer, " at least they are the opinions which I hold now. I am not sure what my opinions will be next year." Another very curious defect in Robertson is that he sometimes quotes Scripture in an inaccurate way. This is the more remarkable as he was a good Greek scholar, a good textual critic, and his opinion on questions of text would be listened to with respect. No amount of scholarship, however, will exonerate any clergyman from the duty of the daily careful reading of Scripture in the English version. It is a fact within personal knowledge that eminent critics who have written excellently on subjects of New Testament criticism have sometimes made mistakes in the text of the

New Testament of which Sunday-school scholars would be ashamed.

We need hardly say that Robertson's verbal errors were not of this serious character. If we come to compare Robertson with other great preachers, the distinctive qualities of his mind come clearly out. It would be doing him an injustice to compare him even with such great pulpit orators as Chalmers in Scotland, or Melvill in England. Perhaps the term orator can hardly be applied unreservedly to these two great men, although it is a term generally so applied. We think it is the very expression most applicable to Robertson. Chalmers and Melvill adhered—we must say servilely—to the written page, yet the written page from their lips achieved some of the finest effects of oratory. Robertson's unwritten sentences have the finest effect of studied composition. The late Archdeacon Sinclair told the writer that he once heard Chalmers speak quite extemporary, the only occasion perhaps when he ever did preach extemporary, and the effect was very remarkable. The Anglican orators as a rule are oratorical from the book. Lord Brougham once wrote a letter to Zachary Macaulay, advising him that his son, Thomas Babington, who showed signs of being an orator, should maintain an entire distinction between his preaching and his writings, and never mix up pen, ink, and paper with his speeches. It was in the spirit and almost in the letter of such advice that Robertson acted.   His notes after preaching might at times be copious, but before preaching they were as terse as he could make them.   He was essentially an orator.   He was no writer—nothing in any fixed literary form was ever produced by him.   At the same time he governed himself by the severest rules of literary art.   He frankly said that he considered the form as being at least as important as the body and substance of the thought.   To Robertson no employment would be more delightful than the construction of sentences.   He must have often tried them till he was satisfied with the form and rhythm. He would no doubt reject them until the sentences were critically perfect.   Such sentences would be essentially oral and not written eloquence, constructed not with an eye to the paragraph, but what the critics call the *periodus oratorica.*   He always spoke direct to the ear, and not to the eye.   His sentences had nothing trite or worn about them, but came fast, sharp, clearly-defined, bright, and glowing as imperial coin fresh issued from the mint.

Let us compare him with other divines whose works have achieved a widespread influence.   The influence of certain great Unitarian preachers was strong upon Robertson.   These were Emerson, Channing, and James Martineau.   Each of these exhibit marvellous thought clothed in fascinating language. Robertson was utterly free from Unitarianism. The difference between his theology and the theology of Unitarianism is as sunlight to moonlight. It has been often remarked that the teaching of Martineau had a great influence over Robertson. There is a cold, impassive beauty about the exquisite sentences of Martineau that contrasts strongly with the powerful, flashing brightness and keen incisiveness of Robertson. There are two living preachers who may well be compared with him—James Martineau himself, and M. Eugene Bersier of Paris. In point of oratorical effect—in the highest, rarest effect, that of the thought and not of the language—we think that neither of these touch Robertson. As a preacher, so far as oratory is concerned, he stands above Martineau and Bersier just as Dean Stanley thought he stood above Newman and Arnold. It is very interesting and instructive to compare different sermons on the same text—let us take St. John xvi. 32—by these three preachers, Robertson, Martineau, and Bersier. In deep feeling, in real thought, in noble imagery, in the fact of being thoroughly *en rapport* with their age, influenced by and influencing the *Zeitgeist* of their time, they are much upon an equality. But the life and fire are peculiarly Robertson's own. The rest bear traces of the study and of the lamp. Compared with the sermons of James Martineau—so remarkable in their way, but at the same time deficient in their scope and wanting in warmth and brightness—the sermons of Robertson to our mind are greatly superior. But the paramount literary excellence seems to belong to M. Bersier, whose eloquent, unfaltering utterances, or impassioned, severe reasonings are set out to the utmost advantage in the clear, diamond-like language of France.

Robertson's great charm is that he goes straight to the human heart. The hearts of his people were swayed by him as the corn-fields are swept by a strong wind from Heaven. We must believe with the heart. Buckle says: "The emotions are as much a part of us as the understanding; they are as truthful; they are as likely to be right. Though their view is different from that of the understanding, it is not capricious. They obey fixed laws; they follow an orderly and uniform course; they run in sequences; they have their logic and method of inference." A curious conversation is related which once passed between Grimm and Diderot. The two men were walking one day in the fields, Diderot had plucked an ear of wheat and a blue cornflower and was attentively regarding them, when Grimm asked him what he was doing. "I am listening," was the reply. "But who is speaking to you?" "God." "Indeed!" "It is in Hebrew; the heart understands, but the intellect is not raised high enough." Robertson helped men to believe unto righteousness by the heart. It is in this absolute fidelity to nature and to truth that there mainly resides the secret of his great strength.

One of the most remarkable characteristics of this wonderful series is the power of illustration. His images possess great variety and beauty. Some of the finest passages in the prose-poetry of modern eloquence may be selected from them. Nothing can be nobler than some of these. Singularly clear-cut, without a redundant word, without a single rhetorical expression, the imagery is of the chastest and boldest order.

We will first, however, say a few words on what may be called the "bibliography" of Robertson. It is very remarkable that he himself never antici-pated any measure of usefulness or fame from the publication of his sermons. Indeed, he never spoke of his pulpit work without some language of weari-ness, disappointment, and disgust. Every reader of the "Life" is familiar with such language. It is believed that in his inner heart Robertson realized the greatness of the honour and privilege that was his in being an accredited ambassador from God to man, for otherwise he could not have felt the respon-sibility so deeply or have fulfilled it so manfully. When Robertson was told that there were members of his congregation who took shorthand notes of his sermons, he did not request them to discontinue the habit, for he had neither the moral or legal right to do so, but he showed plainly that the fact gave him no interest or pleasure. The great mass of his sermons published were due to the shorthand notes of an individual lady. His acknowledgment of her labour of love was somewhat coldly given, and he had not the least idea of the weight of obligation under which this lady was laying himself, his family, and the Christian world at large. When a proposition was made by some friends to employ a regular shorthand writer, he was extremely averse. "I think the plan very undesirable. There are a great many things said in extempore preaching . . . which have not been deeply examined and which will not bear to be coldly scrutinized in manuscript. . . . Add to this that often one at least of the Sunday discourses is insufficiently prepared, the expressions utterly unstudied beforehand, the thing itself poor and jejune and worthless. I should not like to own it. . . . For myself I would far rather that all should perish, except the impression the moment after delivery. I preserve few records myself, except on a few occasions. I can scarcely bear to read over anything I have said. It would be a relief to me to know that no trace subsisted, except a few hints for my own use, and for future development of the thoughts touched on."

The enormous influence of the sermons outside

that circle of immediate hearers on whom they made such a deep impression, was the last thing thought of. The great secret of Robertson's success was his intense vitality, that he threw all the fire and music of his soul into the hour that was passing over him, that he was unfettered by the written page, by the necessity of publication, by the apprehension of the criticism of reviewers. On a reduced scale he reminds us of that great teacher of antiquity, who formed no school, who wrote no books, and yet by his influence on the diverse and conflicting minds of Aristotle and Plato, has so largely influenced the whole current of human thought. A close resemblance, in the judgment of M. de Pressensé, is to be found between his mind and Pascal's in his pointedness, his intensity, his admirable lucidity. There is another point of material resemblance which is well worth noting. I spent some time one day at the Bibliothèque Nationale in Paris, in going over the manuscript of Pascal's wonderful "Pensées," the fragments that were to be consolidated into a work on the "Christian Evidences." There were scraps that had been hurriedly noted down on any piece of paper that came to hand. Some would be on the backs of papers and 'envelopes. Then would come a few pages of exquisite caligraphy in most orderly style. The papers are gathered together on files like so many old bills, and any number of diverse editions is possible, as each successive editor

x 2

may adopt his own scheme of arrangement, and his own plan of the work. Robertson's way of working was not at all unlike this. He jotted down his thoughts on any scrap that came to hand. It might be a piece of paper caught up in his dressing-room, the back of an envelope or the fly-leaf of a letter, even the margin of a newspaper. These scattered memoranda were fused into shape and force during quiet meditative hours at home, or in the course of his rapid walks. After the sermon was preached, often on the very evening of the day, he would make notes more or less full, to gratify some friend, or possibly for his own future guidance. The great difficulty of an extemporaneous preacher is to remember his text, and the treatment of his text. We know the case of a very popular preacher who felt himself obliged to resign his benefice because he could not remember the subject of even a week or two before. Robertson's plan of making notes directly afterwards seems to be the very best that could be adopted. In early days he wrote his sermons before delivery; afterwards he did not, but made notes after preaching them. There is no doubt that there were some few cases in which the sermons were thus deliberately written through from first to last. Mr. Crabbe Robinson states that, owing to the urgent request of friends, he latterly consented to write one of his two sermons. The late Mr. Bowdidge informed me that on his death-bed Robertson stated that there were some eighteen sermons written which he thought might be published for the benefit of his family. As Mr. Bowdidge stated that he found various sums of money put away or lying about, it is possible that these sermons may have been overlooked or lost.

I have now before me a short set of his sermons, copied from his own autograph. One of them, published among the Brighton sermons, was first preached at Cheltenham. Some of the matter at the beginning and end of the Cheltenham discourse is omitted in the Brighton discourse. Now and then a sentence is omitted as superfluous. Now and then a sentence is expanded to get greater clearness. Now and then a paragraph is marked for omission, we expect in case the sermon should prove too long for the auditory. Eloquence lies in the audience as much as in the preacher, and the subtle sense of Robertson could tell him when his people had taken in as much as they could bear. The remarkable fact is that the sermon which excited so much attention at Brighton should have received, comparatively speaking, so little at Cheltenham. But an orator, to do himself justice, requires both a *nidus* and an environment. At Christ Church, Cheltenham, the minds of the people were fixed on Boyd, and save for a few, on Boyd alone. Robertson, as well as the people, was altogether overshadowed by this governing influence. In those few concentrated years at

Brighton, he himself was the soul of his congre
gation.

It will be interesting to our readers if we give
the omitted commencement and conclusion of the
sermon to which we refer, " On the Prodigal Son
and his Brother." They may like to compare these
omitted passages with the sermons as they appear
in the collective edition. We give the exordium.
The part in parenthesis was probably intended to
be left out for purposes of compression :—

"There was one feature in our Redeemer's
character to which, in all indifference to the charge
of repetition, we love again and again to direct
men's attention. It was that singular tenderness
for guilt which brought upon Him the sarcasm of
censorious moralists, and made Him unutterably
dear to every man whose spirit is being crushed
under the weight of his own past excesses. (There
were exclusive narrow-minded religionists for whom
Jesus had no sympathy. There were those who
looked down disdainfully on all who did not adopt
their cant phraseology and did not belong to their
party. We read not of one word of allowance or
excuse which ever fell from the Redeemer's lips for
them—everything which savoured of oppression,
harshness to the poor, insult to the weak, shutting
out hope from the sinful, woke up in our Master's
heart emotions of bitterest indignation, and wrung
from our Master's lips the language of eloquent and

most sublime denunciation. It was by things like these, self-righteousness and oppression, and only these, that the placid current of the temper of Christ was ever ruffled into a storm.

"But, my brethren, when guilt, guilt with its misery and its restlessness, was placed before Him, there was a marked difference in His treatment.)"

The following was the conclusion :—

"I have now to draw from this subject the materials for an appeal to your liberality for Church extension in this diocese. Brethren, there are two classes of persons for whom Church privileges are required. There are the guilty, like the younger son, who need to be reclaimed and to be brought back to God; there are the religious, like the elder son, who need to have their failings rebuked and themselves built up in the right knowledge of God. There are ten districts for which the bishop of this diocese recognizes an immediate and pressing need of Church provision and ministerial instruction. They are all poor districts, utterly unable to provide for the want themselves. Some of them are even in a worse state than that— they do not feel the want of spiritual assistance. In pleading for Church extension let me remind you what is meant. Church extension is not simply building more churches. It is not merely increasing the number of the clerical body—these are not the extension of the Church, only the means of its extension. In these days let us not forget what the Church is—just as a seminary of education means not the masters but the pupils, and the masters for the sake of the pupils, so the Church means the people, and the clergy for the sake of the people. Let the laity of England awake to this conviction that Church extension is their business. They are the Church, not we. To extend the Church is to provide the means, in the shape of buildings and teachers, of doing good to people's souls. And the time has come when the laity must awake from their lethargy, or else the Church's days as a Church are numbered. An immense population, uncared for, unshepherded, has gathered up, as it were, in the night, around us, while men were sleeping, and while the dissenters nobly enlarge their efforts in proportion to their exigencies, and Rome lavishly, and on a magnificent scale, provides for all her needs and all her people. Churchmen up to the last few years have guiltily forgotten that their Church has not grown with the requirements of the day. Brethren, I could wish that this subject had been brought before you by a more powerful advocacy. It is only because no one else could be found in the place of the pastor who commonly addresses you, that I have most reluctantly intruded upon your attention. The power of an eloquent appeal I have not, but I will not do you the injustice to surmise that you will permit this cause to suffer from the absence of your stated minister. This congregation surely needs not to be reminded that contributions are not a tribute to man, but an offering sacred to your most High God. The appeal is made to you as Churchmen, as Christians, as men simply on this ground, to co-operate with your love of God in bringing back to goodness the degraded, the outcast, the ignorant. Grudge not, brethren beloved, to welcome these ones to their Father's feast, lest the rebuke be yours which the elder brother brought upon himself."

It will interest our readers if we transcribe a passage from one of the unpublished sermons, indicating Mr. Robertson's abbreviations and alterations :—

"And now b. you will observe in this the wide diste. wh. there is betw. being forced into w. and selecting w. society. D(avid) had no choice. His poson. was the result of circ. It came in the way of duty : and when it did come the effect wh. it produced upon his spirit was a most painful sense of loneliness. It was in oppon. to every taste of his char. & it left him as in a thirsty land. And suppose that all this is reversed & that instead of compulsion it is by taste and by choice that a man seeks for his relaxon. & his refreshment in the comp^{ny}. of those who care not earnestly for God and then from this passage you
    [two of the evils which belong]   to such compan. [one is]
learn, the conclusion wh. results, It is this

that for a man to delight in the conversion of world.
[The other is that it will dry and parch up what little religion he may have.
With respect to the first of these]
men, is an evidence conclusive of his own irreligion, there cannot be a surer test of spir^y. than the kind of occupon. with wh. men naty. assimilate. By choice a b^r. seeks the society of those who are trenching heavenward. And if this be but an endurance & if a man escape from this to the dissipon. of the world and if you can find him there by choice as loud, as gay, as much in his element as any one of them, you tell us b. can you look on that man and picture to yourselves that he left his chamber after a solemn act in wh. the realities of the trem. fut. were brot. home to his spirit, and that forecasting the temptons. of the day he laid down this as his firm resolve, O God thou art my God. Can you bl. that the man who is so exhib. himself in the evening's revelry spent his morning in rapt and hallowed converson. with heaven. Can you think that he has tasked himself to the nursing up his spirit for eternity? No, my b. there is an incongruity in the thing from wh. the mind recoils as an impossibility [Assocon. with the w. may come in the way of duty but if it comes in the way of taste it proceeds not from a spirit like that of the man who was after GOD'S own heart]. It is not the sinfulness of the act but it is the delib. of the act, wh. makes such associon. so infallible a test of a man's tendencies. There are some sins which

come upon a man, as it were, unawares. The temper may overc. him from time to time and it may lie upon him almost like an invol. spell. Sloth may bind him in its soft chains and though there may be guilt in this, it is not exactly that wh. can be called woeful turning aside from God's service. But when a man throws himself into the vortex of this w. dissipton. the whole trans. is a thing of deliberation. It is the calm balancing of 2 kinds of enjoyment and the deterg. to take that wh. the Scrip. has proved to be enmity with God."

As it is our somewhat ungracious duty to use some language of criticism on some of Robertson's opinions, let us at once adjust some delimitation of the subject, that we may attain to some proportion of things. There were certain views held by Robertson, some in a very positive way, and some in a wavering and tentative way, that the present writer humbly conceives are not in accordance with the mind of the Church, "the blessed company of all faithful people," nor to be reconciled with the language of Scripture, which all Christians hold to be authoritative. It is to be observed, however, that these "arguable" subjects bear only a very small proportion to the vast body of positive truths put forth by Robertson. It was no business of his to stir up controversy, or to disturb faith. He had no desire to preach original doctrines, or to bring himself into any kind of notoriety by sensational or spasmodic preaching. He would not, as the heartless manner of some is, sever the slightest bond that bound any soul to the hope of eternal life. Truth, and not triumph, was always his desire. He never, unlike so many commentators and so many preachers, shirked any difficulty, nor shrank from any expression of any duty. And even when his speculations may be mistaken, we must believe that his honest, diligent search after truth must be eminently acceptable to Him who is truth—the very God of very truth. And so they have been immensely blessed; such blessings ever multiplying and expanding his sphere of usefulness. This accounts for that intense freshness, brightness, and power which, like a stream of oxygen, pervades all his writings, and has quickened and freshened a region of thought which to most minds appears dry and repellent, that queenlike science, the divine philosophy of theology,

> " Not harsh and crabbed, as some men suppose;
> But musical as is Apollo's lute."

The remarkable point about Robertson's system is that for many pages, for many sermons together, we find language that is perfectly consistent with the received theology; and then we suddenly light upon passages inconsistent with that theology, and inconsistent also with opinions that Robertson has elsewhere expressed. It is, however, such passages with which the teachings of Robertson are mainly

identified, and which it is important to examine.
Even when we read them with regret, we are impressed with much that is admirable and beautiful.
Let us first notice his broad, generous, catholic
conception of a Church. He says :—" From all this
we are constrained to the conviction that there is a
Church on earth larger than the limits of the Church
visible; larger than Jew, or Christian, or the Apostle
Peter dreamed; larger than our narrow hearts dare
to hope even now. They whose soarings to the
First Good, First Perfect, and First Fair, entranced
us in our boyhood, and whose healthier aspirations
are acknowledged yet as our instructors in the re-
verential qualities of our riper manhood—will our
hearts *allow* us to believe that they have perished ?
Nay. 'Many shall come from the east and west,
and shall sit down with Abraham, and Isaac, and
Jacob, in the kingdom of heaven.' . . . These, with
an innumerable multitude whom no man can number,
out of every kingdom, and tongue, and people, with
Rahab and the Syro-Phœnician woman, have entered
into that Church which has passed through the centuries, absorbing silently into itself all that the world
ever had of great, and good, and noble. They were
those who fought the battle of good against evil in
their day, penetrated into the invisible from the
thick shadows of darkness which environed them,
and saw the open Vision which is manifested to all,
in every nation, who fear God and work righteous-

ness. To all, in other words, who live devoutly towards God, and by love towards men. And they shall hereafter 'walk in white, for they are worthy.' . . . It may be that I err in this. It may be that this is all too daring. Little is revealed upon the subject, and we must not dogmatize. I may have erred; and it may be all a presumptuous dream. But if it be, God will forgive the daring of a heart whose hope has given birth to the idea; whose faith in this matter simply receives its substance and reality from things hoped for, and whose confidence in all this dark, mysterious world can find no rock to rest upon amidst the roaring billows of uncertainty, except 'the length, and the breadth, and the depth, and the height, of the Love which passeth knowledge,' and which has filled the universe with the fulness of His Christ."

This is a noble passage, and it still comes with freshness and power. But when we come to examine it, there is, in point of fact, no daring novelty about the thought. It can hardly be called an "idea" of his own. It is one which constantly emerges in Christian thought. There is no need of any parade of trumpets to enunciate it. The Fathers of the Church, such as Chrysostom, have dwelt strongly on the idea; and they have only been following St. Paul and St. John. In every nation, he that worketh righteousness is accepted of Him. There is a light that lighteth every man that cometh into the world.

Even to those who never heard of Christ, there was a true *Præparatio Evangelica* which prepared the way for Christ.

It is to be observed that Robertson has only scanty sympathy with the Church of England. Indeed, the associations of his family are mainly Presbyterian. He nowhere shows any special knowledge of its history, archæology, and great Catholic claims. He appears to have had very scanty knowledge of Catholic antiquity. He never seems to have given any serious attention to the writings of the ancient Fathers. He thought he knew them, but there is no evidence that he did. So large a study would have taken up a large portion of his life. Neither does he appear, beyond reading the text-books required by examinations, to have familiarized himself with the great Catholic writers of the Church of England. That intense charm and influence which belongs to an English cathedral seems to have had no effect upon his mind. Robertson nowhere rests upon authority. He has no reverence for the Vincentian canon—*quod semper, quod ubique, quod ab omnibus.* Humble, teachable souls who are willing to follow the guidance of their Church, and at least to study the great master-minds of its history, have saved themselves much of that unrest and disquietude that so often troubled the mind of Robertson.

In his later years Robertson had to take his

theological system to pieces and construct it anew. He started afresh from his own mind and from the Scriptures, disregarding the expansion and development of the Church. In one sense to him, as in the system of Comte, the age of metaphysics and the age of theology was over. He does not like theology: "Theology is very necessary, chemistry is very necessary; but chemistry destroys life to analyze, murders to dissect; and theology very often kills religion out of words before it can cut them up into propositions." He speaks, for instance, of the Sermon on the Mount as "didactic, calm, very engaging . . . which assuredly, if any one were to venture so to speak before a modern congregation, would be stigmatized as a moral essay." Those who speak thus of the Sermon on the Mount—and Charles Dickens has re-echoed Robertson's language—too often forget that, in addition to the morality, the Sermon on the Mount contains the most profound theology. The Lord's Prayer alone, contained therein, involves a whole system of divinity. Perhaps the most startling of all dogmas that could be supposed is that of Robertson, that there are to be no dogmas.

Mentally he swept away whole cycles of religious thought and experiment. He essentially possessed that modern system of impatience of dogmatic theology which has become so strongly accentuated in our time. He again and again flings the dogmatic system to the winds.

Perhaps, however, something may be said on the side of despised dogmatics. A dogma means a decreed truth which has been set forth by the voice of the Catholic Church. The great dogmas of Christianity are the statement of the great facts of Christianity. The dogma of the Incarnation is the statement of the fact of the Incarnation. The dogma of the Resurrection is the statement of the fact of the Resurrection. The dogma of the Procession of the Holy Spirit is the statement of the fact that the Holy Spirit is given to the Church. If we sweep away dogma we go far towards sweeping away the underlying facts on which the dogma reposes, and so rejecting the objective facts of the Christian faith.

In theological discussion there is one subject beyond all others which lies at the root of all teaching. That subject is the effect of the Life and Death of Christ. All religious controversy more or less revolves upon this. Our own may be an age of scepticism, but it is not an age of indifference. The words of Jesus Christ are proved true: " I, if I be lifted up from the earth, will draw all men unto Me." The attraction of the Cross exists, and even when men will not accept the Cross, they are still, by an indescribable fascination, attracted to it. For good or for evil, men will not leave the doctrine of Christ alone. The prevailing method of dealing with the doctrine of Christ in these days is to examine and bring to the test the words and

deeds of Christ.   Since Robertson's day this method
has been pursued with extraordinary minuteness
and enthusiasm.   Some of the best known of our
English theological classics have been devoted to
this object, as in " Ecce Homo," Horace Bushnell
on the " Supernatural," Canon Liddon's " Bampton
Lectures," and other works.

Of course this method has no absolute originality,
but has more or less existed through all ages.
But there has been in our own time a singular
efflorescence of literary discussion on the matter.
Robertson fully recognized that the key to all the
religious discussion in the world lay in the doctrine
of Christ.   As a true theologian, albeit he disliked
the name, he bent his whole energies to the question.   On one occasion he speaks of " the one great
certainty to which, in the midst of the darkest
doubt, I never ceased to cling—the entire symmetry
and loveliness, and the unequalled nobleness of the
humanity of the Son of Man.   Ask me any questions
you will on this, for if there has been anything I have
pondered over and believed in, it is the heart and
mind of Christ."   The most profound impressions
relating to the Humanity of Christ are unhappily
not inconsistent with an elimination of that supernatural element, without which spirituality hardly
rises above the spirituality of Plato.   When the
Divinity is not recognized as well as the Humanity,
we have a Christianity without Christ.

What is the true doctrine of the Person of Christ? Was Christ truly sinless? Was He in any real sense a vicarious victim, a substitute for our sins? What was the effect of the Death of Christ in its relationship to ourselves and to God? Robertson must have known that he, himself, was a born and ordained teacher of men. The one final cause of his human existence was to speak and to bear witness to truth. Now Robertson's treatment of this most important subject is wavering and uncertain. Sometimes his language is as simple and direct as could be framed by any Evangelical teacher. At other times his theory is difficult to be made intelligible to the ordinary understanding. One of his favourite sayings was that the Atonement was an at-tune-ment, a harmonizing of the divine and human. We humbly think that at other times his language respecting the Atonement can hardly be reconciled with the voice of the Universal Church. Robertson says, " The evangelical scheme of reconciling justice with mercy I consider the poorest effort ever made by false metaphysics." He speaks of that scheme as " two gods—a loving god and an angry god—the former saving from the latter." He thinks that the phrase " none but Christ " as used by the Evangelicals is " the sickliest cant that has appeared since the Pharisees." " In proportion as I adore Christ—exactly in that proportion do I abhor Evangelicalism. I feel more at brotherhood with a deranged, mistaken, maddened, sinful chartist than I do with that religious world which has broken Popery into a hundred thousand fragments and made every fragment an entire, new, infallible Pope, dealing out quietly and cold-bloodedly the flames of the next world upon all heretics who dispute their dictum." In the same exaggerated way, he says: "I hold that the attempt to rest Christianity upon miracles and fulfilment of prophecy is essentially the vilest rationalism."

Let us see now what was his view respecting the work of Christ. With his characteristic dislike of dogmatism he says that he determined "to try to fix attention on Christ rather than on the doctrine of Christ." But it is hard to see how Christ and the doctrine of Christ are really separable. Robertson belongs to what De Pressensé calls the Theological Left. In many passages of his writings he seems to have an inadequate sense of the sinfulness of sin, and of the need of an atonement to present us faultless before an infinitely just and holy God. We may not understand the exact mode in which the Sacrifice of Christ propitiates the Divine Mind, and it is rather our wisdom to exclaim with the Apostle: " Oh, the depths. How unsearchable are His judgments, and His ways past finding out." But we may have that broken, contrite heart that owns the presence of sin, and rests its all on the Sin Bearer—the feeling set forth in the old Latin lines,—

> " Quærens me sedisti lassus,
>   Redemisti crucem passus,
>   Tantus labor non sit cassus."

He does not sufficiently realize the infirmity and weakness of man. There is hardly any place for redemption in the view which he sometimes places before us of humanity. His idea of atonement is that Christ saves simply by realizing in His own Person the ideal of humanity—and by the holy constraining influence of His love upon the heart. This presence of evil in the world must have been a sore questioning to Robertson, as it is to so many of us. It is hardly a question bound up with Christianity, for before the existence of Christianity it was one that troubled the mind not only of psalmist and prophet, but of heathen philosopher and poet. It cannot be said that Christianity has solved the enigma, but it gives many considerations which are steps towards the solution. Above all there is one thought, on which Robertson, at least at this time, did not dwell. That is, that the mystery of suffering finds its culmination and its meaning in the Cross of Christ. The old Epicurean idea was that if there were deities they took no real interest in human life, and from their high empyrean enjoyments looked down complacently on the toils, sufferings, and sins of human life. But Christianity, while it brings into sternest relief the facts of sin and death, finds the culmination of suffering in the Cross which takes away the penalty of sin and is the abolition of death. Robertson rightly repudiated the fearful idea of the direct curse of the Father alighting upon the Son, but passes over in silence the mysterious desertion, the anguish of soul which the Master endured, and in which He realized His perfect sympathy with us, all the bitterness of our sin, and recognized God's righteous anger against it. "Robertson," says De Pressensé, "represents the work of Christ as the initiation of a course of reparative effort rather than as the one unique work which it is ours simply to assimilate by a living faith. That such was really his view appears from another sermon on the same subject, in which the principal virtue of the Cross is made to be, that it sets before us an ideal of perfection and fills us with an ardent desire to be conformed to it." He rests upon the original relations between man and God, and greatly overlooks the necessity for the reparative work of redeeming love. His is the religion of a realized ideal, rather than that of redemption and restoration. He does not sufficiently rest on the simple primal doctrines which have been the staff and stay of successive ages of the Church. He complains that only now in the nineteenth century are people beginning to understand Christ, ignoring the multitude which no man can number who have departed this life in His faith and fear.

Some other words of Robertson respecting our Lord must similarly be received with great caution and reservation. He said that if Christ had cast Himself down from the pinnacle of the temple, He would have been destroyed. Some might argue from this on the peccability, or with the Jews, that though He saved others, Himself he could not save. Dismissing these considerations as at least curious, Robertson held that the sufferings of Christ were simply due to natural law, ignoring thereby their voluntary character. " Christ came into collision with the world's evil, and He bore the enmity of that daring. He approached the whirling wheel and was torn in pieces. The sacrifice of Christ comes to be looked upon in the light of a sagacious or ingenious contrivance—a mere scheme. Now remember what law is. Law is the being of God. God cannot alter the laws. If you resist a law in its eternal march the universe crushes you." Now here we demur to the statement that God cannot alter laws. The universe is not ultimately ruled by iron, inflexible laws. Behind the laws there is the Lawgiver. Even man can supersede laws by acts of his own volition, as when he raises the arm which naturally falls, or as when, often in science, he introduces higher law to control or modify the lower law. The life which Christ held was His own ; He had power to take it up, and He had power to lay it down. What Robertson in this passage has left undwelt on is the love of the Great Father in sending His Son, and the love of the Son in coming into the world to die for it. His notion is that Christ having been born into this world, must necessarily take all human consequences which would eventuate in suffering and death. Here we have the fact ignored that the sufferings and death of Christ were according to the determinate counsel and foreknowledge of God, that He was the Lamb slain from the foundation of the world. Here is a shock given to the faithful belief that has pervaded all the creeds, all the churches, all the centuries, until in the nineteenth century new teachers should arise to give a new reading of the import of these awful facts.

His views respecting sin also seem vague and inaccurate, both as regards its nature and its consequences, and then the inadequate idea of regeneration. Just as some persons suppose that as virtue is its own reward, it therefore has no other reward, so Robertson seems to argue that because wickedness is its own punishment, therefore it has no other punishment. Could human society subsist for a week if legislature supposed that thieves and murderers were sufficiently punished by their own remorse, and that there was no need for a system of penalties? He says, "It is the hell of having done wrong, the hell of having had a spirit from God, pure, with high aspiration, and to be conscious of having dulled its delicacy and degraded its desires, the hell of having quenched a light brighter than the sun's, of having done to another an injury

that through time and eternity never can be undone
—infinite, maddening remorse—the hell of knowing
that every chance of excellence and every opportunity of good has been lost for ever." According
to this there is no other penalty than that of self-
consciousness. Then the feeling in the human soul
that behind the laws of God lies all His immeasur-
able power to punish transgression becomes a superstition. There is no need of a deliverer to take
away the penalty of sin, no positive punishment, and
no need of an atonement. But here again Robertson is inconsistent with himself, for in one place,
without any expression of an everlasting hope, he
speaks of the wicked as being fixed in a hopeless
eternity of self-remorse. His difficulty, he says,
was how not to believe the doctrine of eternal
punishment. His views respecting the divine doctrine of the forgiveness of sins, as we sometimes
find them stated, are confused and contradictory.
As we read them we find ourselves asking, " Who
can forgive sins but God?" " God has given to man
the power to absolve his brother, and so restore him
to himself. The forgiveness of man is an echo and
an earnest of God's forgiveness. He whom society
has restored realizes the possibility of restoration to
God's favour." But this is just what human
society cannot do. It cannot forgive or restore. It
cannot make the past as if it had never been. There
was once a criticism passed on a certain system of

judicature that it allowed no place for repentance
and forgiveness. But was there ever human system
that did? Men do not sufficiently grasp the immense
originality of the doctrine of the forgiveness of sin.
Human law has no place for forgiveness. It cannot
gauge the sincerity of repentance or the possibilities
of restoration. Natural law knows nothing of forgiveness. Nature, with all her tenderness and
beauty, is relentless in the operation of her inflexible
laws. So long as we follow in her wake, obey her
hints, imitate her processes, observe her laws, it is
well; but let us violate these, and nature owns no re-
lenting mood; she crushes us with the consequences
of our transgressions. Again, though there may
be sin against the individual, sin against society,
yet the sin in the profoundest aspect is the sin
against God. This is what every Christian heart
feels : "Against Thee, Thee only have I sinned."
It is said that Constantine turned to the religion of
the Nazarene because the heathen flamens told him
that they had no means of absolving him from such
offences as had been his. But God has devised
means whereby He may restore His banished ones.
He is both a Just God and a Saviour. He is just,
and the justifier of him that believes in Jesus. At
the foot of the Cross the burden of sin is taken
away. The handwriting against us is nailed to those
Arms which are stretched out in loving pity to a
weary world :—

" It is the Voice of Jesus that I hear,
His are the hands stretch'd out to draw me near,
And His the Blood that can for all atone,
And place me faultless there before His throne."

Akin to this is his limited teaching on the work of the Holy Spirit of God. He does not present the simple basal truth, which requires to be incessantly represented in its simplest form to simple men, the supernatural, regenerating influence of that divine Spirit, and its effect in giving liberty to the soul. He does not sufficiently recognize the direct, special, mystical operation of the Spirit of God in shedding illumination on the heart. We lay down his sermons which are concerned with this subject not without a feeling of emptiness and disappointment. He does not touch on that one absolute promise of Christ that the Holy Spirit shall be given, that it is the Spirit that teaches us of the things of Christ, that the mind may comprehend those things which are only spiritually discerned. In an earnest, educated congregation such as his no doubt much might be taken for granted, and much might be implied even by a single phrase; but for a preacher not to dwell incessantly on these primal truths is to surrender the simple bread and water, and the light and air, and only to use the artificial combinations that may be formed of them.

So take his treatment of prophecy. Robertson dwells strongly on the fact that the main element in

prophecy is efficient teaching. Prediction is almost
a secondary element. In his time it might be
supposed that because he strongly dwelt on the
preaching, that therefrom he denied the predicting.
This certainly was not the case, if he uses language
in the ordinary way. Lecturing on Jacob's predic-
tions about his descendants, he says: "We are
plainly out of the region of things cognizable by
sagacity, and have got into the sphere of the prophetic faculty." Now what does he mean by this
"prophetic faculty"? "The prophetic power, in
which I suppose is chiefly exhibited that which we
mean by inspiration, depends almost entirely on
moral questions. The prophet discerned large principles, true for all time—principles, social, political,
ecclesiastical, and principles of life—chiefly by largeness of heart and sympathy of spirit with God's
spirit. This is my conception of inspiration."
Now the question arises here, whether the prophetic
faculty was included in the moral greatness, or was
plus the moral greatness. Did he recognize the
preternatural element? If he merely meant moral
greatness, we do not see why inspiration should not
be equally claimed for many great works in literature and art, or why it is to be separated from "the
region of things cognizable by sagacity." He goes
on to say: "That as God communicated facts in
the natural world to the penmen as they are accepted
in the popular mind, not correctly in science, so

His revelation concerning truths of the soul, and its relation to God was communicated in popular and incorrect, not however false, language." It is a very dangerous doctrine that God communicated spiritual and moral truths in popular and inaccurate language. We can understand why God communicated natural facts in a popular and, possibly, in an inaccurate way, though the inaccuracy has yet to be demonstrated. One reason is that it was not the Divine object to instruct men in scientific truth. Another reason was that if the scientific truth were stated in the most absolute complete form, it would probably be beyond the intelligence of any to comprehend it, in the present state of human knowledge, when the aspects of truth are constantly shifting, and the true science has yet to be built up. On the other hand, it was God's design to teach the truths of the soul and its relation to Himself. If we suppose that God did this only in a popular and inaccurate manner, what is to be the standard of accuracy, and how are we to discriminate between what is accurate and what is incorrect? From some other portion of his writings, Robertson would seem to infer that such matters must be settled by the innate moral sense; a moral sense which, as Locke shows in his " Essay," is something that varies in different countries and centuries. We hold that the true doctrine is that the moral sense is to be corrected by inspiration, and not inspiration by the moral sense. Indeed, in the passages above cited, and in others, Robertson is hardly consistent with himself, and had hardly formulated his exact views.

Inspiration was the subject on which he meditated a separate work. He considered it the deepest question of the day, and one underlying all others; yet, when we turn to his sermon on this subject, at the conclusion of the fourth series, we find no repetition of the vague and erroneous views we have mentioned. Indeed, with a happy inconsistency, we find the noblest tribute to the Bible and the amplest recognition that the whole of the Scripture is pervaded by the Spirit of Christ. "Germany and England speak as they speak because the Bible was translated. It has made the most illiterate peasant more familiar with the history, customs, and geography of ancient Palestine than with the localities of his own country. Men who know nothing of the Grampians, of Snowdon, or of Skiddaw, are at home in Zion, the Lake of Gennesareth, or among the hills of Carmel. People who know little about London know by heart the places in Jerusalem where those blessed feet trod which were nailed to the Cross. Those who know nothing of the architecture of a Christian cathedral can yet tell you all about the pattern of the holy Temple. . . . Scripture is full of Christ. From Genesis to Revelations everything breathes of Him, not every letter of every sentence, but the spirit of every chapter. . . .

Every unfulfilled aspiration of humanity in the past; all partial representation of perfect character; all sacrifices, nay, even those of idolatry, point to the fulfilment of what we want, the answer to every longing—the type of perfect humanity, the Lord Jesus Christ."

Coming now to the practical side of the religious system, let us take a few sentences on the subject of devotion which have a kind of autobiographical interest. "By devotional habits we do not mean that a man must have the habit of attending daily prayers or the like; devotional habits depend upon all the varieties of sex, age, and temperament. To one man the devotional habit of every day is to consider a chapter in the Bible; to another man, according to the necessities of his temperament, it may be the attendance on public daily prayer; to another it may be wandering by the sea-shore, calming there his agitated spirit, and throwing open his mind to all the influences which God has shed so abundantly on the world. Sometimes it is a habit like that of Isaac, the wandering alone and meditating in the field at eventide; sometimes it is the voiceless lifting of the solitary soul to God in the chamber, in the crowd, and in society; but unless that habit, whatever it be, is kept up in some way or other, the life will inevitably decay." Here the autobiographical element is very discernible. He is himself the man who will calm his spirit by musing by the sea-side, or will go forth, like Isaac, to meditate in the fields at eventide, and who will lift up his soul to God alike in the chamber and in the crowd. But surely he is not right in placing these devotions in alternation, in supposing that one or the other may be used according to varieties of natural character. Every Christian man will daily read God's holy Word, and daily pass some time in sacred meditation. Robertson could hardly have meant what his words represent him as meaning. We have elsewhere some remarkable language respecting devotional feeling. He had been speaking in one of his letters of devotional reading. "A strong shock," he says, "threw me off the habit—partly the external circumstances of my life, partly the perception of a most important fact, that devotional feelings are very distinct from uprightness and purity of life— that they are often singularly allied to the animal nature," a theory which the writer remembers to have had propounded to him by one of a singularly gifted and pious nature, the late Dora Greenwell, whose "Carmina Crucis" are strains of a singularly elevating and helpful kind. The weak point in Robertson's system of devotion seems to be this, that he hardly seems to be realizing the idea of prayer in its simplest and deepest aspect, of making request unto God, with a definite aim, and the faith that the prayer will be considered and answered.

His idea of devotion is that of a reflex influence. Doubtless there is such a blessed influence, but prayer would cease to be offered, the very idea of prayer would be unintelligible to the masses of the weary and heavy-laden, but for the conviction that in their strong necessity their cry reaches to the throne of the heavenly loving Father. He endorses Tennyson's fine lines—

> " An infant crying in the night,
> An infant crying for the light,
> And with no language but a cry."

And he adds, " I am not afraid of the dark." No doubt there are phases in human life, and times in human history, when men groped in the darkness, if haply they might touch God in the darkness, but for those to whom the Supernatural revelation has authoritatively spoken the darkness is passed, and the true light now shineth. They no longer walk in darkness, but see the light of life.

It seems to us that there was yet another point in which, in his later sermons, he was deficient. Robertson, in his immense power of will, in the strength and fortitude of his character, had perhaps something like contempt for weak natures. This is not only our own impression, but we find it is also the feeling of M. de Pressensé. There seems to us to have been, in his earlier sermons, a strain of sympathy and earnestness for the weak, the failing in moral purpose, the backslider, which is by no

means so apparent in the later sermons. There
is hardly the same dwelling on the seeking, searching,
saving love of Christ. Much ministerial teaching
must ever consist of invitations to those who know
nothing of the power of the Supernatural in their
own hearts, and for whom the language of invitation
and warning must continually be renewed. Those
broad, visible lines of direct teaching, which we
find in the Oxford and Cheltenham sermons, are not
in the same sense and to the same extent discover-
able at Brighton. We find the Rev. A. J. Ross
writing : " He himself walked in such a sunlight of
integrity that any deviation in others from the
paths of righteousness inflicted on him actual pain ;
and not only so—he had such a vivid sense of the
destruction and deadly power of sin, as seemed
quite to have quenched in him the hope that in
certain cases the restorative influences revealed in
Christianity would ever be able to effect any healing."
Now, it is just at this point that we feel the blessed-
ness of the Gospel of Christ Jesus. Robertson
himself had a nature of exquisite moral purity,
of inflexible moral strength. In a touching passage
he says : " I worshipped her only as I should have
done a living rainbow, with no farther feeling. Yet
I was then eighteen, and she was to me for years
nothing more than a calm, clear, untroubled flood
of beauty, glossing heaven, deep deep below, so
deep that I never dreamed of an attempt to reach

the heaven. So I lived. I may truly say that my heart was like the Rhone as it leaves the Lake of Geneva." He reminds us of the knights of the Arthurean legend, who sought, not in vain, the Vision of the Holy Grail, and of the Spiritual City. He could say with Sir Galahad,—

> "My strength is as the strength of ten,
>   Because my heart is pure."

But such is not the blessed experience of the majority of the human race, not even of those whose lives are illumined by the Christian hope. They pass sadly through their "sour-sweet days," with infinite loss and sorrow, with tears and sighs, with feet weary on the shifting sands; with losses and failures and blunders, with the burden of sorrow and sin and care, they struggle onwards to the Infinite, if only they make some advance and win some sure footing, if only they may learn, here a little and there a little; only sustained and comforted by the hope that they are being shaped and disciplined for a higher life and interposing between their frailty and their Judge, the Passion of the Redeemer. It is not theirs with thankfulness to dwell on their purity of heart and the rare heights won by their devotedness. Rather like the unhappy poet, Hartley Coleridge, whose sin-stained soul was not unilluminated by the radiance of heavenly pity and mercy, they meditate on the story of the Magdalen :—

" She sat and wept, and with her untress'd hair
	She wiped the feet she was so blest to touch,
And He wiped off the soiling of despair
	From her sweet soul because she loved so much.
I am a sinner, full of doubts and fears,
Make me a humble thing of love and tears."

With Robertson's pulpit teaching we may compare some of his conversation : " He is a most liberal man—so liberal that I must apply to him the words he has used of Dr. Channing, of whose writings he is a great admirer : 'I wonder how he can believe so much and yet not believe more,' only substituting 'disbelieve' or 'doubt' for 'believe.' I repeated to him yesterday words which I had uttered to Dr. Arnold. 'I am as convinced as a man can be on any matter of speculation, that the orthodox doctrines, *as vulgarly understood*, are false; but I have never ventured to deny that possibly there is an important truth at the bottom of every one of those doctrines of which they are a misrepresentation.' He interposed between the first and second part of this assertion, 'And so am I;' and he said nothing when I concluded. He might have said, and I am perplexed he did not, 'I go farther than saying it is possible; I have no doubt that they are all substantially true.'" It must, however, be remembered that Crabbe Robinson was a Unitarian, and may have been unconsciously biassed into exaggerating the supposed inorthodoxy of his friend. Under

February 15th, 1851, he reports Robertson as saying : " I feel myself more comfortable in the Church of England than I did. I feel I have a *mission,* and then, if I live a few years, it will not be in vain. That mission is to impress on minds of a certain class of intellect that there is a mass of substantial truth in the Church of England which will remain when the vulgar orthodox Church perishes, as probably it soon will." Robinson goes on to say, "*he understands almost every orthodox doctrine in a refined sense, and such as would shock the ears of ordinary Christians.*" Crabbe's next entry is "that Robertson's language was excellent, but too liable to be mistaken." In 1851, he says he heard Robertson preach an extraordinary sermon. " He uttered a number of valuable philosophical truths which I cannot reconcile with Church doctrines, though I have no doubt he does so with perfect good faith. He acknowledges that he is surprised at being so long permitted to preach; he is aware how much he must be the object of mistrust."

"*December 9th.*—My astonishment at this man increases every time I see him. As he interprets the words, ' without blood there is no remission of sins,' they become inoffensive, for it means no more than this—Christ died to exhibit the perfectest Christian truth, that the essence of Christianity is self-sacrifice. It is the Divine principle : God and man are united wherever this principle reigns. I have told him that on Trinity Sunday, if possible, I will go to Brighton, to hear him expound, in his way, the 'Trinity.'"   Again, he says : " I heard a sermon from Robertson marked by his usual peculiarities. . . . Samuel Sharpe told me that people here complain that he unsettles men's minds.   Of course he can be awakened out of a deep sleep without being unsettled."

If the foregoing language be that of an attached friend, a Socinian and an ardent Liberal, one can hardly wonder at the language of distrust and hostile criticism, which went far to embitter Robertson's mind, that was used by the lovers of the old orthodoxy, who had a distinctive dislike of theological novelties. Yet Robertson, though he had only himself to thank for such strictures, had a strong idea that great injustice was done him.   One can hardly avoid seeing a personal reference in such words as these: " Should any of you have to bear attacks on your character or life or doctrine, defend yourself with meekness ; and if defence should make matters worse—and when accusations are vague as is the case but too often—why, then commit yourself to the truth.   Out-pray—*out-preach*—out-live the calumny."[1]   It is rather remarkable that Robertson should have resented language which his own expressions obviously invited.   It is only

[1] Exposition of " St. Paul's Letters to the Corinthians," p. 490.

when we look at Robertson's teaching as a whole—
as embodied in the eight volumes—that we understand how he was refusing to be judged by isolated
passages, but was having regard to his own inner
true self. The intellectual phenomena presented by
his sermons and letters are extraordinary. If ever
he had any idea of publication no doubt he would
have elaborated his own system, and have presented
it in homogeneous form. We have no *novissima
verba*, no ripe results of perfected thought. Each
changeful opinion, each passing emotion, the work
and thought of each fresh week are presented as
they came to himself. Of such treatises the world
has perhaps enough and to spare, but to be admitted into the laboratory of that active brain, to
be permitted to view each thought, each tentative
effort, each passing doubt and difficulty, is a phenomenon almost unparalleled in literary and spiritual
history. We believe it was Mr. H. C. Robinson
who brought together the following apothegms of
Robertson on the subject of

FAITH AND DOUBT.

1.

Some men have never believed enough to doubt.

2.

A sigh shall be given to the doubt of love, which
is refused to the doubt of indifference.

3.

The belief *diabolical* ends in trembling; the belief Christian ends in doing.

4.

We may question the decisions of the intellect; but it is at our peril that we tamper with the verdict of the heart.

5.

To the priestly mind candour seems the first step to unbelief.

6.

You choose a guide amongst precipices and glaciers; but you *walk* by yourself elsewhere.

Two of his aphorisms on Christianity are added :—

1.

It is the part of Christianity to bring out the worth of that which is apparently mean, and the dignity of that which is apparently low.

2.

Paganism held in adoration the characteristics of *man*—courage, strength, &c.; Christianity added thereto the virtues which distinguish and adorn the character of woman.

Mr. Robinson would have been sorely troubled in endeavouring to reduce his friend's views into any orderly form and system. He says that "Robertson was known to declare to his friends that he felt no reluctance to the recital of the

Athanasian Creed, and should not have objected to its being rendered a part of the compulsory weekly service. . . . Mr. Robertson never failed, and we have no doubt, with perfect truthfulness, to assert the doctrines, as he understood them, of the Holy Trinity, Original Sin, the Atonement, the Sacraments, &c." The only way in which these contrasted and antagonistic views could be understood by many of his friends was that these doctrines were held by him in a refined and non-natural sense That is not our view. We believe that, though his mind was often clouded by difficulties and doubt, yet through all he grasped the central truths of revelation, and at the last they were dearer and closer than ever to his heart. Even the most hostile critics declare that though " the tree cast its leaves its substance was in it." He was on the foundation, however the superstructure may have shown hay and stubble mingled with the gold and gems. The marvellous views which we have of his inner life enable him, though dead, to exercise a peculiar and unique ministry, not without tones of warning, but at the same time eminently fruitful and stimulating.

We have dwelt on those points which we consider errors in his popular teaching, in a way that may seem disproportionate to some, but of which the consideration is of the highest importance, and must not be left untouched. The misconceptions, as we consider them, occupy only a small portion of his teaching. It requires indeed some search and analysis, before the latent meaning of his errors is brought out, a meaning which was not always patent to his own mind. But these errors have been laid hold off, and brought out as the essential constructive teaching, as that which was mainly characteristic of the man and the body of his thought. This, however, is not a fair representation. The diligent student of Robertson, if he is sometimes pained and distressed with language which has a disturbing influence upon his mind, which he finds hard to reconcile with revealed truth, and which has been eagerly caught at by those who are hostile to divine truth, will, nevertheless, fall back upon the vast body of positive truth which has been set forth by this great teacher.

On the blazoned window in his honour in the chapel of Brasenose there is the inscription :—" Te Deum laudat Prophetarum laudabilis numerus." The great function of the prophet was not so much in prediction as preaching. This sets forth the righteousness and eternal judgments of God. He applied to the events of his time the immutable Divine principles. In this true prophet spirit Robertson was a teacher and preacher. Milton says :—

> " Till old experience doth attain
> To something of prophetic strain."

And at times Robertson's prophetic glance seems

to stretch forward to futurity, to decipher the signs
of the times, to discern the march of events.
Every true lover of our Lord will desire, while
setting truth above aught besides, in the spirit of
the widest charity and sympathy, to minimize his
differences with this Prince of preachers. Indeed
these difficulties are often neutralized by his own
other language, and probably disappeared in his own
spiritual experience. In these days when the very
bases of religion are threatened and assailed, when
the thought of design is denied, when a natural
religion which knows nothing of a resurrection or
of immortality is offered to us, when there is a bitter
hostility to those who call themselves Christians, it
is time that we should close up our serri d ranks, and
welcome those who are not against us as being with
us. Above all, in Robertson the Christ-like spirit
is ever apparent. No way in which he contem-
plates the atoning work of Christ can obscure the
fact that his whole soul rested upon Christ, His
Sacrifice, and His work. And if ever there lived a
man whose whole life seemed pervaded with the
Spirit of Christ, that man was Robertson. His was
always the fearless, outspoken voice of truth, regardless of all human considerations in comparison
with truth; his the burning indignation against
hypocrisy and cruelty, and injustice, and his the
deep sympathy with all forms of anxiety and heart-
searching, with the unfortunates and outcasts of the

world.   All that we know of his life, so different
from the many disappointments of biography, is in
beautiful consistency with his ministerial life ; his
unsparingness of himself, his loyalty and love, his
self-sacrifice, his stern resolve to do his duty and
his best; the lofty courage and purity of his nature.
He prepared himself and his flock diligently for that
blessed country where there shall be no more moral
failure or intellectual difficulty; where the hunger
and thirst after righteousness will be satisfied :—

Εὕδεις ἀλλ' οὐ σεῖο λελασμένοι ἐσμεν.

THE END.

GILBERT AND RIVINGTON, LIMITED, ST. JOHN'S SQUARE, LONDON.

WARD & DOWNEY'S

NEW PUBLICATIONS.

NEW WORKS JUST READY.

ROBERTSON OF BRIGHTON.

By the Rev. F. ARNOLD, Author of "Turning Points in Life," &c. 1 vol., post 8vo, 9*s*.

THE LETTERS OF GEORGE SAND.

With a Memoir by LEDOS DE BEAUFORT. 3 vols., demy 8vo, with 6 portraits.

GLADSTONE'S HOUSE OF COMMONS.

By T. P. O'CONNOR, M.P., Author of "The Life of Lord Beaconsfield," &c. 1 vol., demy 8vo.

IN AN IRON-BOUND CITY; or, Eight Months of Peril and Privation.

By JOHN AUGUSTUS O'SHEA, Author of "Leaves from the Life of a Special Correspondent." 2 vols.

A LIFE'S MISTAKE.

A New Novel. By Mrs. LOVETT CAMERON. 2 vols., 21*s*.

New Novels.   Price 31*s*. 6*d*. each.

Dulcie Carlyon.   By JAMES GRANT.   3 vols.

At the Red Glove.   By KATHARINE S. MAC-QUOID, Author of " Patty," &c.   3 vols.

Mind, Body, and Estate.   By F. E. M. NOTLEY, Author of " Olive Varcoe," &c.   3 vols.

Lord Vanecourt's Daughter.   By MABEL COLLINS, Author of " The Prettiest Woman in Warsaw," &c.   3 vols.

Where Tempests Blow.   By M. W. PAXTON, Author of " Miss Elvester's Girls," &c.   3 vols.

The Sacred Nugget.   By B. L. FARJEON, Author of " Great Porter Square."   Second Edition.   3 vols.

A Prince of Darkness.   By FLORENCE WARDEN, Author of " The House on the Marsh," &c.   Second Edition.   3 vols.

In Sight of Land.   By Lady DUFFUS HARDY, Author of " Beryl Fortescue," &c.   3 vols.

Price 30*s*.

The Unpopular King: The Life and Times of Richard the Third. By ALFRED O. LEGGE, F.C.H.S. 2 vols., with an etched portrait of Richard the Third, and fifteen other illustrations.

Price 25*s*.

Royalty Restored; or, London under Charles the Second. By J. FITZGERALD MOLLOY. 2 vols., with an etched portrait of Charles the Second by JOSEPH GREGO, and eleven other portraits.

Price 21*s*. each.

From the Silent Past. A New Novel. By Mrs. HERBERT MARTIN. 2 vols.

Leaves from the Life of a Special Correspon-dent. By JOHN AUGUSTUS O'SHEA. 2 vols., with a portrait.

Price 12*s*. 6*d*.

Songs from the Novelists; from Elizabeth to Victoria. Edited, and with introduction and notes, by W. DAVENPORT ADAMS. Printed in brown ink on Dutch hand-made paper. Bound in illuminated parchment, rough edges, gilt top.

" A splendid book."—*Life*.

Price 12*s*. each.

John Ford: His Faults and His Follies. By FRANK BARRETT, Author of " Folly Morrison," &c. 2 vols.

Court Life Below Stairs; or, London under the Four Georges. By J. FITZGERALD MOLLOY. 2 vols.

Price 7*s.* 6*d.* each.

Folk and Fairy Tales. By Mrs. BURTON HARRISON, Author of "Old-Fashioned Fairy Tales." With 24 original illustrations by WALTER CRANE. In cover specially designed by WALTER CRANE, gilt edges.

Japanese Life, Love, and Legend: A Visit to the Empire of the Rising Sun. From the French of Maurice Dubard. By WILLIAM CONN. In specially designed cover.

Comedies from a Country Side. "The Squire;" "The Parvenu;" "The Heiress;" and "The Parson." By W. OUTRAM TRISTRAM, Author of "Julian Trevor."

An Apology for the Life of the Right Hon. W. E. GLADSTONE.

Price 6*s.* each.

Russia under the Tzars. By STEPNIAK, Author of "Underground Russia." Translated by WILLIAM WESTALL. Third Edition.

Victor Hugo: His Life and Work. By GEORGE BARNETT SMITH, Author of "Poets and Novelists," &c.

Court Life Below Stairs; or, London under the First Georges. By J. FITZGERALD MOLLOY, Author of "Royalty Restored," &c.

Court Life Below Stairs; or, London under the Last Georges. By the same Author.

Popular Novels.   Price 6s. each.

David Broome ; or, Out of the World. By Mrs. ROBERT O'REILLY. With illustrations by F. BARNARD.

***That Villain, Romeo !** By J. FITZGERALD MOLLOY, Author of " What hast Thou Done ? " &c.

As in a Looking Glass. By F. C. PHILIPS. With a frontispiece by GORDON BROWNE.

***Coward and Coquette.** By the Author of " The Parish of Hilby," &c.

***Less than Kin.** By J. E. PANTON, Author of " Country Sketches in Black and White," &c.

Viva. By Mrs. FORRESTER, Author of " My Lord and My Lady," &c.

The Prettiest Woman in Warsaw. By MABEL COLLINS, Author of " Lord Vanecourt's Daughter," &c.

Lil Lorimer. By THEO GIFT.

***The Flower of Doom.** By Miss BETHAM-EDWARDS.

Pretty Miss Neville. By B. M. CROKER, Author of " Proper Pride."

Proper Pride. By B. M. CROKER, Author of " Pretty Miss Neville," &c.

Great Porter Square: A Mystery. By B. L. FARJEON.

The House of White Shadows. By B. L. FARJEON.

Those marked * have not been published previously in book form.

Price 4*s.* 6*d.*

A STORY FOR BOYS.

The New River: A Romance of the Days of
Hugh Myddelton. By the Author of " The Hovel-
lers of Deal." In specially designed cover, coloured
edges.

Price 3*s.* 6*d.* each.

Philosophy in the Kitchen : General Hints on
Foods and Drinks. By an old BOHEMIAN.

A Maiden all Forlorn. By the Author of
" Phyllis."

Grif: a Story of Australian Life. By B. L.
FARJEON.

Folly Morrison. By FRANK BARRETT, Author
of " Honest Davie," &c.

Price 2*s.* 6*d.*, in handsomely illustrated cover.

Christmas Angel. A New Christmas Story.
By B. L. FARJEON. With 23 illustrations by GORDON
BROWNE.

Price 2*s.* each, picture boards ; or 2*s.* 6*d.* cloth.

The Outlaw of Iceland. By VICTOR HUGO.
Translated by Sir GILBERT CAMPBELL, Bart.

Honest Davie. By FRANK BARRETT, Author
of " Folly Morrison," &c.

Under St. Paul's. By RICHARD DOWLING.

The Duke's Sweetheart. By the same Author.

Price 1*s.* each.

Eve at the Wheel: A Story of Three Hundred
Virgins. By GEORGE MANVILLE FENN.

The Dark House. By the same Author. 15th
Thousand.

A Deadly Errand. By MAX HILLARY, Author
of " Once for All," &c.

*** This story was published originally under the title of
" Hunted Down ;" but it was found that this title had already
been in use.

A Catechism of Politics for the Use of the
New Electorate. By FREDERICK HOFFMAN, Author
of " Stray Leaves from Gladstone's Diary," &c.

THE POPULAR NOVEL.

AS IN A LOOKING-GLASS.

BY

F. C. PHILIPS.

WITH A FRONTISPIECE BY GORDON BROWNE.

" Clever beyond any common standard of cleverness."
Daily Telegraph.

" Remarkably clever, full of sustained interest."—*World.*

" Marks a distinct epoch in novel-making."
St. Stephen's Review.

" There are ingenuity and originality in the conception of the book, and power in its working out."—*Scotsman.*

" A powerful tragedy, a portfolio of character sketches, and a diorama of society scenes. Its characters are all real and living personages."—*Globe.*

" This original and realistic novel is distinctly clever. As a graphic rendering of some of the most objectionable yet amusing phases of *la vie mondaine*, this book will probably excite considerable attention."—*Morning Post.*

" It will be praised here, censured there, and read everywhere; for it is unconventional and original, and in every sense a most attractive and remarkable novel."—*Life.*

Now ready at all Booksellers'.—Cloth extra, price 6s.

VICTOR HUGO: His Life & Work.

By G. BARNETT SMITH,

*Author of " Poets and Novelists," " Shelley : a Critical Biography,"
&c.*

WITH AN ENGRAVED PORTRAIT OF VICTOR HUGO.

"Excellent. . . . Mr. Smith tells the story of a brilliant but chequered career in his easy manner and with sympathetic discrimination."—*Times*.

"The only book which relates the full story of Hugo's life. . . . He has produced a book that was very much wanted, and the volume is one which no English student of Victor Hugo can afford to overlook. It is dedicated in graceful terms to Mr. Swinburne."—*North British Mail*.

"Vast as is the theme opened up by the consideration of Hugo and his works, Mr. Barnett Smith has so studiously compressed facts that the English public will find in this volume a swift and incisive review that is at once entertaining, instructive, and popular."—*Lloyd's*.

"The book is unique. Notwithstanding the multitude of criticisms which have appeared in our own and other languages upon Hugo's work, this is the only volume which relates the full story of his life. . . . We have pleasure in recommending Mr. Barnett Smith's volume as the fullest and in every way the most satisfactory on its subject that has yet appeared in England."—*The Christian Leader*.

"It is clear and succinct, and contains nearly everything it is requisite for the average English reader to know about the illustrious Frenchman. As a record of his literary and dramatic work it is remarkable for well-ordered completeness, while the account of Hugo in exile is free from the common errors which have disfigured the narratives of the majority of those who have dealt with the subject."
Topical Times.

Just ready, a New and Revised Edition of

PHILOSOPHY IN THE KITCHEN:

GENERAL HINTS ON FOODS AND DRINKS.

BY THE AUTHOR OF

"THE REMINISCENCES OF AN OLD BOHEMIAN," &c.

Crown 8vo, cloth, 3s. 6d.

"The most recommendable book on cookery that has been published in England for many long days."
Saturday Review.

"The recipes in the Old Bohemian's 'Philosophy in the Kitchen' make one's mouth water."—*Graphic.*

"The Old Bohemian is a *cordon bleu* among cooks, and a capital *raconteur.* His chapter on salads alone is worth the price of the book."—*The Lady.*

"A racy, chatty, and instructive book."—*Scotsman.*

"A remarkable book, cleverly written, full of thought, and brimming over with original suggestions."
British Confectioner.

"Excellent recipes, some of which are absolutely new."
Figaro.

"Will quickly take its place among the culinary standards of Brillat-Savarin, Kettner, Fin-Bec, Tegetmeier, and the no less able, but more desultory, George Augustus Sala."
Practical Confectioner.

"An amusing cookery-book, probably the only one in the language. To housekeepers who are not above taking valuable hints as to the preparation of food, to those who look upon eating and drinking as the chief ends of life, and to all and sundry who like useful information none the less because it is lightened with genial gossip and spiced with sparkling anecdote, 'Philosophy in the Kitchen' is a book we can recommend."—*Spectator.*

NOW READY, THE THIRD EDITION OF
Russia Under the Tzars.

By STEPNIAK, Author of " Underground Russia."
Translated by WILLIAM WESTALL.   Crown 8vo, 6s.

" Excessively interesting. . . . We would bear the most cordial testimony to the excellence of Stepniak's work."
Times.

" His vivid and absorbing book should be read and pondered by every one who appreciates the blessings of liberty."—*Daily Telegraph.*

" He exposes the hideous police system, he tells us the secrets of the House of Preventive Detection, of the central prisons, and the Troubetzkoi Ravelin, and gives us graphic sketches of exile life on the shores of the White Sea and in the bagnios of Siberia. . . . For all who would form an adequate idea of the present condition of Russia, gauge its capacity for war, or attempt to forecast its future, Stepniak's work is indispensable."—*Spectator.*

" A remarkable work, and it appears at a most opportune moment. . . . The state of things in Russian prisons, so far as political prisoners are concerned, as revealed by Stepniak, is hideous, if it be true.   If it be untrue the Russian Government ought, for its own honour's sake, to refute his statements. . . . What he describes is terrible."
Athenæum.

" Thrilling pictures of the terrors of prison life. . . . Tourgenieff and Stepniak, indeed, illustrate one another. Naturally the novelist tells nothing of the worst side, the life in a Yakout hut for instance (fancy the flower of a nation being brutalized by treatment of that kind); the riot produced in a Siberian prison that the governor may account for several escapes, due to gross negligence, by saying that "the rules were too easy;" the hunger strikes—prisoners starving themselves to death; the coarse tyranny with its petty tortures ; the comic side of the affair—as when of two Belousoffs the wrong one is seized and can't be set free, for the State can't own a mistake. . . . We have said nothing of the book as a book, because, being Stepniak's, it is, of course, as interesting as a novel.   We fear its thrilling details are true as well as interesting."—*Graphic.*

WARD & DOWNEY, Publishers, 12, York St., Covent Garden.